LOVING IRISH

The Summerhaven Trio

KATY REGNERY

LOVING IRISH

Katharine Gilliam Regnery, publisher

Please visit my website at www.katyregnery.com
First Edition: June 2018
Katy Regnery
Loving Irish: a novel / by Katy Regnery – 1st ed.

ISBN: 978-1-944810-30-6

Many a time a man's mouth broke his nose.
It is not a secret after three people know it.
—Traditional Irish sayings

In memory of
Pauline Katharine Kelley Tapley
xoxo

the plan

(Part 1)

Ten years ago

"Tonight's the night!"

Almost seventeen-year-old Hallie Gilbert fell dramatically onto the lower bunk as the screen door of the cottage slammed shut behind her.

"Really?" cried Brittany Manion, her best friend, who suddenly appeared from above, her pretty face upside down. "Oh, my God! For your birthday? That's *so* romantic, Hallie! Are you *sure* you're ready?"

"I'm in love," said Hallie with a sigh. "He's the one."

"The...*one*?" Britt's eyes widened before she swung her legs over the bed and jumped down onto the bare, wood plank floors of the cabin they shared at summer camp. "Tell me everything."

Hallie sat up, patting the comforter beside her to invite Britt to sit down. "Where are Tate and Chelsea?"

"We're meeting them at dinner."

"Perfect."

Hallie loved their other two roommates, but she hadn't filled them in on her secret summer romance with Ian Haven. Britt was the only one who knew, and it needed to stay that way.

Once Britt was cross-legged across from her, Hallie recounted the steps of her epic summer love affair. "The first week of camp we kissed, right?"

Britt, who was Hallie's biggest supporter in all things romantic, nodded earnestly. "Right."

"That's first base. The second week, he...well, you know."

"Touched your boobs," said Britt, trying not to giggle.

"Exactly," said Hallie matter-of-factly, accustomed to the way her friend occasionally blurted things out. "And last week, we..."

"—did everything *but* the deed!"

"Yes," sighed Hallie. In various make-out sessions over the last several weeks, she'd become accustomed to the weight of Ian's muscular body on top of hers, felt his panted breath on her throat as his lips dragged across her hot skin, and watched the drunk expression in his emerald eyes when she touched him "down there." She felt both powerful and vulnerable in his arms, her body coveted and beloved, her heart safe in his keeping. "And so tonight it's time to..."

"DO. THE. DEED," said Britt in a dramatic whisper.

"Voilà," said Hallie, grinning at her friend.

"You love Ian?" asked Britt. "You *really* love him?"

"I *really* love him," said Hallie, her voice soft and fervent because she really did. She was utterly and totally in love with Ian.

Ian Haven, the son of the camp owners and the same age as Hallie, had been her from-a-distance crush since she'd first attended Summerhaven Camp at age thirteen. With jet-black hair, sparkling green eyes, and a teasing smile he lavished on the female campers, he was the hottest boy she'd ever seen...not that he'd *seen her* in return.

In fact, for her first three years at Summerhaven, Hallie, and her best friend, Brittany Manion, had commiserated together about how Ian—and his equally good-looking brother, Rory—hadn't seemed to notice them at all.

But something had changed this year, at least for Hallie.

Maybe it was the fact that she had grown out her long, straight dirty-blonde hair, or that she'd finally convinced her parents to let her start wearing contacts. She'd also lost the last of her baby fat, had her braces removed, and noticed that her breasts, which had been slow to develop, were perfect B-cups for filling out bikini tops now. Or maybe it was that she'd finally garnered the notice of the boys at her Boston private school, who'd invited her to dances and on dates, boosting her confidence.

Whatever the reason, the moment she'd stepped off the bus in June, Ian had finally noticed her. Blinking in surprise, his smile had grown from small to teasing to full as he reached out his hand and helped her down the stairs. And the moment her hand had touched his? She'd known. She'd known it as certainly as her name or her reflection in the mirror or anything else that was intrinsically hers: Ian Haven *belonged* to her. And she belonged to him.

"More details!" said Britt. "It's clear that Rory is *never* going to notice me. I'm going to have to live vicariously through you, Hal."

Hallie sighed happily, thinking about the note she'd just found under their "special rock," behind the public phone booth. It read,

Happy almost birthday.
You and me.
The barn.
Tonight.
9:00.

ILY.

—Irish

Her stomach fluttered with butterflies as she reached for the note in her back pocket and passed it to Britt.

Brittany read the note once and looked up with puppy eyes, then read it again with soft mewling sounds, and then she read it a third time, *whooshing* forward on the bed to throw her arms around her friend as soon as she finished.

"Oh, my God!" whispered Britt. "I can't *even*!"

"I know," said Hallie, her voice breathless.

"It's so...*perfect*."

Hallie held out her hand for the note, folding it before sliding it under her pillow.

"Are you nervous?" asked Brittany.

Hallie thought about this for a second.

She'd never had sex, but she *had* made out with two boys at school, and she knew that Ian was bigger than average. From what she'd gathered, reading books and watching movies, it was going to hurt when he put it in the first time. But after that? By all accounts? It would be heaven. Besides, she loved Ian. She trusted him. She wanted her first time to be with him.

"No," she said. "It just feels right."

"*So* right," agreed Brittany, just as the camp bell rang to announce dinner.

The girls jumped off Hallie's bed, checking their faces in the small mirror over the bathroom sink.

"You'll cover for me tonight? At the campfire?" asked Hallie, catching Brittany's eyes as she swiped on a little mascara.

"Of course. I'll say you have 'cramps' and you're resting

in bed. Mr. Haven won't touch that with a ten-foot pole." Brittany winked at Hallie and giggled. "What time will you be home?"

"Before the breakfast bell, for sure," said Hallie. "But I want as much time with him as I can get. When the sun rises on my birthday, I'll wake up in his arms, Britt."

Brittany gasped, her eyes filling with tears. "I just…I just can't *even*! This is so romantic!"

"C'mon. You told Tate and Chelsea we'd meet them." Hallie reached for her friend's hand, pulling Brittany out the door of their cottage, Lady Margaret.

They joined the wave of other campers migrating from Oxford Row to the dining hall, smiling at friends along the way. Outside the cafeteria, a group of four girls that Hallie and Britt referred to as "the Fakes," were on "greeting" duty tonight.

Vicky, Lea, Tasha, and Christine stayed in the cabin next door to Brittany and Hallie—Pembroke Cottage. Because of the way a certain exhaust pipe was positioned in Pembroke's bathroom, the girls in Lady Margaret could overhear a lot of their neighbors' nightly conversations wherein they verbally brutalized other girls at camp.

Vicky was the "Queen Bee," but Tasha was the most vicious, with Lea and Christine mostly acting as a fervent audience to Vicky and Tasha's razor-sharp meanness. No one else knew what went on in Pembroke—the Fakes were too clever for that. Outside of their safe space, they acted like everyone's best friends with eager smiles and syrupy-sweet compliments.

"The hottest girls at camp have arrived for dinner!" exclaimed Vicky, checking off Brittany and Hallie's names on her clipboard with a wide smile.

"Hey, y'all," said Lea, who was from Charleston. "Lookin' good tonight."

"Thanks, Lea," said Brittany with chipper smile, playing along. "You too. Christine, your hair's, like, perfect. For reals."

"Staaaaaahp," said Christine, putting her hand on Britt's arm. "*Yours* is *amazing*!"

"Oh, *my God*," said Vicky, elbowing her friend, "just take a compliment, Chris!"

"You're so right, Vicks." She turned back to Brittany. "Thanks, Britt. You're the sweetest."

Hallie flicked her eyes to Tasha, whom she caught with a sour look, checking out Hallie's new DKNY swimsuit cover-up. It was a navy-and-peach-colored, strapless Lycra dress with a sash that accentuated Hallie's slim hips.

"Tasha?"

She changed her expression quickly, brightening her face with a huge smile and gesturing to Hallie's outfit with a flick of her chin. "New?"

Hallie nodded. "My Mom sent a box of stuff for my birthday."

"OMG! It's your *birthday*?!" exclaimed Vicky. "That's so *cool*! We'll make everyone sing for you tonight, Hallie!"

"You guys are the *best*," said Brittany sweetly, tugging Hallie into the dining hall with her. She leaned closer. "Ugh, those four. I feel dirty now. Where's the shower?"

"Tonight, Tasha will be talking about how ugly she thinks my dress is. Make sure you take notes."

Brittany squeezed her friend's hand. "Forget it. You'll have to ask Tate or Chelsea. I'm putting on headphones and tuning them out. I can't *even* with the meanness."

Hallie grinned at Brittany before looking up to find Ian Haven walking toward her from across the great room, his muscular chest covered by a royal-blue Summerhaven Camp polo shirt, his tan legs corded with sinew, his calves flexing with each step.

Tonight. Tonight. Tonight.

With his eyes locked on hers, he touched the skin behind his ear with two fingers, a coded gesture that meant, *I left a note for you.*

She wet her lips with her tongue. *I got it.*

He bit his lower lip, then raised his eyebrows. *Yes or No?*

She nodded at him, a gesture so subtle it would be missed by anyone but him. *Yes.*

He never slowed his pace, passing her without incident, careful not to touch her, careful, *as always*, not to draw attention to their fierce, thriving love. It was the most important rule of their relationship: his parents could never find out. Dating campers was totally forbidden by Mr. and Mrs. Haven, and while Ian didn't seem to mind breaking the rules, he didn't want to be caught and punished for it either.

"You two," murmured Brittany from beside her. "I could literally *feel* that."

Me too, thought Hallie, weak with desire as Brittany pulled her toward the salad bar. As she took a chilled plate from the stack, she flicked her eyes in Ian's direction, watching as he stood at the entrance with the Fakes for a few minutes, talking to Vicky and Tasha before tossing back his head with full-bodied laughter.

It didn't make Hallie jealous. If anything, it made her smile to watch him laugh. *Because*, she thought, *let's face it: in three hours, it won't be one of their bodies he's worshipping.*

It'll be mine.

Happy birthday to me.

***

Ian Haven made it a point to deflect attention away from him and Halcyon Gilbert by flirting with other girls—*any* girls, it really didn't matter whom—after every time he saw her.

Just in case someone had noticed the quick, hot look they'd just shared, he needed to be sure that it appeared that he didn't have a favorite. Because shite, if his parents caught wind of what was going on between him and Hallie? His goose would be cooked. Nah. Worse. His mother would draw blood if she knew what Ian had planned for tonight.

"...a Rory and Ian sandwich!" finished Vicky Lafontaine, winking at Ian as her friends tittered around her.

He had no idea what she'd just said, and frankly, from the tidbit he'd caught at the end it sounded pretty disgusting, but he threw back his head and laughed. "Damn, Vicks!"

"Vicky, you're pure evil," purred Tasha.

"I'm just sayin'," she said, ignoring her friend, eyes only for Ian, "you and Rory are *scorching hot* this summer."

"Takes one to know one," he said suggestively, letting his glance flick to her full breasts before catching her eyes again.

Vicky's cheeks flushed as she laughed breathlessly. "You're the worst flirt, Ian Haven."

Ian winked at her. "I have it on good authority that I'm the best, actually."

Vicky gasped softly, licking her lips and taking a step toward him. "Wouldn't mind finding out for myself."

Shoot. This is going too far. Ian chucked her under the chin like he did with Tierney sometimes.

"'No datin' the campers, Ian,'" he said in his best Irish brogue, imitating his mother.

"I wouldn't tell," said Vicky, her eyes wide and dark as she cocked her head to the side.

Ian took a step back from her, straightening his expression. "Rules are rules."

"...and made to be broken," persisted Vicky.

He should have known better than to choose Vicky for his deflection tactics. She was increasingly bolder this summer. She didn't need his encouragement.

"Ian? Ian! I need your help."

Thank God.

He looked up to see his sister, Tierney, standing nearby with an armful of towels that she could easily handle on her own.

"Duty calls!" he said, winking at the girls before sprinting away.

Tierney gave him a look as he took half of the towels from her. "You're playing with fire."

"Nah. It's nothing."

"Ten bucks says that Vicky's parents file a complaint by August."

As they started walking side by side, Ian flicked a glance over his shoulder, only to find Vicky watching him thoughtfully from the dining room door. When they locked eyes, she smiled widely and winked at him. Ian turned quickly, though he had a sense that Tierney might be right. Fuck.

"For what?"

"Disappointed expectations," said Tierney.

"I don't *like* her. Not like that."

"Yeah. I know," said Tierney matter-of-factly, "but *she* doesn't."

Ian's neck felt itchy, but his hands were full of towels so he couldn't scratch.

He should have flirted with one of the other Pembroke girls, but Hallie's sky-blue eyes had distracted him so thoroughly, their plans for tonight so filling his head, he hadn't been on his game.

Hallie. Halcyon Gilbert.

The old Webster's dictionary in his parent's living room said that "halcyon" was an adjective that meant happy and golden, and damn, but it was the perfect name for her. Everything about her—everything about the way she made him *feel*—was happy and golden.

He was so in love with that girl, he didn't know what to do with himself.

"Speaking of…" said Tierney as they continued walking toward the Cambridge Row cabins, "who *is* your flavor-of-the-month? Rory and I can't figure it out."

"I think that's a good thing."

"Is it?" Tierney was quiet for a moment. "I know you're with someone. I can tell. How come you haven't told us who?"

It was a good question, a fair question, because Ian was usually forthcoming with his siblings about whom he was dating…or fucking, for that matter. But this time? It all felt different. He hadn't told *anyone* about his feelings for Hallie. They were too sacred. Too special. He couldn't risk them by speaking of them—not even to the people he trusted most in the whole world.

"I…can't. Not yet."

"Huh," murmured Tierney. "Does that mean it's serious?"

"Yeah, Tier," he said softly. "It does."

She didn't press him further as they walked silently to the row of cabins and changed out the used towels for new.

It was something that Ian dearly loved about his sister—that she would keep his confidence, even though she didn't have details. She knew that whomever Ian was seeing, the girl was important to her brother, and that was enough for her.

Halcyon Gilbert had been on Ian's radar for years—her bright smile free of any machinations. She was genuine and deep, authentic in a sea of girls who often seemed shallow and self-serving. He'd always *liked* her, but he hadn't been *attracted* to her until she stepped off the bus from Boston in June. And then? Holy Lord, his whole world had come to a screeching stop.

Now the girl who he'd always considered a cut above her peers in personality was scorching hot to boot, and he couldn't tear his eyes away or stop his body from wanting her on the spot. That said, Hallie wasn't the type of girl with whom he could have a summer fling. The way her eyes held his, the careful way she chose her words and the earnest way she delivered them, even the sassy way she called him "Irish"—everything about her was *girlfriend* material, and for the first time in Ian's life, he loved the idea of being someone's boyfriend. He didn't want to be a conquest or a bit of summer fun. He wanted something far deeper altogether. He wanted to *belong* to her.

"Ian, whatever you're doing," said Tierney as they placed the last of the clean towels in the final cottage, "be careful, huh?"

"Yeah. Yeah, of course."

Tierney's green eyes, identical to his own, searched his with worry. "I mean it."

"I know you do," he said, looking away, putting his hands on his hips.

He felt a little defensive, which was unusual for Ian. His personality didn't lend itself to high-strung traits—he was too laid-back to let most things raise his dander. But this was different. This was Hallie. And he loved her madly.

"Okay," his sister whispered, her voice filled with uncertainty.

Ian watched her walk away, an unfamiliar—and wholly unlikable—feeling of anxiety leeching into his heart as he thought about his plans for later: tomorrow was Hallie's seventeenth birthday, but they would be celebrating tonight. All night long.

In an old picnic basket hidden on the upper level of the barn, he'd already stashed two bottles of white wine from his parent's stock, wineglasses, her favorite cookies, a couple of soft, fleece blankets, candles, condoms, and his gift for Hallie in a little white box. It had cost him half of his summer allowance, but it was worth every penny. She deserved such a fine gift, and he couldn't wait to see her blue eyes sparkle when she opened it. He'd pick her some wild flowers from the east side of camp on his way to the barn and arrange them when he got there.

It wouldn't be Ian's first time tonight, but it would be hers, and he wanted it to be as perfect as possible, in part, because Ian though of this summer—of every moment he spent with Hallie—as a beginning of something much bigger. He wasn't given to feelings as serious as the ones he had for Hallie, but he also couldn't deny them. He wanted their relationship to last beyond Summerhaven, beyond New Hampshire, strong enough to withstand their separation in September when she left for Stanford and he'd be starting at Boston University. Ian wasn't delusional. He knew that it would take effort to turn a summer love into a forever love, but he couldn't even picture a girl he'd want or love—*ever* want, *ever* love—as much as he wanted and loved Halcyon Gilbert.

One day, she'll be Halcyon Gilbert Haven.

He gazed at the lake as he repeated the words over and over again in his head, promising them to himself with every throbbing beat of his seventeen-year-old heart and hoping that tonight was another step toward making that dream come true.

CHAPTER ONE

Present Day

"Mr. Haven? Darn it all, is this thing working? Mr., um, Haven? Are you somewhere out there? Over?"

Ian smiled at the familiar voice of Miranda Toffle, the longtime receptionist of the Summerhaven Conference and Event Center, as he reached for the walkie-talkie sitting on the sunny dock.

He pressed down on the side button with wet fingers. "Here, Ms. T. Whassup?"

"Oh! There you are. Mr. Haven, your cousin has arrived. Over."

"Fin's here? Damn! He's early!"

"Yes. A full day early. He flew space-available from Shannon this morning and called an Oobuh to get here from Manchester. Over."

Ian chuckled, wondering if Mrs. Toffle had any idea what an "Uber" was and guessing the answer was probably no.

The lake water swirled around his waist, not as cold as the air, but quickly getting there with each passing day. By the end of October, it would be too cold for these kinds of jobs, and with Rory spending more and more time in Boston and on the road, Ian and his assistant manager, Doug, just weren't able to handle everything. His cousin, Finian, arriving on a six-month work visa from Ireland, would be welcome help.

"Tell him to cool his jets, Ms. T....or better yet, tell him to get his jet-lagged ass—er, um, *butt* down here and help me get this dam—um, *dang* dock out of the lake."

"I will relay your message. Over." After a pause, she spoke again, but not to Ian. "Hmm. Come again, Mr. Kelley? I didn't get that. Once more?" Finian's accent was strong, and Ian imagined Mrs. Toffle squinting her eyes at Fin as she tried to make out what he was saying. "Yes. Yes, I understand. Mr. Haven? Mr. Kelley says to tell you, *póg mo thóin*. Over."

Ian guffawed with laughter. Somehow, his cousin had just gotten straight-laced Miranda Toffle to say "kiss my ass" in Irish. *Damnú!*

"Tell him I'll be up in a little bit," he said, choking back more laughter.

"Very good. Over and out."

Placing his hands flat on the boards of the dock, Ian lifted his body from the lake—all two-hundred-and-twenty-five pounds of muscled flesh, tanned from a summer of working outside. As the water sluiced down his body, pooling beside the walkie-talkie, he pushed it gently away, reaching for the towel he'd brought along.

It was sixty-six degrees in the bright afternoon sun, but it was supposed to go down to fifty flat tonight, and before the lake started to freeze, he needed to get the last of the docks hauled onto land.

This was precisely the sort of job that Finian could give Ian a hand with tomorrow.

"Fuck it fer now," he muttered, rubbing the water from

his legs, stomach, chest, and arms. His bathing suit trunks would dry quickly as he walked back up to the office, and he threw a sun-warmed Summerhaven polo over his head, sighing with pleasure at the heat against his cool skin.

Because today was a Wednesday, he and Fin would head over to Tierney's place for dinner tonight. Hopefully Tierney and Burr wouldn't mind hanging out with their young cousin while Ian attended his weekly AA meeting at eight o'clock in Sandwich.

It was six months and two weeks since Ian had arrived on Tierney's doorstep on April 1st, tearing her place apart after she'd poured out the vodka he'd brought with him. With the help and support of his siblings, Ian had made a fateful decision that night: to pursue sobriety. In two more days, Ian would meet the two-hundred-day mark—the longest he'd been sober since he started drinking ten years ago, the summer he was seventeen years old.

He was grateful for the love and encouragement of his siblings, but even more, he was proud of himself. The road to sobriety was a perilous journey, a day by day—sometimes even hour by hour or, when cravings hit, minute by minute—challenge that many a recovering addict couldn't walk. But through the grace of God, Ian was walking. One foot in front of the other. One day. Five. Fifty. One hundred. Two hundred. Almost there.

"I'll never go back," he said softly, watching the way the sunlight danced like diamonds on the surface of the lake. "Never."

Balling up the damp towel in his mitt-like hands, he reached for the walkie-talkie and clipped it to the waistband of his wet trunks, then headed up the path to greet Fin.

***

"When'll Rory be back, now?" asked Finian, sitting across from Ian at Tierney's kitchen table.

Ian looked to his right, raising an eyebrow at Tierney, who had gotten into the habit of talking to Rory's fiancée, Brittany, almost every day.

"On Saturday. And they plan to stay local 'til the wedding."

"Saturday," said Fin. "That's grand. Haven't seen Rory in ages."

"Not that they'll come up for air for a day or two," said Ian, giving Finian a look. "There's a lot of love going on in that old chapel apartment. I like to bang pots and pans as I arrive so I don't walk in on anything."

"You're so gross," said Tierney to Ian. Then she turned to Finian with a cringe. "But Ian's right. To be safe, always assume they're…*busy*. And never, ever walk in without knocking. You're liable to get an eyeful."

Tierney's boyfriend, Burr, who was a police officer in nearby Center Harbor, chuckled as he winked at her from across the table. "Same rule should be followed here, boys."

Ian snickered as his sister's cheeks flared with heat, two bright spots of red coloring her milky skin.

"*Is minic a gheibhean beal oscailt diog dunta,*" she warned her boyfriend in sharp-tongued Irish, which only made him smile wider. *Be careful your open mouth doesn't catch my fist.*

"Ha!" said Burr, raising his glass to Tierney with an adoring smile, which was totally at odds with the fierceness of his tattoo, which peeked out of the neckline of his white T-shirt and read *Destroyer*. "What a woman."

"Ya' let her talk t' ya' like that?" asked Finian, who, at

twenty-four, was a few years younger than the twenty-seven-year-old Haven siblings.

"Boyo, she can talk to me however the hell she pleases," answered Burr, still holding Tierney's eyes across the table. "I belong to her."

"Ugh!" cried Ian, gagging. "First, Rory and Britt, and now you two. I'm surrounded by saps. Will you two get a room already?"

"Great idea," said Burr, pushing away from the table.

"I was kidding," said Ian. "Actually, I have to get to my meeting. I was hoping one of you could give Fin a ride back to camp when he's ready."

"'Course we can give him a ride," said Tierney. She turned to Ian, her green eyes the same shade and color as his. She reached out and took his hand, squeezing his fingers. "Proud of you, Ian. So proud."

That was Tierney.

Always supportive.

No matter what. No matter how many times Ian had fucked up over the years, his sister had always been there for him, and he'd go to his grave wondering how someone as good as Tierney had ended up in the same womb as him. But he'd also be on his knees in thanks that it was so.

He kissed her cheek, high-fived Burr and told Fin he'd seen him back at camp, then headed to his truck.

Ian rolled down his window on the way to Sandwich, familiar with the route he'd taken every Wednesday night since he'd started attending Alcoholics Anonymous meetings back in April. He attended a meeting in Moultonborough on Monday night, Tuesdays and Thursday nights in Laconia before hockey practice in Gilford, Wednesdays in Sandwich, and the Wolfeboro meeting on Friday. In the beginning, he'd also attended meetings on Saturday and Sunday nights, but after six months, he'd allowed himself to drop weekend meetings, and so far, so good. If he ever felt the inclination to backslide, he'd add those meetings back into his schedule.

Many recovering alcoholics, upon joining AA, were surprised to learn that the organization suggested "a meeting a day" for the first ninety days of recovery, which led to the sort of habit-making that created a lifelong attendee. For Ian, the meetings were nonnegotiable. His siblings were amazing, but it was the people he met in AA—at all stages of their recovery—that most strongly impacted his sobriety and will to continue.

In part, his co-survivors acted as a reminder of what lay in wait, should he resume his alcoholic lifestyle. They were people like Ian, who had lost their jobs and found themselves living on the streets. Or others, who'd lost spouses or children because of destructive behavior. Some had driven while drunk and hurt someone. Some had been arrested multiple times for drunken disorderly behavior, disturbing the peace, public urination, or worse.

The life Ian had rebuilt for himself in New Hampshire was clean and neat—he had a good job managing Summerhaven, a nice apartment, and biweekly family dinners with his brother and sister. He fostered dogs for a local shelter when needed and played goalie on a hockey team he loved. It would be easy to trick himself into believing that the sweet life he had now had always been his; but if he did that, one day, after a winning game, he might have a beer with his teammates. Why not? Just one. Just one beer like a normal guy with a normal life couldn't hurt.

Except it would.

It would ruin his life all over again. It would undo all the work he'd done in achieving and maintaining his sobriety. Meetings reminded him that he was only one sip from relapse. Did it suck to have to remind himself daily? On one hand, yeah, it did. Sometimes he was in a great mood around seven forty-five, and he didn't want to go to an overlit church basement for an hour and listen to someone talk about their upcoming divorce, or the fact that they couldn't see their kids anymore, or that the bank had just repossessed their house, or that they'd been fired for coming in late one too many times.

It was depressing as hell—and just plain sad. There were many, many nights he'd prefer to skip a meeting and just linger at Tierney's table or sack out in front of the TV at his apartment.

But he was also certain that skipping meetings would be the beginning of the end for his sobriety. He needed to remember his drunk life, his addict life. He needed to remember sleeping on sidewalks, being kicked in the gut by passing college kids for fun, and throwing up in the gutter. He needed to remember the worried looks in Rory and Tierney's eyes and that when his mother had had her stoke several years ago, they hadn't been able to find him for days. He needed to remember the way his principal looked when he fired Ian from his coaching job—sorry as hell but left with no options after Ian had arrived drunk to a high school match.

Sure, Ian was in recovery *now*. But he needed to remember *then*.

And meetings helped him to remember.

He parked his car in the church parking lot and headed down the now-familiar stairs to the basement, waving hello to familiar faces and pouring himself a cup of coffee before taking a seat.

"Hey, Ian," greeted his friend, Shandie, with whom he'd gone to high school. "How was your week?"

"Real good," he said. "You?"

"Okay," she said, but he could tell from the way she averted her eyes that it wasn't.

He patted the empty seat beside him. "Tell me what happened."

She sighed, sitting down and twisting the wedding ring on her left hand. "Dale got a new job."

"That sounds like good news, actually."

She looked up, her eyes bleak. "His new boss sent a bottle of champagne to the house."

"Oh," said Ian, grimacing at his friend. "So...what did you do?"

"I brought it inside, and I stared at it. I mean, I stared at the shiny, red-and-white Bollinger box. My mouth was watering. My hands started to shake."

Ian nodded with understanding and empathy.

Shandie had stopped drinking six months ago after her husband, Dale, had threatened to take away their toddler, Lucy, and start divorce proceedings. The saddest thing about her story was that she'd started drinking *after* having her daughter. She'd been lonesome at home, with only her baby for company.

Once she started making friends with other at-home moms, cocktail hour had figured prominently into their gatherings. At first, it was harmless. A glass of bubbly to celebrate getting through another tough day of motherhood. Maybe two. But over time, Shandie found herself opening three bottles, four, five, and finishing most of them on her own. She found herself driving home intoxicated with Lucy in the back seat. As she made dinner, she'd drink more, slurring her words by the time Dale got home from work.

Little by little, she'd lost the few friends she'd made—embarrassing them with her behavior. They stopped inviting her to playdates and "cocktail hour," but that didn't stop Shandie from drinking at home, alone. One day, Dale came home to find her on the kitchen floor—a pool of blood around her head. She'd started drinking in the morning and had probably fallen around ten, hitting her head on the kitchen counter and passing out with a concussion. Lucy had screamed from her crib for hours, hungry and dirty, but Shandie hadn't heard her daughter's cries.

Two days later, with a bandage on her forehead, she'd walked into the basement of the Moultonborough Methodist Church.

Six months later, she was sober, but gifts—like an unexpected bottle of champagne—could ruin all the progress she'd made, and Ian was worried for her.

"What next?" Ian prompted her, bracing himself for the worst.

She gulped. "I took it out of the box, you know? I put the bottle on the living room table, and I sat down on the couch and I stared at it. I touched it. Like, I caressed it—the *glass*, which is fucking nuts."

"No, it's not."

"It was cold. The—the, um, glass bottle. It was so cool under my fingertips, I guess because they'd delivered it to the front door, which is in the shade. Anyway, my mouth started to water because I remember how good it was—I mean, I didn't want to, but…"

"Shandie, did you—?"

"No!" she said, shaking her head. "I picked it up, took it out to the garage and put it in the garbage. I took Lucy to the park, called Dale, and told him to get rid of it."

"And he did?"

"Of course. He came home from work and took it away. Texted me to let me know when the coast was clear."

"Good man," said Ian.

"Yeah," she whispered, tears filling her eyes. Her shoulders drooped, and her voice dropped to a horrified whisper. "But I came *so close*, Ian. So close. I thought about it. The bubbles on my throat. The sweetness. The coldness…"

"Okay. But instead, you were strong."

She cleared her throat and nodded. "I really need this meeting tonight."

"Why didn't you call Maevis?" Her sponsor.

Shandie shrugged. "She's out of town visiting her grandkids."

"You could've called me," said Ian.

She looked up at him "Really?"

"Of course."

She grinned at him. "Call the cute guy from high school to come to my rescue? Yeah. Dale would've just loved that."

"Okay. Okay." Ian chuckled. "Doesn't have to be *me*. But you can always call someone from this group. You don't have to wait for the meeting to talk it out. That's what we're all here for."

"Yeah," she said. "You're right. I know. I just…I'm six months clean, you know? I didn't think it would be this hard after six months."

Ian nodded at her. His recovery time was almost identical to hers, so he understood completely. It was a blow every time you realized that it would be a lifelong battle. Not just achieving sobriety but, more important, maintaining it when alcohol was part of almost every social celebration imaginable.

"I know," he said. "But you did good. You were strong, Shandie. You're okay."

"Thanks, Ian."

Just then, the leader of their meeting stood up at a podium in the front, and the group greeted her in unison after she announced:

"My name is Kim and I am an alcoholic."

***

Another important part of Ian's recovery was getting up early in the morning and taking a jog around the Summerhaven campus. He'd been doing it every morning, regardless of the weather, since the second week in April when someone at the Laconia AA meeting had made the connection between spiritual and physical wellness. If you work out, you're liable to fall asleep faster, sleep more soundly, and feel more rested when you wake up. Not to mention, recovery is all about change: dropping bad habits and replacing them with good ones.

When Ian had lived on the streets of Boston for the last two months of his life before arriving at Tierney's, he'd often sought shelter in the triangle created by Trinity Church, the Boston Public Library, and Old South Church, which also had the benefit of a park in the center. Six blocks away, on West Newton, was a 7-Eleven that opened at 6:00 a.m. and sold beer at 8:00 a.m., per state laws. And that's where Ian found himself most mornings in those days: purchasing a six-pack of whatever was cheapest to get him through the morning.

When he'd shared this with Tierney after that particular AA meeting, she'd handed him a pair of Rory's old sneakers and told him that there was no need to cut out the morning walk, just the reason for taking it.

Ian had needed to dig deep and find a new reason for putting on sneakers and getting his ass outside. The one he chose? Health. Wellness. Taking control over his abused body and bringing it back to life.

Six months later, he was in amazingly good shape. Yeah, his liver would probably need the rest of his life to unpickle, but between jogging, hockey, and manual labor around Summerhaven, the rest of him was more fit than he'd been since college. And damn, but it felt good. It was a different kind of rush, a better sort of high, and Ian looked forward to his run every morning.

Last night at the meeting, Kim had asked all the attendees to reflect on where their addiction had started, and why, hoping that some of them would share their stories over the upcoming weeks. And as Ian's feet hit the path in familiar, rhythmic thumping, musing over the question, he found himself running in the opposite direction: west instead of east, along the shoreline instead of through the woods.

The land on which the Summerhaven Event and Conference Center had been built at the turn of the last century was prime lakefront real estate. Bordering the camp land on either side was private property.

At one point in history, little vacation homes, called "cottages" or "camps," had dotted the shoreline. These homes were generally painted dark green or brown to blend in with nature, and the architecture was that of rustic cabins. Traditionally, they had a great room with a cooking and dining area, and anywhere from two to six bedrooms—a few private bedrooms for married couples and one or two larger bedrooms filled with bunkbeds for grandchildren, nieces, nephews, and other young visitors. They were simple places, some even without electricity or running water, that were closed up from Labor Day to Memorial Day and only used during the warm, lovely summer months when loons called and the lake water was bath-warm.

Now two- or three-million-dollar lake homes with stories of balconies, sweeping decks, swimming pools, and custom-built boathouses had replaced the traditional lake camps. Almost all the little summer cottages that used to flank the Summerhaven campground were gone now. All, in fact, except one: Colby Cottage, the summer cottage of the Gilbert family.

Every so often, Ian would take a walk or run over to the little structure, which had seen much better days in its one-hundred-year history. Once a place of storybook-style charm, it was badly run-down now. The front garden was overgrown, and the picket gate hung unevenly on one hinge, creaking eerily with the breeze. Several of the windows were cracked or broken, and the moss-covered roof looked ready to fall in.

A "For Sale" sign out front waited for a rich businessman to buy up the property and knock down the old cottage in lieu of a spectacular summer place, but there hadn't been any bites over the summer. Ian knew this because he checked out the real estate transactions in the newspaper every week. Just to be sure.

Once upon a time, he'd known one of the Gilberts personally.

Loved her madly, even.

And whatever remained of that love meant it hurt Ian to see the old place fall to ruin. He'd even thought about tidying up the garden or fixing the gate, but he had no right to touch any of it. Honestly, he tried to avoid it and all the painful memories the old place conjured.

But when Kim asked the question last night—how Ian's addiction had started and why—he'd seen Hallie's sky-blue eyes in his mind. Immediately. Without hesitation.

All these years later, and he could remember Halcyon Gilbert's face with a level of detail that should drive a person insane.

Rounding a bend at the Summerhaven-Gilbert property line, Ian slowed his pace, approaching the cottage gingerly, like being there was forbidden, like he was trespassing or in danger. He gulped as it came into view—the crumbling chimney against the brilliance of a New Hampshire sunrise. Stopping in front of the gate, he stared at the cottage, remembering how it had looked ten years ago when he'd run to it the morning of Hallie's seventeenth birthday. He'd raced through the pristine white gate, sweating and panting from his run, banging on the front door and calling her name, but there'd been no answer. Not then, and never again.

Taking a shaky breath, he turned to leave, but

something caught his eye: the bright-white realtor signpost beside the front gate was empty. The last time he'd come to see the cottage, a "For Sale" sign had swung gently back and forth in the breeze. Now? The post was empty. The sign was gone.

Had someone bought the property? No. Ian wouldn't have missed the property transfer notice in the local paper.

If it hadn't been sold, then it must have been taken off the market, which meant...what? That the Gilberts weren't selling Colby Cottage after all?

Since learning two weeks ago that Halcyon was returning to Summerhaven for Rory and Brittany's Thanksgiving wedding, Ian had refused to think about her. Even in quiet moments, when his brain tried to turn to thoughts of her, he'd shut it down, desperate to keep her out of his mind. Ten years hadn't changed anything. She'd hate the sight of him just as much at Rory's wedding as she had a decade ago.

He'd stay out of her way out of respect, and she'd avoid him, leaving for Boston after the wedding. And Ian's life, and his dogged pursuit of sobriety, would continue undaunted.

But standing before her family's crumbling cottage—his curiosity piqued about the status of the property, his memories blending with unpleasant thoughts of their impending reunion—Ian couldn't help but wonder if fate had something else in store for him. And if life wasn't about to get a wee bit more complicated than he'd planned.

chapter two

There was no way to sugarcoat it:

Hallie Gilbert's life was in shambles.

It all started on February 10th when she'd visited her gynecologist for a checkup. She was having some groin irritation and wanted to clear it up before Valentine's Day.

After taking a look, her doctor had leaned away, glancing up at her face with worried eyes.

"UTI?" she asked. "Thrush?"

Her nursing background meant that she knew the common causes for such rashes.

"No." He cleared his throat, averting his eyes and shaking his head. "No." He cleared his throat *again*. "Um, Mrs. Silveira, I'm sorry to ask, but…do you have any sexual partners *other* than your husband?"

Her face had flushed uncomfortably as the doctor looked up at her. She scanned his face, trying to process why he would ask such a question.

"N-No."

He took a deep breath, reaching for a prescription pad on the counter next to him. "Antibiotics will clear up the infection in a few days. But you need to have a frank talk with your husband. I think—I think it's highly likely that *he* may have sexual partners other than you."

That's how Hallie found out that her husband was cheating on her.

Feet up in stirrups, sitting mostly naked on a piece of tissue paper in her doctor's office, Hallie's entire marriage—her entire *world*—had crumbled before her eyes.

Much like the way her husband of five years, Sergio, had crumbled when she confronted him that evening.

"I am sorry, *meu amor*," he'd said, his tanned, handsome face genuinely sad. "But I have too much love in my heart, in my body, for only one woman."

"What does *that* mean?" she'd yelled.

"I adore you, *querida*. You are the mother of my child. But one woman forever?" He opened his hands, palms up, and shook his head forlornly, like fidelity was an impossible foe he should never have tried to conquer.

"Why didn't you just ask me for a divorce?" she cried as tears streamed down her face.

"Such an ugly business." He shrugged with ennui. "We are comfortable, yes? We are mostly happy? Maybe we can—"

"You're cheating on me with someone who gave you a venereal disease!" she shrieked. "This *is* an ugly business! We are *not* comfortable, and we are *not* happy, Sergio!" Swiping her tears away, she'd added in a fierce whisper, "We're *over*."

She'd thrown him out of their apartment that night—no, not *theirs*. *Hers*, because she'd purchased it with her *own* money before their marriage—and found a good divorce lawyer the following day. What she hadn't known then, was that she was at the beginning of a horrible journey filled with appalling discoveries of her husband's extracurricular activities.

Not only had Sergio Silveira been cheating on Hallie since the birth of their daughter, Jennifer, four years ago, but he had regularly solicited the charms of prostitutes and escorts, which had racked up an almost-unbelievable amount of debt.

By May, she'd learn that he owed almost two hundred *thousand* dollars on about ten different credit cards he'd taken out on his own—and about which Hallie knew nothing. How had he accrued such debt? Well, unbeknownst to her, he'd lost his job the previous fall, likely due to his proclivities. Every day from October to February, when he left for "work," he'd party the day away with his whores. And all of those "business trips" to New York and Chicago? Those had been binge weekends in Florida and California, where bottles of *Cristal* were charged to cards guaranteed by Hallie's once-impeccable credit rating.

And just when she thought it couldn't get any worse? In September, Sergio stopped showing up for court appearances and weekend visits. It wouldn't take long for her to figure out why. He'd returned to his native São Paulo, and according to his sister, Catina, he had no plans to return. He did, however, ask—through Catina, because he was too much of a coward to get on the phone himself—if Jenny could come and visit him in Brazil at some point, which had almost fried Hallie's already-frazzled mind.

The Boston family court had awarded Hallie her divorce and full custody of Jenny, but it had also held her responsible for the debt incurred by her husband during their marriage. With her bank accounts empty, Hallie had no choice but to sell her Boston apartment. She received a little over three hundred thousand dollars for it, which paid off Sergio's debts. But after realtor fees, conveyance taxes, and moving expenses, it didn't leave Hallie nearly enough to buy a decent place for her and Jenny.

Her parents, who owned a beachfront condo in Palm Beach, invited Hallie to move in with them, but giving up her independence was the last thing she wanted. What Hallie really wanted was a fresh start: a home of her own—a safe place where she and Jenny could start over.

And that's when she'd remembered Colby Cottage on Squam Lake.

The modest, cabin-style vacation home had been built by Hallie's great-grandparents in the 1930s, then passed down through Hallie's maternal grandmother to her mother, who'd decided to sell the never-visited house last summer.

Hallie, herself, hadn't set foot in New Hampshire since the morning she'd left over ten years ago, promising herself that she'd never return. But she'd already be breaking that promise when she returned to Summerhaven in November for Brittany Manion's wedding. Not to mention, beggars couldn't be choosers. Although she gathered that the cottage was in a state of some disrepair, it was also empty and rent-free, and Hallie had enough furniture from her Boston apartment to furnish it. If she banked the remaining money from the apartment sale and made updates on the cottage frugally, she and Jenny could live there comfortably until she found another job.

And so she'd quit her nursing job, hired a handyman she'd found over the internet to get started on repairs, packed up their belongings, and today was the day—she and Jenny were moving.

"Hey, Jen-Jen," she said, looking in the rearview mirror at her daughter, who was small for her age and still sat in a five-point harness car seat, "I promise you're going to love it in New Hampshire. Our new house has the prettiest garden in the front yard, with beautiful bright flowers, and do you know what's in the backyard? A lake! A big lake with a dock where we can swim next summer. We're going to be happy there, baby. I promise."

Jenny glanced at her mother briefly, holding her eyes for about two seconds before turning to look out the window and slowly feed Goldfish crackers into her mouth.

Hallie took a deep breath and sighed.

Of all the destruction Sergio's behavior had wrought, none hurt Hallie as much as the way Jenny had withdrawn over the past three months. For all that he'd been a horrible husband, Hallie had to grudgingly admit that Sergio had been a decent father to their daughter. Not that he'd ever changed a diaper or made her a meal himself, but he'd loved Jenny, and Jenny adored her father.

It was hard enough when Hallie had thrown Sergio out—Jenny had grabbed onto her father's leg, begging him not to go, and she'd blamed Hallie for making him leave. And when Sergio had stopped showing up in September for their weekly Saturday visits, it hadn't stopped Jenny from sitting on the love seat in the front window for hours, waiting for him. Even after Hallie explained that "Papa moved away to Brazil," showing her daughter the distance between Boston and São Paulo on a map, Jenny still sat on that damned love seat every Saturday, insisting to Hallie that "Papa is coming."

But the worst was when Hallie told Jenny that she needed to sell their apartment and that they'd be moving to New Hampshire. The four-year-old had screamed so long and so loud, she'd lost her voice for three days after. And since then, Jenny hadn't said much of anything, though her blue eyes, identical to Hallie's, said it all: *You did this, Mommy. You ruined my happy life. You drove my Papa away. I blame you. I hate you.*

Hallie had taken her daughter to the pediatrician, who'd advised Hallie not to push Jenny too hard.

"Kids process loss in a lot of different ways. She's grieving the loss of her father, the loss of your family."

"She hates me."

"She *needs* you," the doctor insisted, "more than ever."

"She blames me."

"One day she'll understand what happened here; she'll see the simple truth: that your husband left and you stayed."

"And until then?"

"Help her."

"How?"

"Can she talk to your ex-husband on the phone? Skype with him? Letting her communicate with her father may make her feel less isolated from him."

The mere idea of reaching out to Sergio made Hallie's stomach flip over and skin crawl, but if it was the right thing for Jenny, she'd figure out a way to include him in their daughter's life. "I'll think about it."

"Listen," the doctor had continued, "this is Jenny's way of having a little bit of control over what's going on. She can't make her father come back. She can't undo the divorce. She can't make you stay in Boston. But she doesn't have to talk. It's all she has right now."

"She has *me!*" Hallie insisted.

The doctor regarded her with sympathetic eyes. "Then be patient. Try to understand. Kids are resilient. She'll come around eventually. Let her decide how to communicate and when she wants to start using her voice again."

Hallie was trying—Lord, she was trying so hard to be patient and understanding, but after the last six months of awfulness, it hurt that Jenny was so furious with her. She couldn't explain to a four-year-old that she was actually blameless and Sergio, the rat, had ripped their family apart, then run away. Anyway, Hallie wouldn't do that to her baby. No matter what else Sergio was, he was Jenny's father, and Hallie would protect her daughter's right to love him. If he became a villain in Jenny's eyes, it wouldn't be because Hallie had purposely poisoned the well.

"Jenny? You want to stop for McDonald's soon? Chicken nuggets? You know you love them!" She glanced into the rearview mirror, but Jenny didn't meet her eyes this time; she just continued staring out the window, methodically eating from her little carton of Goldfish. "We'll stop in a little bit. Until then, Mommy's going to put on some music. You can sing along if you want, okay?"

Leaning forward, Hallie pressed play on the SUV's CD player and lowered her window as Aladdin started making promises to Jasmine about a "whole new world" waiting for them.

Right. Liar.

You're a big fat liar, Aladdin.

She pictured Aladdin and Jasmine sitting on the magic carpet together. He was pretending to be a prince, and she was buying it hook, line, and sinker. Only later would the duped princess discover that the man she'd fallen for wasn't a prince at all. He was a guttersnipe, a petty thief, and a liar.

And that's the problem with men, thought Hallie acidly. *They all made promises they didn't keep. They all lied to get what they wanted. They all used women for their own means and discarded them—or replaced them—when it suited them.*

She pictured Sergio's handsome face briefly, but it was quickly supplanted by the emerald eyes of a man who'd engineered the original, and most bitter, betrayal of Hallie's life.

No, she thought, banishing him from her mind. *He's in the past. Leave him there.*

Except Ian Haven wasn't entirely in the past.

In fact, his presence loomed in her future like another dark cloud in a series of hundred-year storms. Whether she wanted to or not, she'd have to see him at Brittany and Rory's wedding.

But that didn't mean she had to like it.

Nor did she have to look at him, talk to him, or acknowledge his presence.

She'd lived the last ten years with the sharp sting of Ian's treachery in her heart, and she'd lived the last six months with Sergio's infidelity piled onto that original pain.

Hallie Gilbert had had enough betrayal from men to last her until the end of her days. The only answer was to stay away from them. The only answer was to refuse to have anything to do with them so that she could heal her broken heart and concentrate on her daughter.

No more men. No more lies. No more betrayal. No lovers. No male friendships. Nothing. No one. No more. Please God, no more. I can't bear any more.

Blinking back her tears as she rolled up the window, she glanced into the mirror again to see her daughter's lips moving to the words from *Mulan*'s "Reflection":

Who is that girl I see, staring straight back at me?

Ignored by her daughter, Hallie caught her own eyes in the mirror and wished she could answer such a simple question. *Who am I? Who are you?*

But no answers appeared in her mind.

The truth was, *nothing* felt simple anymore.

***

After dinner at McDonald's, Jenny had fallen asleep, and the sun was setting by the time Hallie arrived in Sandwich, leaving just enough light to see that yet *another* man had betrayed her trust.

She knew from her parents and their realtor that Colby Cottage had been in a state of some serious disrepair, but she'd found a handyman on the internet two weeks ago, signed a contract for his services, and wired him ten thousand dollars so he could get to work on the place.

Now that she'd arrived?

It was clear that neither he nor anyone else had done the slightest bit of work on the cottage.

What was once a driveway was now overgrown with shrubbery, so she parked on the road by the front gate, which hung from one rusty hinge.

A haunted house.

They were the first words that passed through her head as she cut the engine of her car, stepped from its warmth, and stood facing the decrepit house that had been the place of so many wonderful childhood memories.

The small structure was dark and foreboding; nothing about it ringing out the joy she'd found there in her youth. The white picket fence out front was missing spindles, the paint cracked and uneven, and the path to the house was barely passable, covered with high grass and overgrown greenery.

Using her purse to push aside thorny vines and sharp branches, she made her way to the door, reached into her pocket for the key with a shaking hand, opened the front door, and stepped inside.

It smelled all wrong.

When she was young, the cottage had smelled of decades of burned fire wood combined with the pleasant, slightly musty essence of the surrounding forest and lake.

But now? She covered her nose against an assault of staleness and decay. Something must have died there recently because the smell was eye-watering. Reaching for the light switch to her right, her shoulders sagged in relief when the stag antler chandelier, hanging from the great room ceiling, turned on without delay. At least they had electricity, which meant light, base board heat, and—*hopefully*—a working kitchen.

Leaving the front door open so she could hear Jenny if she called out, Hallie stepped into the empty cottage, fumbling in her hip pocket for her phone.

She dialed the handyman's number, unsurprised when her call was answered by a recorded message saying that the number was no longer in service. Grinding her teeth, she blinked back her tears and hit the "End" button. All his good reviews must have been fake, and his listed number was just a temporary ruse to trap an unsuspecting victim like her—someone who had local property that needed work but who wasn't, in fact, a local.

Mr. Smith of AAA HandyMan was a crook, and Hallie was the victim of a scam.

"Shit," she muttered. "Shit, shit, shit, shit, shit. Stupid, Hallie! You're so stupid!"

Her realtor had put her in touch with a reputable local handyman, but Mr. Carlson from Carlson & Sons Contracting had sent her a quote wildly over her budget, whereas Mr. Smith had promised to work within her means.

Right. All he'd done was sell her a pretty line…and it had cost her ten thousand dollars.

She inhaled sharply, swiping at her burning eyes and stepping into the dilapidated space.

It was a square building with two floors. The bottom floor had an *L*-shaped great room, dining area, and kitchen, and the square inside of the *L* consisted of a private bedroom with a tiny bathroom en suite. The wooden floors were dusty with leaves strewn about, like a window had been left open or leaves had made their way down the chimney, but she saw no evidence of nesting. *The owner of the terrible smells must be living upstairs*, she guessed.

Making her way to the ground-floor bedroom, she opened the door to find the windows closed and unbroken, and the smell musty but tolerable. *Thank God for small mercies.* She'd set up beds for her and Jenny there tonight. It was cold, but she'd brought an electric heater that would make the room toasty in no time. And as soon as the rugs arrived on the moving truck from her apartment, they'd cut the draft in half.

She closed the bedroom door behind her as she backed out of the room and headed for the stairs. They surprisingly sound—creaking with her weight but otherwise strong, which was encouraging. It meant that the old bones of the place were still good.

At the top of the stairs, the bathroom door was open to reveal a floor covered in leaves and debris, an open window over the bathtub the culprit. She closed the window, then the door without further inspection and turned right to look into the bedroom that had been the guest room. Another broken window had ensured that the floor was littered with leaves and twigs. There was animal scat on the floor, and a smell of urine so overwhelming that she covered her nose and mouth, trying not to breathe.

"Disgusting!" she muttered, pulling the door shut with a resounding slam and staring at it like it might pop back open of its own accord. "You're a bastard, Mr. Smith of AAA HandyMan." Shaking her head with disdain, she added, "That's probably not even your damned name!"

Backing away, she turned to the bedroom, which had once been hers, crossing in front of the bathroom and stairs and opening the door to find the setting sun blazing into the room…through a large, jagged hole in the ceiling. A large branch caught in the hole betrayed the culprit of the damage, but animals had done the rest. There were at least two nests in the room, which was littered with debris and scat, the smell even more noxious than the other bedroom. Distracted by the soft sound of chittering, she turned slowly to the left, where she found a hissing raccoon, its yellow eyes focused on hers and back hair straight up.

"Ahhh!" she screamed, jumping back into the dark hallway and pulling the door shut.

She placed her hand over heart and pressed her ear to the door. *Holy Lord!* She heard a frantic scrambling and leapt away from the closed room, wringing her hands.

The place was unlivable.

For anyone *except a desperate single mother at the end of her rope*, the place was unlivable.

Lifting her chin, Hallie headed back down the stairs, through the great room, and out to her car, swiping away overgrowth along the path with her bare hands. Once there, she opened the trunk and pulled out two tarps she packed in the back. She'd intended to use both in their bedroom, under their air mattresses, until the rest of her furniture arrived, but they'd have to make do without them.

Grabbing a toolbox she'd purchased at a hardware store in Boston, she marched back into the house and nailed the tarps over the stairs' opening. She used way more nails than was probably necessary, but when she was finished, the stairs were completely covered and nothing was getting through, headed up or headed down. If anyone needed to get into those rooms for any reason, they could use the outdoor staircase for now.

Once finished, she headed back out to the car and pulled the two air mattresses and air pump from the trunk. It was just *luck* that the downstairs bedroom was habitable, but at this point, she'd take what she could get.

After she had both beds inflated, she returned to the SUV and grabbed two sleeping bags, two duffel bags full of clothes, a lamp, and the heater.

She plugged in the heater and made the beds, thanking God that Jenny was still asleep and wouldn't see the cottage in its dark, creepy glory. When the bedroom was ready, she returned to the car, unsnapped Jenny's harness and gathered her daughter into her arms.

"Mommy?" asked a soft, groggy voice.

Hallie's heart stuttered. It felt like ages since she'd heard her daughter's voice.

"I'm here, baby," she whispered.

"Where's Papa?"

"He's…" Hallie looked down at her daughter's long, dark lashes, closed over her eyes. "He's asleep." *Somewhere.*

"I…miss…him," her daughter sighed, nestling more deeply into her mother's arms.

Hallie's eyes prickled with tears, both for the pain Jenny was suffering, but also for the now-rare show of affection for her. She savored the weight of her child against her chest, walking slowly and carefully through the brush to the front door, through the great room to the bedroom. Settling Jenny on the bed, she reached down to take off her shoes, then set her in the sleeping bag and zipped her up, safe and sound. Jenny sighed, rubbing her head against the pillow before falling into a deep sleep.

Hallie only left the room to close the doors on the SUV and lock the front door of the cottage, then returned to the dark bedroom, pitifully lit with the single bulb from a lamp that had decorated Jenny's room in Boston. Hallie had hoped it would lend some familiarity and cheer to their makeshift bedroom, but all it did was remind her that she'd uprooted her daughter from their home and brought her to this—this—*haunted house* in the middle of nowhere. She closed the door, stuffed towels in the crack between the bottom of the door and the floor, then turned around to look at Jenny.

Maybe I should find a motel? she wondered. But saving money was crucial. Now more than ever. She'd have to call Mr. Carlson in the morning and see when he could get started on repairs. Besides, this room wasn't fancy, but it wasn't dangerous or dirty either. Frankly, it wasn't any better or worse than a cheap motel.

A cheap motel.

She cringed.

"This is my life," she whispered. "My choices are a dilapidated haunted house or a cheap motel. Hallie Gilbert, how did you sink so low?"

Suddenly overwhelmed with loneliness and uncertainty, Hallie withdrew her phone from her back pocket and opened a new text message.

HALLIE: Britt…surprise! Long story, but J and I are staying at Colby for a while. Don't know if you're up here right now, but if yes, pls let me know. Could really use a friendly face in the AM. —H

She stared at the message until she knew it had been sent, then placed her phone on the floor beside her bed. A beam of moonlight shone down on Jenny's little face, and Hallie reached up to wipe away twin tears that coursed down her own cheeks.

"*Please* let this turn out to be a fresh start," she said softly to any higher being that might be listening. "*Please* tell me I'm doing the right thing."

Her answer was the lonely call of a loon on the lake, which only served to amplify her doubts as she kicked off her shoes, turned off the light, and slipped into the sleeping bag beside her daughter.

the plan

(Part 2)

Brittany, Tate, and Chelsea had left ten minutes ago for the nightly campfire, leaving Hallie alone to get ready for her date with Ian.

Hallie didn't have "special" lingerie from Victoria's Secret or anything like that, but she *did* have a matching white-lace bra-and-panty set that she barely ever used because it was too itchy. But for tonight? It was perfect because it was extra pretty. Stripping down in the tiny bathroom, she shaved her legs in the shower, spraying her pulse points with perfume borrowed from Tate. Then she put on her underwear and opened her bureau drawer to decide what to wear.

She chose coral-pink shorts and a white halter top. The white against her tan skin would pop, and the spaghetti straps made the top the sexiest thing she had. Adding pearl studs in her ears and a silver charm bracelet on her wrist, she checked herself in the mirror and smiled. She looked ready; not a super model, by any means, but solidly pretty, which made her grin wider.

She knew that tonight wasn't Ian's first time.

First of all, he had a certain reputation around camp, and Hallie knew all the girls he'd dated in the past three years. And second of all, he'd already told her that he'd been with several girls. But in the same breath, he'd told her that while he hadn't loved any of them, he did love her.

And Hallie believed him.

She knew it in her bones and with every breath she took: she was special to Ian Haven, just as special to him as he was to her.

So even though it wasn't Ian's first time tonight, in a way it was. It was the first time he'd be *making love*. And she wanted it to be perfect for him too.

Checking her watch, Hallie realized that she still had thirty minutes before she needed to leave her cabin for the barn, and she sat down on her bed, jittery with excitement.

Knock. Knock knock.

"Hallie? Baby?"

M—Mom?

Her neck whipped to the side, staring with confusion at the cabin door.

"Honey? It's us!" said her dad's voice. "Where's our birthday girl?"

Jumping up from the bed, she crossed the room and opened the door to find her parents standing on the threshold. *Oh. My. God. My...parents.*

"Mom?" she asked dumbly, blinking at her mother and wondering if she'd somehow missed a message telling her that they were coming up for a visit.

"Sweetheart!" she exclaimed, stepping forward to throw her arms around Hallie, her only child. "Happy birthday!"

Over her mother's shoulder, she looked up at her dad's smiling face. "Surprise!"

"What...What are you doing here?" she asked, feeling utterly bewildered but forcing a smile as she leaned away from her mother, looking back and forth between her parents.

"We're surprising you! We've come to take you for a dinner cruise over on Lake Winnipe—"

"But I've already *had* dinner," she blurted out, her heart racing. *And I have plans. Big plans.*

"Well, no matter," said her father. "You can have a *second* dinner. We have tickets on the nine o'clock cruise!"

"On Winnipesaukee," her mother added. "Remember? We used to go when you were little?"

"Swinging to the oldies!" her dad added with a grin.

"It'll be lots of fun," said her mother. "We need to hurry, though. It's already eight thirty!"

"Hit some traffic on the way up from Boston."

"But…" stuttered Hallie. "I didn't—I mean, I had no idea you were coming."

"Honey!" Her mother scanned Hallie's face. "Are you—Are you unhappy to see us?"

As their only child, Hallie felt the responsibility to be *everything* to her parents, and she couldn't bear to see the hurt that was about to cover her mother's face. Her parents had, apparently, driven up from Boston to surprise her with tickets on a local dinner cruise, and her less-than-warm reception was about to hurt feelings.

She smiled at them. "No! It's—I'm just so surprised!"

"We found Britt at the campfire," said Hallie's father. "She said you were a little under the weather?"

"But you look wonderful, darling!"

"I…" Oh, Lord, what could she say? She was sworn to secrecy where she and Ian were concerned. Not to mention, her parents would be wholly disapproving of their daughter's plans to lose her virginity tonight. She was stuck. One hundred percent stuck. "I…rested. I'm feeling better."

"Great! Grab your things," said her father. "Let's go!"

"Just let me go to the bathroom," she said breathlessly, heading into the little room and closing the door.

Shit, shit, shit. Ian would be waiting. Ian would be in the barn waiting for her, and she had no way to let him know that she couldn't make it. He'd think she decided not to come. That she didn't want to be with him.

I have to let him know. I have to let him know that I can't—

Brittany. Brittany could tell him. But her friends were a ten-minute walk away at the Friday night campfire. If she insisted on going to Britt, it would take twenty minutes. They'd miss the cruise.

Oh, God. What should I do? What can I—

"And that dress? I mean, are you serious with that?"

"Tash! You're the worst!"

Tasha's and Vicky's voices sailed through the vent from the cabin next door, and Hallie darted her eyes up to the metal grating, a desperate idea unfolding in her head.

She flushed the toilet and exited the bathroom, flashing a smile at her parents as she stepped out of the cabin. "I just need to tell my friend Vicky something, okay? One sec!"

Running over to the cabin next door, she knocked, waiting for one of the girls to answer. Finally, Vicky, wearing a nightgown and a blue clay face mask, appeared at the door.

"Hey, Hallie. What's up?"

"Vicky, I—I need a favor. My parents just showed up and—"

Vicky looked over Hallie's shoulder, smiling cheerfully at Hallie's parents, who attended the same country club in Boston as the Lafontaines. "Hey, Mr. and Mrs. Gilbert."

"Hello, Victoria," said Mrs. Gilbert. "How are your

parents?"

"Just fine," she said with a smile.

"Tell them we say hello!" said Hallie's dad.

"Will do!" She slid her eyes to Hallie. "Come in."

Hallie stepped into the cabin, looking to her right to find Tasha lying on her bed, a current copy of Cosmo in her hands.

"Hey, Tasha."

They weren't in public now, as they'd been at the dining hall. Tasha didn't mince words. "What do you want?"

Hallie blinked at the unfriendly note in Tasha's voice, turning her glance back to Vicky, who looked at Hallie curiously. "You said you needed a favor?"

A chill went down Hallie's spine.

Is this a mistake?

Hallie had promised Ian never to tell anyone about their relationship. But the thought of him waiting for her, thinking she'd stood him up on such an important night? She couldn't bear that.

She gulped and blurted out the words: "I'm seeing Ian Haven."

"What?"

"I'm *seeing* him. Dating him."

Vicky's eyes narrowed. "Is that right?"

Hallie nodded. "We've been together since June."

Vicky straightened her expression. "I had no idea."

"We've kept it a secret."

"Apparently," said Tasha, swinging her legs over the side of the bed and joining the other two girls in the doorway. She crossed her arms over her chest, standing behind Vicky like a sentry.

"We have a date—I mean, we're supposed to get together tonight at the barn. But..." She gestured to her cabin. "My parents just surprised me. For my birthday. They're taking me out to dinner so I can't—"

"... meet Ian," said Vicky, nodding as she put the pieces together.

"No," said Hallie. "And I was wondering—hoping—"

"You need one of us to let him know you can't make it."

Hallie nodded. "Exactly. He'll be waiting for me in the barn at nine. Maybe you could...I mean, could one of you...?"

"Of course," said Vicky. If Hallie hadn't been so distracted by everything, she might have noted the hardness around Vicky's eyes, but she didn't. She concentrated on Vicky's smile instead. "I'll do it myself."

"You will?" Hallie sighed with relief. "Thank you!"

"No problem."

She reached for Vicky's hands. "Just—just tell him we can meet tomorrow instead. Same plan. Okay?"

"Will do," said Vicky, sliding a glance to Tasha. "We'll take care of it, right, Tash?"

"Right," she said. "We'll get him the message."

"Thank you!" Hallie said again. "I owe you! Big time!"

"Have a *great* time with your mom and dad," said Vicky, her smile widening just a touch. "It's not every day a girl turns seventeen, huh?"

Hallie nodded, squeezing Vicky's hands once more before turning and heading back out the door.

It would all be okay. As okay as it *could* be.

Hallie wasn't a fool. She didn't trust Vicky and Tasha to

keep her secret—heck, the news that Hallie Gilbert and Ian Haven were a couple would likely be the talk of camp tomorrow—but at least Ian wouldn't be waiting for her. At least he'd know why she wasn't coming. They could deal with the inevitable gossip later.

It'll be okay. It'll all be okay.

She let the door to Pembroke slam closed, walked back over to her parents, and smiled. "Let's go!"

chapter three

"Oh, my God!"

Ian's neck snapped up, and he looked at Rory's girlfriend, Brittany Manion, who was leaning against the kitchen counter, staring down at her phone in surprise.

His brother and *almost*-sister-in-law had returned home to Summerhaven last night and Brittany had made a traditional Irish breakfast for the brothers at Ian's place this morning while a jetlagged Finian slept in.

"Everything okay, *mo mhuirnín*?" asked Rory, who sat at the table across from Ian, looking at his fiancée with concern.

When she glanced up from her phone, she stared hard at Ian before sliding her eyes to Rory.

"Yeah." She cleared her throat, flicking another look at Ian. "Um. Just a text."

"About…?"

There was no point keeping a secret that was bound to come to light sooner or later. She sighed. "Hallie's here."

"Already?" asked Rory.

"Wait. What?" cried Ian, as Brittany's words surged through him like a preternatural force. *Hallie's here. Hallie's here. Hallie's here.* "What do you mean 'Hallie's here'? The wedding's not for a month!"

"I don't have a lot of details," said Brittany, taking a sip from her coffee mug, before looking back at her phone. "I just got a text from her. She sent it last night. She's says she's staying at the cottage for a while."

"Shit," muttered Ian, wincing as he recalled the condition of the cabin when he'd jogged by it yesterday. "At *Colby* Cottage?"

Brittany nodded. "Yep. She said it's a long story, but she and Jenny are staying at Colby and—well, and she said she could use a friendly face if I was around."

Ian pushed away from the kitchen table and stood up in pajamas and bare feet. "Let's go."

"Whoa, there," said Rory, who was still seated with a full plate of eggs in front of him. He shoveled another spoonful into his mouth. "We're eating breakfast."

"Not to mention," said Brittany, moving from the sink to stand behind Rory, across from Ian. "No offense, Ian, but I'm not sure *your* face qualifies as 'friendly.'"

Ian clenched his teeth together, taking a deep breath through his nose and nodding. "Yeah, okay, fine. I'm not her favorite person. But that place is a piece of shit. You haven't seen it."

Brittany cocked her head to the side. "It can't be *that* bad. She's had someone working on it."

"I saw it *yesterday*, and I promise you, no one has been working there," said Ian. "It's—it's *bad*, Britt. She can't—I mean, it's practically falling over. She *can't* live there. Not with a kid. Not at all!"

"Well, she is."

"That's insane," insisted Ian, running a hand through his shoulder-length hair. "It should have been condemned. Doesn't she have somewhere else to go?"

"I didn't tell you how bad it got for her in Boston. But

her ex-husband went back to Brazil, leaving her to clean up his mess. And I mean *mess*." Rory pushed his plate away and pulled Brittany down onto his lap as she continued. "He didn't contest the divorce, thank God, but he left her hundreds of thousands of dollars in debt on joint credit accounts. She had to sell her apartment to pay them off. And then—well, she wasn't left with many options. She could have rented a crappy place in Boston or moved in with her parents in Florida, but then she remembered that Colby was sitting empty up here so—"

"So why didn't she?" demanded Ian.

"Why didn't she *what*?"

"Go to Florida!" he growled.

"Because she's a grown woman. She doesn't want to live with her parents," said Brittany.

"Why didn't she rent a place in Boston?"

"For a lot of reasons. She's a single parent now. Staying in Boston would have meant putting Jenny in childcare while she worked, and she didn't want to do that. Not after everything she's been through." Brittany shrugged, her face concerned. "Jenny stopped—she stopped talking when her father left."

"Fuck," muttered Ian.

Brittany nodded, her eyes severe. "Hallie hasn't exactly had the best luck with men."

Her double meaning wasn't lost on Ian; he was on the list of men who'd hurt Hallie Gilbert. He knew it, and it twisted like a knife in his heart.

That said, however, the place she'd chosen to live was a hovel. Ian flicked a glance at his brother. "Rory! You've *seen* that place. We need to help her."

"I agree," said Rory, staring thoughtfully at Ian, "but upsetting her isn't going to help anyone."

Ian could see the unasked questions in the mossy depths of Rory's eyes: *What happened between you two? And how come I still don't know about it?*

For the same reason then as now, thought Ian.

Because Hallie Gilbert was special. Because she was too special to talk about with Rory and Tierney. Because no matter what had happened between them, the love they'd shared was the best, most intense, most *real* feeling Ian had ever known and keeping it to himself protected it.

"I don't want to upset her," said Ian softly. "I just want to help her."

"I tell you what," said Brittany. "Why don't you drive over there with us...but if she's uncomfortable, you'll go. Deal?"

Ian hated her terms, but they were fair enough, all things considered. "Deal. I'll get changed."

He left the kitchen, heading back to his room where he shut the door and leaned back against it, staring at the ceiling before closing his eyes.

Hallie.

Hallie's back.

His hands fisted by his sides, and his heart thrummed behind his ribs. He'd felt it the moment Brittany had said the words—the instant rush of excitement, of wonder, that the girl he'd loved so desperately was here. So close. Only a mile away.

He wasn't certain why he'd been so bullish with Brittany about joining them at Hallie's place this morning. Maybe because making amends was such an important part of the AA steps, and this was a rare chance to do some small thing to set things to right. But he suspected his motives were deeper and more visceral than that. He wanted to see her. He *needed* to see her.

Pushing away from the door, he crossed his room and opened his bureau drawer, taking out a clean pair of boxers. He pushed down his pajama pants and pulled on the underwear, then grabbed a clean pair of jeans from the second drawer and slipped them on too.

Staring at his reflection in the mirror on the back of his closet door, he considered the changes in his body in the ten years since he'd last seen her. His chest was broad and muscular, though it wasn't intricately cut like a body builder's. He was just strong. Like a bear. Like a truck. Much bigger than he'd been as a teenager, with sinew showing the contours of his arms and a farmer's tan speaking to a summer of hard work.

His eyes were the same, weren't they? Though they'd seen some truly horrible days and muddled nights of dirt and desperation. His lips—the lips she'd kissed a hundred times—they still remembered how hers felt beneath his. Would she recognize him? Would she still hate him?

Reaching up, he touched the skin behind his ear with two fingers. *I left a note for you.*

Inhaling sharply, he grabbed his hair and twisted it into a bun, securing it with a black rubber band on the nape of his neck, then taking a clean T-shirt from the pile next to his jeans. It was black and had a four-leaf clover on the front. Half of the clover was red, white, and blue, and the other half was green, white, and orange. Irish-American. *Just like me.*

His beard was black and bushy, and he reached for the scissors in his desk drawer, snipping off some of the longer growth so it wasn't as unruly. Scowling at himself, he wondered if he should go to the bathroom and shave the damn thing off all together, but he could only imagine what kind of ribbing that would get him from Rory, who'd asked no less than four hundred times for Ian to shave it.

Instead, he turned away from the mirror in a huff, slipping his mammoth feet into a pair of leather flip-flops that had seen better days, and concentrated on quieting the wild flutters in his stomach. After a minute or two, he gave up. The reality was that they weren't going anywhere soon.

Hallie Gilbert was the only true love of Ian's pitiful life.

The one and the only.

And after a decade apart, he was about to see her face again.

***

"Wake up, sleepyhead," said Hallie, pouring Frosted Flakes in two plastic bowls and covering the cereal with whole milk.

Before leaving Boston, she'd packed a cooler with milk, yogurt, cheese, and butter, and two reusable grocery bags with cereal, bread, bottled water, and other essentials. Because they didn't have a kitchen table yet and the entire cottage was covered in a decade's worth of dust, she decided to serve breakfast in bed. Even in the daylight, this room was the least scary of the bunch, although the great room would be much improved with a thorough cleaning and the arrival of their furniture. For now, spiders (and their many webs) still held dominion.

Jenny had slept in a little, allowing Hallie to bring in the cooler and groceries, relieved that the refrigerator was both working, *and* spick-and-span inside.

A week ago, she'd asked the realtor to take the cottage off the market and requested that the electricity be turned back on. It had been beyond humiliating when she heard back from the realtor that the electric company had refused to turn on the power. Hallie's credit score was so low, she'd need to send a money order with six months of utilities prepaid upfront. She'd overnighted the money so that Mr. Smith would have electricity for his tools, but it had stung—and driven home the circumstances of her new life.

She had about forty thousand dollars left in the bank, but she needed a job. Without it, she'd have no insurance and no income. But she'd already decided—until the new year, she was focusing on two things and two things only: one, Jenny. She needed to spend as much time with her daughter as possible, letting her know she was safe and loved and helping her adjust to their "new normal" in New Hampshire. And two, Colby Cottage. Every inch of the old place needed to be cleaned, drafty or broken windows needed to be replaced, and—when she was ready—she needed to deal with the disaster upstairs.

The immediate problem with this plan? When she called Carlson & Sons this morning, Mr. Carlson informed her that he was already booked for the next three weeks. And while she wasn't willing to take a chance on anyone else, Hallie wasn't exactly handy.

That said, necessity was the mother of invention. She was practical, smart, and capable. She had access to the internet via her phone. Until she could get on Mr. Carlson's schedule, she would figure out what she could handle and get started. If memory served, there was a nice little hardware store down in Moultonborough; she and Jenny could take a trip down there later today.

And when January rolled around, Hallie could find a nursing job locally and a good nursery school, day care, or childcare provider for Jenny. It would be okay. *It'll all be okay.*

"Mommy? Where are we?" asked Jenny, blinking at her mother from the sleeping bag.

Hallie savored this sleepy version of her daughter, who still spoke to her. "We're at the lake, baby! Want some breakfast? I have your favorite. Frosted Flakes!"

Rubbing her eyes, Jenny sat up and looked around, her lips tilting down until they were a perfect upside-down *U*. Tears flooded her eyes, and she inhaled raggedly, her little chest heaving against the tears she was so desperately trying to swallow back.

"Oh, Jen. Come here."

Hallie opened her arms, but Jenny didn't budge. She remained in her bed, still wearing the clothes she wore last night in the car, her face a mask of sheer misery. She shook her head back and forth, reached for her plush Luna doll, and hugged it to her chest.

Hallie pursed her lips, blinking back her own tears, and picked up the cereal bowl, offering it to her daughter wordlessly. Jenny smacked it away, causing some of the milk to spill onto her sleeping bag.

"Hey! Don't!" yelled Hallie. She placed the bowl on the dirty wooden floor, frustration and sadness getting the better of her. "You've got to cut me a break, Jen!" Standing up from her own bed, she crossed her arms over her chest. "I know you hate me. I get it. But baby, I'm all you've got!"

Jenny looked up at her mother, her blue eyes sparkling

with tears, then bolted from her bed, running barefoot to the door of the room and throwing it open. Startled, Hallie watched her run before chasing after her.

Luckily, she didn't need to go far. She found Jenny standing in the center of the great room, looking out the dozen windows that faced the lake, which was only about thirty feet away, and at least fifteen of those feet were the great room and deck just beyond.

Jenny was frozen, still clutching Luna. Without looking at her mother, she asked softly, "The lake?"

"The lake," said Hallie, trying not to get her hopes up but encouraged by the fact that Jenny was speaking to her, even if she probably didn't mean to.

"Pretty," Jenny whispered.

"Yeah," said Hallie from behind her. "*Really* pretty. And so much fun in the summer."

The sound of a truck pulling up in front of the cottage distracted her from Jenny, and Hallie turned to look out the little window beside the front door. Probably the realtor coming to check on her, or Brittany. She hoped for the latter. She wasn't kidding about needing to see a friendly face.

"Jen, I think Auntie Britt might be here. Want to say hello?"

Though Jenny adored Brittany, she shook her head silently, captivated by the lake.

"Okay." Hallie looked at the sun sparkling on the water. She'd need to get Jenny swimming lessons as soon as possible. "Jenny, listen to me. You never, ever go near the lake without Mommy or another grown-up, okay? Nod so I know you heard me, baby."

Without looking at Hallie, Jenny nodded. Turning away from her daughter with a sigh, Hallie crossed the room and opened the front door.

"Hallie!"

"Britt!"

In a hot second, Britt had her arms around Hallie in a legendary Brittany Manion–style hug, and Hallie closed her eyes, letting her weary body relax against her friend. She smelled like warm breakfast and expensive body wash, and Hallie breathed deep, relieved for the friendly face, the company, the hug, the love and support when she felt so uncertain and lost. *Thank God for you, Britt.*

"Thanks for c-coming," she said, her voice catching in a small sob as she rested her head on Britt's shoulder.

"Hey…hey, now," crooned Britt, squeezing tighter. "It's okay. It's all going to be okay."

"I k-keep telling myself that," said Hallie, "but my whole life is sh-shit."

She felt Britt giggle against her, and joined her friend, laughing through tears as they clutched each other.

"Don't laugh!" said Hallie.

"I can't help it," said Britt. "You know I laugh when I don't know what to say."

"I know," said Hallie, blinking back more tears and sniffling. "I appreciate you coming, even if it's to take pleasure in my horrible life."

"I take no pleasure in your horrible life," said Britt, "and you may not thank me when…" Her voice trailed off.

"When what?" Hallie opened her eyes, leaning back to look into her friend's face.

"You might not thank me when you see who I

brought."

Hallie lifted her face, looking over Britt's shoulder.

And there they were—side by side, leaning against the truck parked in front of her dilapidated cottage: Rory and Ian Haven. Tall and strong with their trademark jet-black hair and green eyes, Hallie would have known them anywhere, after any length of time.

She looked at Rory first, clean-cut and sheepish, raising a hand in hello, before sliding her eyes—*slowly, so slowly*—to his brother.

Ian.

Irish.

She gasped so softly only Britt would have heard, but it was like all of the air in the whole world had been sucked away from her, and she grappled to fill her lungs as her eyes met his. A small sound escaped from her throat, and Britt squeezed her hard, forcing her to inhale a mouthful of air, but she didn't look away. She couldn't, even if she wanted to.

His hair was pulled back and his black beard was full, but she *saw* him—the boy from her dreams, the shattered love of her life—in his eyes. She knew from Britt that he'd battled addiction in the years since their romance, and she could see it in the lines of his face, but the changes in him captivated her just as much as the familiar.

She had loved him.

She had loved him with a depth and intensity that was *only ever* rivaled by her love for Jenny.

He straightened up as soon as she looked at him, his ivy-green eyes locking like lasers on hers. But as he took a step forward, she recoiled, drawing back from Britt and crossing her arms over her chest protectively.

"The Havens," she murmured, finally dropping Ian's eyes and looking into Brittany's.

"I'm sorry," whispered Britt, her face contorting into a cringe.

In Hallie's peripheral vision she could see the brothers, like statues, by the truck, but she refused to glance at them again. She wouldn't give Ian the satisfaction of seeing her ogling him like a lovesick teenager, and anyway, she didn't trust herself. She'd sworn off men forever, but it was still possible that after all these years, Ian Haven could be her kryptonite. She wouldn't risk finding out by giving him the time of day.

"Yeah, you are," said Hallie, her lips pursed.

"This place is a *wreck*," said Britt, opening her arms to gesture at the overgrown garden and chipped paint. "Didn't you tell me you had someone working on it?"

She shook her head. "I thought I did. Turned out I didn't."

"What do you mean?"

"I didn't think I could afford my realtor's contractor, Mr. Carlson, so I found this guy on the internet. He had decent reviews. He answered my call right away and faxed me a contract that looked legitimate..."

Brittany's face fell. "Oh, hon...what happened?"

Hallie looked over her friend's shoulder at the overgrown front walkway and broken gate, careful not to make eye contact with Ian or Rory. "Nothing. Obviously. I signed the contract, he took my deposit, and now I can't get a hold of him. His number's been disconnected. I checked the internet this morning to find his mailing address, and it's like he never existed."

"Hallie," said Brittany. "I'm so sorry."

"Me too. Just what I needed…more bad luck."

"Let me help."

Brittany Manion was an heiress—she had millions at her disposal. But Hallie had integrity, and part of the reason that Hallie and Britt had stayed friends for so long was that Hallie had never taken advantage of Britt. She'd never asked for a dime, and that's how it was going to stay.

"I can manage."

"How?"

"I'll…do what I can until Mr. Carlson can help me. He's got an opening in his schedule in three weeks."

"*Three weeks?*" said Britt, shaking her head. "No. You *can't* live here. Come and stay with me and Rory."

"In your love nest? No, thanks."

"Okay," said Britt, like she'd almost expected Hallie to refuse her, "then I have another idea."

"Am I going to like it?"

"Probably not."

Hallie took a deep breath. "Tell me."

Brittany looked over her shoulder at the Haven brothers. "Let *them* help."

Absolutely not. "No."

"They'll work for free."

"No."

"Hallie, think of Jenny!"

Hallie winced, flicking a glance at Rory before turning back to her friend. "I don't care if Rory stays, but his brother isn't welcome here."

Her friend scrunched up her nose, then grinned like she had a great idea. "Hey. I brought two folding chairs, a bottle of Prosecco, a jar of fresh-squeezed orange juice, and the biggest, best blueberry muffin you've ever seen for Little Miss Jenny. Forget about them. Let's put the chairs in your crappy living room and have a mimosa. We can talk about my wedding while they take a look around. You won't even know they're here."

Right.

But free help? She simply wasn't in a position to turn it down.

Twitching her lips, Hallie nodded once. "Fine. Thank *Rory* for me."

"Eeeep! Yay! I will." Britt clapped her hands, turned around, and hurried back to the truck while Hallie, without meaning to, lifted her eyes to Ian.

He was watching her intently, with a fierce expression on his face. In return, she narrowed her eyes, then turned her back to him and marched back into her cottage.

Standing just inside the door, she took a deep breath, wishing her heart would stop racing.

He just *had* to be built like some superhuman action hero, complete with impossibly long, black eyelashes and the greenest eyes God had ever made.

"Damn it," she muttered. "You couldn't make him just a little ugly? Some scars? Or a hunchback?" She shook her head. "Maybe he limps. Or has some disgusting flatulence problem." Thinking about Ian walking around with a cloud of fart smell following him made her grin.

"Who's that?"

Hallie looked down to see Jenny at the window, staring at the Haven brothers, who appeared to be getting a lecture from Britt.

"Um, well, that's Auntie Britt, of course, and...see the man in the white shirt? That's Rory. You can call him Uncle Rory after the wedding."

"No, not him. Who's *that*?"

Pressing one stubby finger against the window, Jenny pointed, unmistakably, at Ian.

"Him? Oh. He's no one."

"He's someone, Mommy," Jenny insisted. "He has black hair...like me."

"Yours is dark brown."

"Who is he?" she persisted.

Of course Jenny would notice Ian, *the bane of my existence. Can nothing go my way?*

"His name is Ian. M-Mr. Haven. But really, baby, he's no one. He's just—he's just Rory's brother."

"See? He *is* someone," said Jenny, turning to look up at her mother with a stern expression.

Oh, man. I can't win with you, kid.

"Look!" said Hallie, changing the subject. "Here comes Auntie Britt. She has a muffin for you. Blueberry. Your favorite."

Britt swept into the cottage, carrying two folding chairs and a picnic basket, but dropped all of it to the floor and squatted down to give Jenny a bear hug. And to Hallie's relief, Jenny went willingly into her godmother's arms.

"How's my Jenny?" exclaimed Britt, showering the little girl with kisses. "Oooo! I missed you! I missed you! I missed you! And you smell like sweet sleep. You'll be lucky if I don't take a bite!"

"No, Auntie Britt!" cried Jenny, dodging more kisses and giggling for the first time in days. "I'm not for

71

breakfast!"

Britt chuckled right along with her goddaughter before reaching into the basket and pulling out a muffin the size of Jenny's face. "No...but *this* is!"

"Yum!" yelled Jenny, grabbing the muffin and scampering off to sit with Luna on the porch steps.

"No going near the water!" called Hallie before turning to her friend. "You really are the best."

"Forgive me for bringing Ian here?"

"No," said Hallie, her smile slipping as she picked up the two folding chairs and carried them to the center of the empty great room. "But I'm grateful for any help or advice Rory can give."

Britt gave her friend the side eye. "You know...I mean, you know Ian lives here, right? Next door? At Summerhaven. You might—" She shrugged. "—bump into him now and then."

"Not if I don't want to," said Hallie, unfolding the chairs. "He can live wherever he wants, Britt. It's none of my business, and I don't care."

"*Much*," murmured Britt from behind her.

Hallie chose to ignore her friend's comment. Sure, she'd lost a bit of her composure coming face-to-face with Ian after ten years, but now that their first meeting was out of the way, she'd be fine. He was no one to her, just as she'd said to Jenny.

They sat down side by side and Britt took out two champagne glasses, filling each with half wine and half juice. Handing one to Hallie, she asked, "What should we toast to?"

"Something happy," said Hallie. "How about...your

wedding!"

Britt beamed back at her, taking a teeny sip before putting her glass on the floor. "That's all I can have."

"But you love—Oh, my God! Wait! Are you—Are you—"

Britt nodded, her smile blinding. "Yep. Knocked up."

"Brittany! Why didn't you tell me?"

She shrugged. "I don't know. I'm getting married again. Baby on the way. New company Rory and I are starting together. My life…"

"…is good," said Hallie.

"And yours…"

"…sucks," said Hallie with a self-deprecating chuckle. "But I'm *happy* for you." She reached for Britt's hand and squeezed it. "You don't have to keep things from me."

"I know," said Britt, reaching up to wipe away tears. "But I'm so happy, and you've been so sad. I didn't want to add to your—"

"Stop! I *need* to hear about good things. I swear! It gives me hope in a sea of despair," she said.

"Speaking of despair…have you heard from Sergio?"

Hallie shook her head. "Nope. I think I told you that I talked to Catina? His sister? Yeah. That's about as close as I've gotten to talking to him. At least he sent back the divorce papers quickly. I half expected him to try to get more money out of me before signing."

"Such an asshole!" exclaimed Britt. "How's Jenny doing? She seems okay."

Hallie took another sip of her drink. "Yeah? Maybe for you, but not for me. She hates me."

"She's just sad. So much change, so quickly," said Britt.

"She'll come around."

"Her doctor said that I should find a way for Jen and Sergio to connect. Skype or something. I just don't know if I can bear it."

"Maybe it would be a good job for a doting godmother?" Britt squeezed Hallie's hand before letting it go. "If you won't take my money, you'll have to take this instead. Give me Catina's contact info. I'll track him down and set up a time for them to Skype. And I can sit with Jenny while she talks to him to make sure everything goes okay."

"You'd do that?" asked Hallie. "Are you sure?"

"Absolutely. In fact, *please* let me do it. I'd feel better if I could help."

Hallie nodded, saying a silent prayer of thanks for Brittany's friendship. "You've always been there for me."

"Well, I love you, silly."

Hallie sniffled back some tears before shifting her glance to the porch, but Jenny, who'd been sitting on the steps a moment ago eating her muffin, had disappeared.

"Where's Jenny?" she said, placing her glass on the floor and standing up to get a better view of the porch and lake beyond. "Britt, did you see where she went?"

"N-No. I…she was just there, wasn't she?"

"Jenny!" cried Hallie, crossing through the porch and stepping down onto the lawn. "Jenny? Jenny!" She turned to her friend as panic quickly set in. "Britt, she doesn't know how to swim!"

"Don't worry. She's only been gone for a minute." Britt called from the porch steps. "Jenny? Where are you?"

"I'm going to the lake," Hallie yelled over her shoulder.

"Will you check the front?"

Running toward the dock and the small, caving-in boathouse, Hallie felt a sharp pang of terror. What if she'd fallen into the lake? Or wandered into the woods? There were bears and maybe wolves in these north country woods. *Oh, God. Please, please let my baby be okay.*

"Jenny? Jenny!" she called. "Where are you?"

A little face peeked out from the boathouse entrance. "Right here."

"Jenny!" Hallie shrieked, racing down the splintered planking of the dock to the boathouse and swooping her child into her arms. "I was *worried.* Baby, I told you not to go near the lake without a—"

"But there *was* a growed-up here," said Jenny.

"Sorry we scared you," said a masculine voice.

Hallie lifted her eyes from Jenny to find Ian Haven standing in the boathouse doorway.

"*You,*" she snarled.

"Mommy, lemme go!"

"What the hell were *you* doing with her?" Hallie demanded, trying to hold a wiggling Jenny closer.

Ian raised his hands palms-up in a pacifying gesture. "Nothing. She must have seen me checking out the boathouse and wandered down to—"

"Stay away from her!" Hallie cried. "From *us!*"

"Stop, Mommy! Down!"

The crease between Ian's eyes deepened as he looked back and forth between raging Hallie and her howling, squirming daughter.

"Hey," he said, the familiar rumble of his voice making the hairs on Hallie's arms stand up, "I didn't mean any harm.

75

I was just checking out the beams in the boathouse. I turned around and there she was. I promise you—"

"Don't you *dare* make me any promises!" hissed Hallie. "You listen to me: I don't want you *near* my daughter! Do you understand me? If you so much as—"

"Stop yelling at him!" Jenny screamed at her mother, the pitch so high and blood-curdling, Hallie stopped speaking midsentence, blinking at her daughter. "You're *yelling*," Jenny sobbed, still struggling to get away from Hallie. "Like you yelled at my papa and made him leave! I hate you! I hate you!"

Hallie gasped in pain at the furious words, her arms loosening reflexively. Jenny used the opportunity to slide down her mother's body and scurry back toward the house with Luna clutched tightly to her chest. The porch door slammed shut, and Hallie turned to Ian, so furious she didn't trust whatever would come out of her mouth next.

Ian put his hands on his hips, shaking his head back and forth. "This place is a mess. You're in *way* over your head, Halcyon."

When people got shot on TV in slow motion, you saw them recoil inward, almost folding into themselves from the shock and pressure of the bullet. That's how it felt to hear Ian Haven call her "Halcyon."

He was the only man in her life who'd ever used her full first name, and only then when they were…when they were…*together.*

Kiss me, Halcyon.

Halcyon, I love you.

She stared at his lips, her memories rushing back like an assault: his full lips claiming hers, the heat of them sliding down the column of her throat, the way they pursed around the puckered buds of her nipples then skimmed lower to—to—

She gasped at the vividness of the unwanted memory, lifting her furious eyes to his and saying, "Stay. Away. From. Me."

Then she turned away from him and ran back up to the house to check on her daughter.

chapter four

Well, fuck.

Yesterday sure hadn't gone too well.

Ian stared at the pad of yellow paper sitting in front of him on the kitchen table, which listed everything that needed fixing at Colby Cottage.

It was way worse than he and Rory had originally thought.

Plumbing.

Her water was a brownish color, which either meant that her well was running dry, and therefore dredging up mud, or her pipes were completely rusted. Either way, it would need to be dealt with sooner than later or she and her daughter would be buying bottled water and trying to bathe in a freezing lake.

Glass.

Ian and Rory had counted six broken windowpanes upstairs and two downstairs. All would need to be replaced, especially before the first snow, which would arrive in four to six weeks.

Roof.

While the roof was surprisingly sound over most of the cottage, a large limb had crashed through the roof into one of the upstairs bedrooms at some point, and it would need to be removed so that the roof could be patched and reshingled.

Wildlife.

Rory had almost lost his shit when they entered one of the bedrooms to find a family of raccoons living there. While Ian had hooted with laughter at the time, the fact remained that the animals needed to be trapped and returned to the woods as soon as possible. They'd also found a bird's nest in the upstairs bathtub and mice droppings just about everywhere, which meant a trip to the hardware store in Moultonborough for traps.

Trees.

The trees around the cottage were too close and way overgrown. One had already fallen through the roof in a storm, and if she didn't remove some of the others, or at least cut them back, it was going to happen again.

The dock and boathouse, unfortunately, were unsalvageable. When she was ready, Ian could recommend a local carpenter to rebuild one or both. But the existing structures would need to be pulled out, broken down into manageable pieces and carried to a dumpster.

He picked up the pencil and made a note: *Rent dumpster.*

The front garden, with its vines, branches and thorny roses, was a hazard, though one that could—mostly—wait until spring. For now, he'd clear the front path with a chainsaw and rake, and deal with making it pretty at a later date.

And if that stubborn woman intended to spend all winter in that goddamned deathtrap, it needed to be winterized. That meant a shit ton of new insulation and a chimney sweep to clean out and inspect the hundred-year-old chimney. Not to mention, he'd noticed a funny odor when they'd tested the baseboard heat. Could be a family of mice living—or dead—inside of it. That might need some maintenance too.

Honestly? She'd be better off knocking the whole thing over and rebuilding, but it didn't appear that option was available to her.

Nor did it appear she was at all interested in free help.

At least…not if it was coming from him.

He put down his pencil and raised a cup of coffee to his lips, taking a sip of the hot, bitter brew.

Hot and bitter.

Much like Halcyon.

With her dirty-blonde hair and bright-blue eyes, he'd have known her anywhere, and his heart had leapt with something that felt very much like joy when he'd laid eyes on her again. Beautiful? Absolutely. But ten years and one child later? Scorching hot to boot. She'd only gotten more stunning with time, losing her slightly coltish gait and moving her body like she was used to it now.

Damn, but he'd like to feel that body moving beside his.

No. Fuck, Ian. No. She can barely look at you.

Thoughts like that weren't much use when the object of them still hated your guts.

After she'd freaked out at him on the dock, she hadn't come out of the house again, so Brittany had acted as intermediary between them to arrange for Ian to help her. Unfortunately, Rory wouldn't have a lot of time to help out with his wedding fast approaching and his new business just getting off the ground. But Ian could make time. With Doug and Finian handling the off-season maintenance at Summerhaven, he could concentrate on Colby Cottage for the next few weeks and get it in some sort of livable shape before winter set in.

That is, if she'd let him.

Brittany had disappeared inside the house for a good half hour, emerging only to say that Hallie would accept Ian's help if—*and only if*—he agreed to two conditions:

1. Hallie insisted on paying him. She couldn't afford much, and frankly, Ian didn't want a dime, but she said she wouldn't accept his help unless the relationship between them was strictly business.

2. Along the same lines, she asked that they avoid each other as much as possible. If he'd leave weekly invoices in her mailbox, she'd pay them. Otherwise, she hoped they'd have little cause for interaction.

He'd had half a mind to barge back into her shithole cottage and tell her to shove her conditions where the sun didn't shine.

However, he'd remembered her eyes when she'd told him he couldn't make her promises.

Fuck his life, but she'd looked beautiful, blazing with anger.

But she'd also looked...broken.

And man, but Ian hated to see it.

Reminding himself that she'd just been through a horrible divorce, lost her home, moved herself to an almost-uninhabitable summer cottage, and been duped out of her deposit by a piece-of-shit con man, the last thing she needed was shit from him. So he'd swallowed his comments, and pride, and nodded at Brittany, saying that she'd have a "damned invoice" in her mailbox on Friday.

"Mornin'."

Ian looked up to see Finian standing in the kitchen doorway, wearing boxers and a T-shirt and scratching his balls like it was a medal-round event.

"Do you mind?" Ian asked, grimacing.

Finian gave him a look. "What? Yer balls don't itch in the mornin'?"

"Might be you should get that checked out," said Ian.

"*Dúil mo bod*," said Finian. *Suck my dick.*

"*Dún do bheal*," answered Ian. *Shut up.*

Fin sauntered over to the counter, took a cup from the cupboard over the sink and poured himself a cup of black coffee. "I really prefer tea."

"Then bloody well make some," said Ian.

He hadn't seen Finian in a couple of years, and his cousin seemed more coarse and bullish than he'd been as a teenager. But then, he'd skipped college to make money, and he'd been working at a garage in Dublin over the past five or six years. By all accounts, he knew his way around every nook and cranny of an engine, but it was manual work with only other men for company. And it hadn't done a thing to soften his manners.

He took a loud sip of coffee, smacking his lips before belching.

"What a shock no girl's snapped you up yet."

"Eh. Girls is trouble," said Finian. "Had a mot. Broke it off before I come here."

"Bet the tides wouldn't take her out," said Ian.

"Lick me bag," suggested Fin, clutching at his crotch.

Ian chuckled, because crudity aside, his cousin was pretty damn amusing. "So this girl. She had a name?"

"Yeah. Cindy."

"Cindy?"

"Cynthia."

"Okay. And what happened with Cynthia?"

"Bleedin' weapon." Finian sat back in his chair and ran a hand through his unruly light-brown hair. "Nothin'. D'ye have anythin' for breakfast?"

Ian knew that a "weapon" was slang for a woman who was disagreeable, but how or why this Cynthia turned out to be a weapon was for Fin to tell. It didn't appear that he planned to, and frankly, Ian was too preoccupied with a woman of his own to pursue the matter.

"Cereal in the cabinet over the microwave. Milk, eggs, and bread in the fridge. Help yourself."

Finian got up to inspect Ian's cereal options, looking over his shoulder to ask, "What are we up to today?"

"You and Doug are going to get the rest of the docks out of the lake. Haul 'em up on the shore, into the brush, then cover 'em with plastic tarps."

"Great," said Fin, pouring Cheerios into a bowl. "Hangin' out in a freezin' lake all day. My balls thank you."

"Your balls aren't my concern."

"Right," said Fin, opening the fridge and bending over to look for milk. "*Your* concern is some slag and her git over on the—"

Ian reached for the saltshaker and launched it at his cousin, hitting him squarely in the ass.

"What the fuck?" demanded Fin with a yelp, turning around to look at Ian with narrowed eyes.

"You won't talk about them like that."

"Christ!"

Ian lifted the peppershaker, aiming it at Finian's

precious balls. "I mean it."

His cousin covered his crotch with his hands. "Fine. Jaysus, but you're feckin' touchy, Ian."

"Nah. Just making a point. You'll talk about her with respect or not at all." He rolled the glass shaker back and forth between his fingers. "We good?"

"Yeah. Fine," said Fin, pouring the milk and adding, "*Craiceáilte.*"

Ian took a deep breath and sighed as his cousin rejoined him at the table with his bowl of cereal.

"No, I'm not crazy. And yeah, I'll be looking after Hallie's cottage for the next few weeks. You, me, and Doug will meet in the mornings to go over what I need you two to do, and we'll touch base again at the end of the day."

"With all due respect," said Fin, his voice thick with sarcasm, "what's the deal with you and the—*Hallie?*"

Ian blew out a long breath. "I knew her a long time ago."

"She fucked you over, then?"

Ian picked up the peppershaker and threw it at his cousin's head, trying not to laugh when it bounced off Finian's temple and elicited a yelp from his cousin. "*Damnú air!*"

"I warned you."

Finian rubbed the side of his head, frowning at Ian before taking a bite of Cheerios. "Please, sir, Mr. Haven, sir. What happened with you and the honorable Miss Hallie once upon a time?"

Ian flashed back to an evening—one of many—they'd spent together long ago. He'd rowed her out to the raft at Loon Island in a canoe. Once there, they'd tied the boat to a raft and laid down on their backs, side by side, staring up at the dark sky, at the millions of stars overhead.

It was one of their earlier dates, and he'd reached down for her hand, touching her fingers gingerly, waiting for a sign that holding them would be okay. Her fingers had entwined with his, and happiness had sluiced through his body like liquid fire, warming him from the inside out.

"Halcyon," he'd whispered into the darkness.

"Hmm?"

"I'm crazy about you," he'd said softly, the words sacred because they'd never been said.

"Me too," she said, her fingers adjusting so that their palms were flush. "Me too, Irish."

Suddenly his mind changed gears without warning and the sound of her words from yesterday echoed in his mind like a slap across his cheek:

Stay. Away. From. Me.

He cleared his throat, shaking his head. "Nothing good."

"So why do you want to help her so bad?"

"Because..." He drank the last of his coffee, then stood up to place the mug in the sink. "You know I'm an alcoholic, right?"

"Everyone's an alcoholic," said his Irish cousin matter-of-factly. "Just different degrees."

"Well, I'm a bad one."

"Yeah. Okay. So?"

"So part of AA is making amends."

"Amends."

"Righting past wrongs."

"I'm not a bloody eejit. I know what 'amends' is."

"You asked why I want to help her, and that's the best answer I can give you." Ian leaned against the sink. "I'm making amends."

"By fixin' her shit-heap house?"

Ian nodded. "Yep. By fixing her shit-heap house."

"Musta been bad...whatever you did to her."

"Yeah. It was," said Ian, reaching up to grab his chin with his thumb and forefinger, and rubbing his beard. He winced at the memory of her face yesterday. *It was bad enough, in fact, to make her hate me for life.*

"Well...go then," said Finian. "My balls'll thank ya kindly for leavin'."

"Mrs. Toffle downstairs has a to-do list for you and Doug. Touch base with her by eight o'clock, okay?"

Finian nodded before plunging his spoon back into his cereal. "Yeah. We'll be grand. Go, now."

Ian headed out of the room, but at the last minute, he turned around. "Hey. What happened between you and...Cynthia?"

"Go fuck yourself. That's what happened," said Finian amicably, before giving Ian the finger and continuing his breakfast.

***

Since the incident on the dock with Ian yesterday, Jenny had doubled down on not speaking to her mother. No matter what Hallie had said or done for the rest of the day, Jenny wouldn't utter a word—just looked at Hallie with mistrust and fury, which hurt Hallie to the quick.

You're yelling! Like you yelled at my papa and made him leave! I hate you! I hate you!

As Hallie lay awake for hours last night, forbidding

herself from thinking about the broad, muscular wall of Ian Haven's chest, she made an effort to see things through her daughter's eyes.

Jenny was too young to understand that charming Sergio had cheated on her mother. Too young to understand that he'd run up unimaginable debts that had killed their comfortable lifestyle. She was too little to see that once things had gotten really bad, Sergio had left them. Voluntarily. Of his own free, cowardly will.

That first, terrible evening in February, after Hallie had picked up the antibiotics she needed to remedy the STD she'd been given, yes, she'd screamed at Sergio. She'd called him names and yelled terrible things, and eventually demanded that he leave.

That's what Jenny had seen and heard: her mother driving her father away. Cause and effect. Hallie had yelled. Sergio had left. It was black and white to a four-year-old child. No room for gray.

Seeing Hallie yell at Ian had triggered something in Jenny: a flashback to that awful night. But it made Hallie wonder if there wasn't room—here and now—to help Jenny understand the entire picture, just a little better. She wanted Jenny to understand so goddamned much, in fact, she was willing to allow Ian Haven—a man she swore she'd never speak to again as long as she lived—near her, if he could help further Hallie's cause.

It wasn't Brittany's cajoling that had made Hallie give in to Ian's help. It was the fact that if Jenny never saw Ian again, it would mean she was right: Mommy drove Mr. Haven away, just like Papa. But if Ian came back today to work on Colby Cottage? Maybe it would plant a seed of doubt in Jenny's mind. Mommy yelling at Mr. Haven *didn't* drive him away. *He* came back.

Flicking a glance at the clock on the kitchen wall, she realized it was seven fifty-five and her heart skipped a beat, stuttering before resuming a faster pace. Part of that reaction was due to the fact that she was still affected by Ian, no matter how much she despised him…but the other part was excited, that maybe—with Ian's unwitting help—Hallie could reconnect with her daughter today.

As she rinsed their cereal bowls in copper-colored water that, frankly, troubled her a little, Hallie glanced over at Jenny, who was watching *Doc McStuffins* on Hallie's iPad at the kitchen table.

"Hey, Jenny," she said, trying to sound casual. "Did I tell you that Mr. Haven is coming over this morning? Yep. He is. He should be here any minute."

She watched Jenny's face whip up, her eyes wide and animated, a smile about to spread across her face before she purposely stopped it and switched gears to scowl at her mother instead. Hallie could almost hear her daughter's inner thoughts: *We'll see about that, you homewrecker.*

"We made a really good dent in the cleaning yesterday, didn't we? The living room has no more spiders, the floors down here have all been swept and scrubbed, and we're ready for our furniture to arrive later today. But we need help with some of the bigger stuff, don't we? Yep. We do. I don't know how to fix windows or roofs. So Mr. Haven said he'd help us. Nice, right? Even though Mommy yelled at him, he's still coming back. He knows that mommies get mad sometimes. He's tough enough that it won't make him run away." …*unlike other people we both know.*

Part of her hated that she was singing Ian's praises like this, but in fairness, she really *wasn't*. She was using him for her own means, the same way he'd probably used her that whole summer.

As if on cue, she heard the hum of an engine drawing closer, the crunch of tires over a gravel-and-dirt road, and ignoring the pitter-patter of her own traitorous heart, she slid a glance to Jenny, who reached forward to shut off her show. She stood up at the table, looking at her mother *without* scowling, then grabbed Luna and ran to the front door.

"Jenny, wait!" said Hallie, drying her hands on a paper towel and following her daughter.

But Jenny had already opened it and was standing in the doorway, waving at Ian, who parked his truck and waved back through the open passenger-side window.

"Morning, Jenny."

"Mr. Haven!" she cried, jumping up and down. "You came back!"

Hallie's heart clutched.

And as much as she hated to admit it, in that moment, something happened that she never, ever could have anticipated: in that split second, she was *grateful* to Ian Haven. Grateful to the boy who'd broken her heart. Grateful for his shaggy black hair and big body pulling up in front of her cottage. She shook her head in bemusement. *Life never ceases to amaze.*

Ian stepped from the truck, walking around the hood and stopping in front of the one-hinged gate. "Morning, Halcyon."

She tightened her lips.

Gratitude or not, this *was* Ian Haven.

But just as she was about to turn and march back into the house without greeting him, Jenny's head turned, her eyes locking with her mother's and her expression begging her mother to welcome Ian.

Hallie sighed. "Good morning, Ian."

The sides of Ian's mouth twitched in a tiny victory as he looked at the cottage before glancing back to the mother-and-daughter pair.

"Thought I'd start by getting those critters out of the upstairs rooms, and get the windows covered with tarps. I'll take some measurements and then head down to the hardware store in Moultonborough to order replacements. Sound good to you?"

Jenny nodded her head vigorously. "Can I help you?"

"N-no, baby. Mr. Haven needs to—"

"Jenny," said Ian, pivoting to grab a metal trap from the bed of his truck and holding it up. "I tell you what...I'm going to go upstairs to catch the raccoons right now. If you'll get dressed and put on some sneakers, you can help me release them back into the woods."

"Yes!" said Jenny, turning to run past Hallie and go get dressed.

"Oh, but wait!" said Ian, his voice stopping her. "You'll have to ask your mom's permission first. Can't help me with anything unless your mom says it's okay. That's a rule whenever I'm here working, okay? Mom's permission comes first."

Jenny froze in place, and Hallie could *feel* her daughter's dilemma: her desperate desire to spend time with Ian would come at the price of voluntarily speaking to her mother. She bunched up her little shoulders, looked up at Hallie slowly and blinked.

Hallie raised her eyebrows, staring down at her daughter, determined not to be the one to break the silence.

"Mommy?"

"Yes, Jenny?"

"Can I?"

"Can you what, baby?"

"Can I help Mr. Haven with the raccoons?"

Hallie raised her chin and tapped it twice. "Hmm. I'm pretty sure that question was missing something important."

Jenny's brows knitted together in consternation for a moment before a triumphant look replaced it. "Can I *please* help Mr. Haven with the raccoons?"

"Yes," said Hallie, grinning at her. "You can. Go choose an outfit."

"Thank you!" cried Jenny, racing past her mother to get dressed…and leaving Hallie and Ian alone.

He stood beside the broken gate, the metal cage in his hand, staring at her. And she leaned against the battered cottage doorway, staring back. Between them were tangled rose vines barbed with sharp thorns, unruly and angry.

Hallie took a deep breath and held it, her eyes still locked on his.

What in the world do you say to the man who was once your whole world, your first love; the boy to whom you were going to joyfully surrender your virginity? What do you say to him ten years after he betrayed you, flaying your soul, pulverizing your heart? What do you say when he has clearly noted the friction between you and your daughter and offered—of his own free will—some small gesture to help? Do you start to trust him? Do you soften toward him, even though you desperately want to stay hard?

"Don't overthink it, Halcyon," he said softly, his baritone rich and familiar in her ears and, though she didn't want to admit it...welcome.

"I'm not."

"Yes," he said, with a very small smile, still stationed by the broken gate. "You are."

"I don't like you being here."

"I know."

"I really don't want you near me...or her."

"I know that too."

"But she's been through so much, and she seems to—I don't know...*like* you."

"I'm likable," said Ian, his eyes bright as emeralds in the sun.

"Yes," she said sadly. "You always were."

"We don't have to be friends," said Ian. "We could just—"

Her stomach tightened. Her heart raced.

"We *can't* be friends," she blurted out. "We can't be *anything*."

He stared at her hard, then nodded once, his eyes losing most of their sparkle. "Fair enough."

Hallie cleared her throat, wishing they could go back in time, wishing they could make different choices and choose each other.

"Your room's okay?" asked Ian.

She nodded. "It's livable."

"Then I guess I'll tackle what's not." Ian sighed, then gestured to the outdoor stairs with his chin. "I'm going to go catch the 'coons. I'm thinking there's two or three—maybe a mother and two kits—and they should be asleep now that it's daytime. Did you hear them last night?"

She nodded. "They were scrambling around up there."

"Probably using the tree branches poking through the roof to get out at night to eat. You gotta take down some of these trees. They're too close to the house."

Hallie nodded. She didn't know what else to say and wanted to go back inside the house. It was awkward standing here, a riot of confusing, conflicting emotions as she and Ian talked about—of all things—raccoons and trees.

"Anyway, um, I guess I'll get to it," he said, giving her a grim half smile before heading around the house to the outside stairs and leaving Hallie alone.

She put her hands on her hips and huffed in frustration, tears burning her eyes as she watched him walk away. Where her tears came from, she had no idea. Their exchange had been civil enough—no raised voices, no old recriminations. And yet, everything about it made her feel so empty, so hollow and hopeless, so incredibly sad.

Turning away from the door, she closed it behind her with a resounding click and went to go help Jenny get dressed.

The plan

(Part 3)

After building the campfire for "Sing-Along and S'mores," a Friday night tradition at Summerhaven, Ian went home to get ready for his date with Hallie.

Showering off a day's worth of sweat, he also shaved extra close so he wouldn't scratch her sensitive skin. He borrowed a little of his father's aftershave and clapped it on his cheeks, hoping Hallie would like the smell.

Ian dressed casually, but with care, in a pair of khaki shorts and a blue button-down shirt, rolled at the cuffs. His navy-blue belt had the Summerhaven logo embroidered on it. On his right wrist, he wore the watch his parents had given him for high school graduation, and on his left, he wore a white braided rope bracelet, the type favored by sailors. Hallie liked it; she often touched it while they talked, her fingers tracing the braids and occasionally slipping to his skin, the fleeting touch sending good shivers down Ian's spine.

He'd already pre-hidden the picnic basket in the loft of the barn, and now he checked his watch. With flowers to pick and candles to light, he needed to get moving.

Leaving a note for his parents that he was going to a party in nearby Weirs Beach and might stay overnight at a friend's house, he headed out into the evening, butterflies filling his stomach as he imagined spending a night with Hallie for the first time.

He'd been with other girls, sure, but Ian had never been in love. Everything was different where Hallie was concerned, and more than anything, he wanted tonight to be special—no, *perfect*—for her. So he went over some ground rules for himself on his quiet walk to the barn:

Go slow.

Be gentle.

Put her needs first.

Make sure you ask.

Make sure that she says yes to everything.

Stop if she says "stop."

It's not about you; it's all about her.

It's your responsibility to make this the best night of her life.

He stopped on the way and picked some yellow and blue irises, her favorite, bunching them in his sweating hand before continuing.

By the time he arrived at the barn, the butterflies in his abdomen had turned into some sort of large bird—eagles, maybe—and he rubbed a hand over his queasy stomach. He took a deep breath, which filled his lungs but didn't mitigate the uncomfortable feeling.

"Man up," he muttered to himself, opening the door to the dark barn. He turned on a light, grabbed the broom just inside the door and headed up the stairs to the loft.

Why was he so...so...*nervous?*

It was partially emotional—he loved her and wanted tonight to be the best night of her life, which placed an enormous amount of pressure on his young, broad shoulders. Compounding his nerves was that—despite all his good intentions—Ian was uncertain about his talent as a lover.

Yes, he'd slept with four girls before Hallie—a girl from his high school whom he'd dated for most of his junior year, a girl who came to camp two summers ago, and two more girls from last summer—but the truth was that Ian was only seventeen, and while he had more experience than Hallie, with the exception of Mina, his high school girlfriend, the others had been one-night stands.

And frankly, things between him and Mina had been, well, pretty lackluster. They'd get together, barely talk, fuck for five minutes, she'd moan "Oh" once or twice, he'd come, they'd watch TV for an hour, then say good-bye. Not that he hadn't enjoyed it—he *had*, but he hadn't gained some amazing insight about the wants and needs of women either. And the girl last summer? The girl he'd slept with once? She'd actually *stopped* things before they really got going, wincing in pain and calling him "way too big."

What if that happened with Hallie?

What if he was "way too big" and hurt her?

Fuck!

He didn't want to mess up tonight. He really, really didn't. He didn't want to let Hallie down.

Using the broom, he swept the floor carefully, leaving all the debris in one corner since he didn't have a dustpan. Then he pulled the basket from underneath the garbage bag where he'd hidden it and withdrew a fleecy blanket. He spread it on the wooden planks, straightening it carefully.

Next came the candles, scented like vanilla and fir trees—a little of him and a little of her—and he placed them carefully around the blanket with the irises. He'd used ice packs to keep the wine cold, and even though they were mostly melted now, the bottles were still cool.

Ian wasn't a drinker, really. He'd had a sip of champagne on New Year's Eve with his brother and sister, but his maternal grandfather had waged a lifelong battle against the bottle back in Ireland, and Ian's mother was a conservative drinker as a result. She had made it clear to her boys and girl that if she caught them coming home drunk, she'd take the spoon to their arses and redden them right.

Still, it was Hallie's birthday tonight, and it felt celebratory—and mature—to offer her wine. He'd brought two bottles because one was called Riesling and one was called Chardonnay and he didn't know which one she'd like. He figured it was best that she have a choice.

He set up the two bottles and glasses in one corner of the blanket, then checked his watch.

8:50 p.m.

She'll be here any minute.

He tossed the other blanket loosely to the side of the one on the floor in case she wanted it—for modesty or warmth—then tucked two condoms under the blanket. He placed her favorite cookies, Scottish shortbread, beside the glasses on a small flowered plate he'd stolen from his mother, then reached into his back pocket for a lighter.

As he lit the candles, he thought of the final object sitting in the bottom of the picnic basket: in a small, white ring box was a promise ring.

Made of sterling silver, it held a small ruby, Hallie's birthstone, and a small emerald for Ian. He'd ordered it two weeks ago from the Kay Jewelers up in North Conway, and he'd chuckled softly when he picked it up. It looked like a Christmas ring rather than a promise ring, but maybe that was okay too. He was hoping that when Hallie returned to

Boston at Christmastime, they'd still be together and make plans to see each other again. Maybe Christmas colors would help remind her of his love during the long months apart.

Ian's reality was that everything stopped with Halcyon Gilbert.

No woman had ever come close to her spot in his heart, and he was certain that no woman ever could. And while he knew they were too young to become engaged, tonight—especially tonight when she was giving him something so precious—he wanted to be certain that she knew what she meant to him. The ring was a symbol of his promise to her and for them: that no matter what, he wanted to be with her forever, even if they'd need to wait a few years for forever to formally begin.

When the candles were lit and the ring box was open, he turned off the light downstairs, sat down on the wooden planks of the old barn loft and waited.

She'll be here any minute.

Any minute.

Any second.

Except…she wasn't.

By nine fifteen, she *still* hadn't arrived, and Ian's nerves, which had been growing steadily all day, were hitting a pretty high pitch.

Maybe she got held up.

Maybe my dad saw her leaving her cabin and ushered her to the campfire instead. In that case, she won't arrive until a little after ten.

Or maybe she's not—

No. She's coming. She's definitely coming.

His hands were sweating, and he wiped them on his shorts, leaving two handprints. Great. So much for being the cool, calm, and collected one of the two.

He walked down the barn stairs, peeking out the window but careful not to call attention to himself. If his mother or one of the other camp employees saw him, his plans would be busted wide open, leading to embarrassment and punishment. And worse still, possible separation.

She's just a little late. You need to calm down.

Heading back upstairs, Ian nodded at the setup he'd so lovingly created, his glance lingering on the unopened bottle of Riesling.

Everyone knew that alcohol "took the edge off," right?

And right here, right now, Ian needed a little help with his own, personal edge. Untwisting the cap, he poured himself a glass and lifted it to his lips, letting the sweet, delicious wine fill his mouth and sluice down his throat. Unaware of how thirsty he was, he immediately poured himself another full glass and drank that one too.

It was like ginger ale or Sprite—but with a little kick and an aftertaste of honey. As he finished the second glass, he looked at his watch again.

Nine twenty-five.

Did she decide not to come, after all?

No. No. The campfire. My father probably made her go to the campfire.

But she was going to say she had her period. My dad wouldn't have made her go.

So why isn't she here yet?

Maybe she isn't coming.

The butterflies immediately returned with a vengeance, and Ian's eyes slipped to the bottle again. He poured himself a third glass, trying to sip it this time, but more and more agitated by his thoughts.

Did I miss something today at the dining hall?

She seemed fine, smiling at me and nodding about coming tonight.

But should I go check and see if she left a note canceling? No. No. Someone could see me. How would I explain why I'm not in Weirs Beach?

Does she have her period? Maybe that's why she isn't coming?

No. Fuck. You're getting confused, Ian. She doesn't have *her period. She was just going to* say *that if the need arose.*

Without realizing it, he'd finished the third glass of wine, and he checked his watch again.

Nine forty-five.

Fuck.

He poured the rest of the bottle into his waiting glass and, standing up from the floor, was surprised when the room suddenly spun around him and he lost his balance, staggering into a low ceiling beam.

The weird thing?

Even though touching his forehead proved he'd received a little lump, and his fingertips were smeared with blood, it didn't hurt.

Not at all.

In fact, it was a little silly that he was bleeding from something that didn't hurt, so he started laughing, his wine sloshing over the rim of his glass and extinguishing a couple of the flickering candles with a soft hiss.

Hiss.

Hiss.

Fucking wine.

"Fucking wine," he said with another chuckle, throwing back the half-full glass in his hand and downing the contents.

"Hisssssss. Hisssssss."

He belched loudly, the sound bouncing off the rafters, and he laughed again, turning around to look at the blanket and few remaining candles.

"Not c-coming?" he asked into the quiet candle-lit room, hiccupping softly. "Well, tha's ok-kay. Your l-losssss, Hal-ceeeeeee-on. Your...l-loss."

He didn't feel any pain in his forehead, and it occurred to him that he'd been able to numb the pain in his heart too, for the most part. Except now, in saying her name, it came back.

Falling to his knees and knocking over two more candles, which were doused by their own wax, he reached for the other bottle of wine.

"W-Why...aren't you...c-coming?" he murmured, blinking his eyes. They were burning. Probably because of the goddamned candles, which he sort of hated now. A lot. He rubbed his eyes hard, willing the burning away. Hating it. Hating the candles and the flowers and the stupid promise ring. Hating the way it was all making him feel.

As he drew his hands away from his face, he caught a glimpse of the time: *Ten fifteen.*

"She's n-not...c-coming," he whispered through hiccups, turning the cap on the second bottle and sloppily filling his glass to the brim.

"Hello?"

A girl's voice sounded from somewhere far away. He squinted, looking around the room, but seeing no one.

Halcyon? asked some semi-alert part of his brain.

"Um...hello?"

No, he thought with bitter disappointment. *It wasn't her.*

"There's...n-no one...here," he told himself, taking a gulp of wine.

But the girl's voice without a body spoke again.

"Um...Ian? Hello?"

"Hello, Ian," he answered, finishing his fifth glass of wine and lying back, half on the fleecy blanket and half on the broom-swept floor.

The ceiling was mostly dark except for a circle of light that seemed to get bigger and closer with each step.

Step?

Whose step?

Oh, no. Staring up at the light made the room spin like crazy. His stomach had horses in it now—colts and mares and thoroughbreds, their hammering hoofs making it hard to hear anything but the whooshing and whirling.

He groaned softly, closing his eyes and relieved to find that it made the spinning stop just a little, just enough to breathe.

"Oh, wow," said the girl's voice, first surprised, then amused. "Oh, Ian. What's going on here, huh?"

"N-Nothing," said Ian, feeling petulant. "N-Nothing...is g-going on...h-here." *Except hiccups. Hiccups are definitely going on.*

"Someone's a drunky skunky," said the voice.

Hilarious. The disembodied female voice was hilarious. Ian laughed, trying to say what she'd said, without luck. "D-Dunk...d-dunk the...dunky sk-skunk..."

"Shit, Ian. How much did you...Oh, my. A bottle and a half? Whew."

"Lotsa...b-bottles," answered Ian. "F-For. Hallieeeeee. Hallie's b-birthday."

"Yeah. Well, sorry, Romeo. That's not happening…"

She continued talking, this she-devil, this harpy harbinger of horrible news, but all Ian heard in his head were the words "not happening" over and over and over again.

Not happening.

Not happening.

Nothappeningnothappeningnothappeningnothappening.

Hallie is not happening.

Ian is not happening.

Promises are not happening.

Nothing is happening.

His eyes burned so terribly this time that they were wet when he reached up to rub them, and someone—no doubt the *someone* attached to the fucking voice that had destroyed his dreams and shattered his heart—touched his face, gently pushing his tears away.

"Hey," she said, "it's okay."

"It's n-not," he sobbed through another fucking hiccup. *Not happening is not okay.*

"Ian," she said, "maybe you should sleep. Sleep will help."

He felt the *whoosh* of a breeze over his face as she covered him with a blanket, but he couldn't bear to be alone. Hallie was warmth and light and everything he wanted in his future. If she wasn't happening—if she didn't love him—he was alone. And his once-beautiful future would be dark and grim, and so fucking lonesome, he'd rather die.

Not happening.

"S-Stay," he said to the body with the voice, reaching up blindly until she took his desperate hand in hers. "Stayyyyyy…w-with…m-me, babyyyyy." *Oh, Halcyon. Happen and stay.*

"Are you sure?" she asked. "I mean, I *want* to, but Ian…"

The whirling in his head wouldn't quit, and her voice was so far away he could barely hear her anymore.

Not happening.
Not happening.
So very far away.
So far away.
So far…
Away.

chapter five

"Two weeks ago, I asked you all an important question," said Kim. "Your first binge. The birthplace of your addiction. Where did it all begin? Does anyone want to share?"

Shandie was sitting beside Ian again, and she raised her hand, along with five or six other people seated in the circle.

"Jonah, why don't you start. Tell us your story."

The remaining hands lowered, and Jonah, who was four years sober, cleared his throat, and started at the beginning: an abusive father, an absentee mother, and a childhood seeped in poverty.

And this was the reason Ian *hadn't* raised his hand: because he'd had a loving, if stern, mother, a kind father, and two devoted siblings. Their apartment at Summerhaven wasn't fancy, but it was comfortable, and Ian liked sharing a room with Rory. He had plenty to eat and new sneakers whenever the old ones wore out. He did well in school, was taken to Disney World in Florida twice before the age of twelve, and went to Ireland every other year to see his grandparents and cousins.

Ian hadn't been abused or mistreated. He'd been cared for and loved.

But he'd *still* become an alcoholic.

Why?

Because one glass of wine to "calm his nerves" had led to five in under ninety minutes.

And in the morning? When he realized what he'd done? The only remedy for the fierce and relentless pain in his heart—*and* his head—was more wine.

At first, he'd been good at hiding it. For the rest of the summer, he'd stolen bottles from his parents little-visited wine cupboard and liquor cabinet. When he went to parties in Weirs Beach, he'd volunteer to work the keg and drink two Solo cups for every one he poured. Rory and Tierney had noticed his hangovers, of course, but they'd kept mum, advising him to keep his new habit from their mother, who'd skin him alive if she found out. A month later, his parents drove him to college in Boston, and that's when all hell had broken loose.

Beer was everywhere on campus: at fraternity parties, in his friends' minifridges, and at the off-campus convenience store that sold beer to minors at a significant markup. It wasn't a habit that sneaked up on Ian quietly—it was a fast and furious descent. He was probably a full-blown alcoholic by Columbus Day.

But that didn't matter to him, because there was no girl coming home to Boston that Christmas wearing his ring. There'd been no promises or love made. There were only shattered dreams and love lost. And Ian continued to drink.

He was a textbook "functioning alcoholic," someone who binge drank and who used alcohol for coping with unpleasant feelings. He would occasionally set boundaries for himself, but he'd always be unable to stick to them for any prolonged length of time. He was arrested by campus police more than once for public urination, nudity, and disorderly behavior, but he was also one of the star hockey players of the college team. That went a long way in keeping him from being expelled, which—in retrospect—might have saved him. Instead, he attended weekend rehab where he'd dry out for a few days before returning to campus and resuming bad habits all over again.

Ian slipped through college and somehow sobered up enough to shine at job interviews for high school coaching jobs. Genial and handsome, he was offered three great opportunities after graduating, but the "real world" proved to be Ian's ultimate downfall.

Continued partying with friends meant that he was often late to work and drunk at practice. It was an embarrassment to the school district when Ian was arrested for DUI one Saturday night. He was promptly put on probation and ordered to undergo both rehab and counseling. Upon his return to work two weeks later, he was sober. Barely. And not for long. At the next matchup between his team and that of a neighboring town, he arrived late and drunk, pushing a ref on a call he didn't like.

And that was the end of coaching. He'd been fired the next day.

Ian found a job at a local Boston ice rink, doing maintenance and driving the Zamboni, until one night he drank a couple of 40s on the job and drove it into the boards. When the rink manager found him the next morning, passed out in the cab of the machine with empty bottles by his feet, he was fired from that job too.

After that, Ian lost his apartment, selling most of his belongings and refusing to tell Rory and Tierney how bad things had gotten. He found himself napping in doorways at churches and libraries, his life a dismal failure, his heart numb to hurt and shame except when the buzz was wearing off.

In those spare moments of utter despair, one hurt after another would bubble to the surface like scum on a pond. And there was one that always trumped the rest.

Halcyon. Her face. The look on her face that morning. When she found him...*them*—

"No!" he shouted.

Shandie's hand landed on his thigh.

"Ian," she said gently—the room had gone silent and still, Jonah's narrative temporarily on hold—"it's okay. You're okay."

Ian blinked, looking around the circle, his eyes landing on the group leader, Kim, for a moment. She tilted her head to the side, her dark eyes kind. "Are you all right, Ian?"

He gulped, nodding his head. Shifting his eyes to Jonah, he shrugged. "Sorry, man. Bad memory."

There were mumbled *It's okay*s and *Been there*s from the group, other members nodding their heads with understanding.

In some ways, Ian had beaten the odds. Since relapse was most likely in the first three months after recovery, making it to six months sober meant that Ian had achieved abstinence and was now tasked with maintaining it.

And frankly, he knew better than to go down the Hallie Gilbert rabbit hole. He couldn't change the past. Thinking about it—torturing himself about it—would depress him and make him susceptible to relapse. But on the other hand, being around her again made it next to impossible not to think about the past.

"Please. Go ahead," said Ian, gesturing with his hands for Jonah to continue.

"What was the memory?" asked Jonah, taking a sip of his coffee.

"I hurt someone," Ian answered.

Jonah nodded. "You were drunk?"

"Yeah. First time."

"Are you powerless over your addiction?" asked Jonah, referencing the first step.

"Yes," answered Ian.

"Do you believe God can help?"

"I do."

"Have you given God permission to help?"

Ian nodded. "I have."

"Have you taken a personal inventory?"

Again, he nodded. "Yes."

When he'd tackled step four, Ian had literally sat at his dining room table with a pencil and yellow pad. He'd started the list with Hallie, then added his parents and siblings, college friends he'd hurt or embarrassed, his hockey team, his coach, the school where he'd worked and the kids he'd let down. At the end, he had a long, long list of people who'd suffered because of his addiction.

"Have you admitted it?"

"Yes."

In fact, Ian had read the list aloud at a different meeting—the one in Moultonborough that he'd first attended with Rory, two nights after he'd arrived at Tierney's on a bender.

"Have you asked God to correct and/or remove your shortcomings?"

Steps six and seven.

Ian nodded. "I have."

"Have you made a list of wrongs?" asked Jonah gently.

"Yes," said Ian.

"And have you reached out to those you harmed to make amends?"

Step nine: Amends.

Make amends.

And there it was: the sticky wicket.

The contradiction of Ian's life right now was that on one hand, being around Hallie hurt, but on the other hand, being around Hallie, whom he harmed first and most of all, was the only way to make amends for his wrongdoings.

He blinked at Jonah, feeling the sting of tears behind his eyes. Looking down at his thigh, he saw Shandie's fingers tighten a little, just to remind him that he wasn't alone.

Taking a deep breath, Ian looked up at the group. "I'm trying."

"Keep trying," said Jonah. "Making amends, and *living* amends, means genuine change." He paused for a moment and then added. "You might doubt it at times, Ian, but amends are the key to serenity. You cannot go through life avoiding those you hurt. By making amends fully and completely, we don't have to avoid people or places. We don't have to regret or try to forget the past. We can allow it to be part of the fabric of our lives. We can live *with* it, instead of in fear *of* it."

Ian clenched his teeth together and blinked again, but it didn't help. A tear slipped down his cheek, hiding in his beard on its descent.

"Thanks, Jonah," he whispered, unable to say more.

"Anytime, man. Work the steps. They work," said Jonah, before picking up where he'd left off in his own story.

Ian thought about Jonah's advice, tasting it, weighing it, deciding whether or not he liked it.

Wouldn't it be something not to regret the past? Ian asked himself. *Wouldn't it be something to be free of it? To live with it? To somehow find a place for it that didn't hurt?*

Shandie's hand squeezed his leg again before she lifted it away.

She leaned close to him and whispered, "How about a coffee after the meeting?"

But Ian shook his head.

You cannot go through life avoiding those you hurt.

There was somewhere else he wanted to be.

***

Hallie lay next to Jenny in the darkness, listening to the night sounds of the lake through a half-opened window and feeling—for the first time in so long—a small measure of peace.

Colby Cottage was finally coming together, mostly thanks, she had to admit, to Ian. In the week that he'd been working at her cottage from sunup to sundown, he'd gotten a lot done.

The raccoons were gone, and the upstairs floors and walls had been thoroughly cleaned and disinfected. After a fresh coat of paint, the rooms would feel new. He'd gutted the broken glass from shattered windows and covered panes with heavy tarps and masking tape until new glass could be installed. The tree branch that had protruded into the guest bedroom was gone, and a piece of plywood and a royal-blue tarp covered the hole in the roof. Ian had three roofers coming to give Hallie estimates next week.

Hallie's furniture had arrived, two days late, and the

workers had claimed she only paid for delivery, not unloading. Giving the guys a look that would curdle butter, Ian told them to wait in the cab of the truck and unloaded it all himself, helping her unroll the living room rug before bringing in her sofa and chairs and putting together a full-sized bed in her and Jenny's bedroom while she plugged in lamps and unwrapped framed pictures in the great room.

She'd almost asked him to stay for dinner when the movers finally drove away. They'd barely exchanged a word since she'd informed him on the first day how much she didn't want him there, but dinner seemed like the least she could do after all that heavy lifting. However, by the time she'd mustered her courage to ask him, he was already calling out "See you tomorrow" and driving away.

For all she knew, he had a girlfriend in town.

Or two.

Or twenty.

In any case, he certainly seemed like he had somewhere else he needed—or *preferred*—to be.

"Mommy?"

"Yes, baby?" asked Hallie.

"Mr. Haven sure is strong, isn't he?"

She glanced over at Jenny's little face, brightened by a beam of moonlight. "Yes, sweetheart. He is."

While Hallie was grateful for Ian's help, and their cottage was much cozier and safer now than it was when they first arrived, the greatest development since he'd started working for her, was the effect of his presence on Jenny.

Since his arrival, Jenny spoke more often and even, sometimes, when she was lost in thoughts about Ian, with sweetness.

Having Ian around was good for Jenny.

And no, it didn't make Hallie like him (much) or trust him (at all) but she couldn't challenge the strong stirrings of gratitude deep inside that wouldn't quit. So she'd stopped fighting them. She was grateful for Ian Haven, whether she liked it or not.

But she refused to let her feelings for him go any further than gratitude, and on that point, she would be unyielding.

Fool me once, she reminded herself, *shame on you. Fool me twice, shame on me.*

"Is Mr. Haven married, Mommy?"

Hallie took a deep breath, realizing that she didn't know—with total certainty—the answer to this question. Could he have a wife somewhere? She supposed he could and was surprised by the sharp twist in her heart when she imagined Ian belonging to someone else. It's not that she wanted him—*not at all*—but she didn't love the idea of him with somebody else either.

"I don't know," she answered. "I don't think so."

"Are you ever gonna love Papa again?"

"No," said Hallie firmly.

"Well…maybe you could love Mr. Haven instead."

I did, she thought. *Once upon a time, I loved Mr. Haven very much.*

"No, Jenny," she said gently. "Mr. Haven just works for us. He can be your friend, but that's all."

In response, Jenny huffed out the breath she'd been holding before flipping over to present her back to her mother.

Hallie sighed. *So much for sweetness.*

Swinging her legs over the side of the bed, she stood up and leaned over to kiss Jenny's cheek. Then she turned to the door, closing it halfway, and headed for the kitchen.

She took the dinner dishes from the white-painted, round kitchen table, and pushed in the sweet white chairs, which had cheerful blue-and-white-gingham cushions. Under the table was a blue, gray, and white braided rug, and once she painted the brown kitchen cabinets white, the little kitchen's transformation would be complete.

Turning on the faucet, she was relieved to see that the water had turned from coppery brown to a light yellow. To test the plumbing, Ian had insisted she run the water in all faucets for over two hours. He told her that it would either run out, indicating that her well was dry, start edging its way toward clear, which meant that the plumbing had just been unused for too long and needed a good flushing, or stay brown, which would mean pipe galvanizing. Because option three would require the replacement of her pipes at great expense, she'd checked on the water regularly that day, relieved beyond measure when it started lightening from brown to tan and, now, to light yellow. She'd still boil it before drinking just to be safe, but at least it didn't appear that she'd need to pay for new pipes.

Just as she placed the clean dishes in the drying rack, she noticed headlights brightening up the road out the window over the sink. And since she was the final cottage on a dead-end road, it was likely that it was someone coming to see her.

Maybe it was Brittany stopping by for a chat or to ask wedding advice. If Ian was the best thing about moving for Jenny, then Brittany was the best thing for Hallie. Having her friend so close meant that Hallie felt more supported and loved than she'd felt in a long time, and no matter how much heartache she'd experienced in her own life, planning a wedding was just plain fun. Hmm. Maybe Britt was coming over with more magazines with bridesmaid pictures. Last time, they'd *almost* narrowed down the choices to eighteen, she thought with a chuckle.

After wiping her hands on a dish towel, she walked to the front door, opening it to find the Summerhaven truck parked just outside the white gate. Though the paint was still peeling on it and it was missing a picket, it hung on two new hinges now, and Ian had made quick work of clearing the front path with a chainsaw and rake.

But it wasn't Britt who rounded the truck and stood on the other side of the gate, hesitant to step through it.

It was Ian.

And her heart—her stupid, ridiculous, pathetic heart—leapt, as it always had, as it likely always would, at the mere sight of him.

He held up his hand. "Hi."

"Hey," she said, stepping out of the house and crossing her arms over her chest.

"You're still up."

She nodded. "Night owl."

"Me too."

"Did you, uh…" She saw his jaw flex and tilted her head to the side. "…forget something today when y—?"

"I'm sorry," he blurted out.

Her breath caught. Her heart galloped.

"What?"

"I'm sorry."

"For what?"

"For everything," he said, his voice gruff with emotion. "I never got to say that to you—that I was so sorry, so *fucking* sorry, for what happened between us."

"Oh," she murmured, clasping her arms so tightly her shoulders brushed her ears. "Okay."

"By the time I got here that morning, you were gone."

"Yes."

"And I...God, I just wanted to...to..." He was still standing on the other side of the gate, his eyes intensely focused on hers. "...die."

She gulped, looking away from him as her own eyes flooded with tears.

"You need to know that, Halcyon. You need to know that I *never* meant to betray you."

But you did.

"I *never* meant to hurt you."

But you did.

"If I could go back in time and do it all over again, I'd—I'd—"

"You can't," she said softly.

She heard him take a deep breath, the sound accompanied by a small whine of pain in the back of his throat that sounded like a wounded animal, like a creature caught in a trap. It fisted around her heart, that small, sad sound, but the same heart had also learned, long ago, not to trust him.

"You should go," she said. "Our agreement—"

"This is penance," said Ian, gesturing with both hands to her house. "You see that, don't you? I'm making amends."

She looked up at him and nodded. "I see that."

"I can't take money for it."

"But we agreed—"

"I *can't*," he insisted. "I *won't*."

She would find a way to pay him later. For now, all she could do was gulp softly and nod.

He continued. "I'm making amends to show you that I'm a changed man, but also because it's all I can do. I can't change my wrongdoings. I can admit them. I can apologize for them. But that's not enough." He stopped for a moment, as though to gather his thoughts before continuing. "If I stole twenty dollars from you when I was drunk, it's not enough to say I'm sorry for stealing. I need to make a commitment to myself, and to you, never to steal again. And then I need to return your twenty dollars to you, no matter how many years have gone by since I stole from you."

She stared at him, trying to follow what he was saying but having trouble. He hadn't stolen money from her. He'd broken her heart.

"I'm saying I need to...to...fix things between us. To repair them...as much as I can."

Repair them? *How?* What did he even *mean* by that? Was he saying that he wanted to somehow work toward restoring the same level of love and trust that they'd shared the day before her seventeenth birthday? Did he actually think such a goal was within the realm of possibility? It was such a ridiculous notion that a small, bitter chuckle escaped from her lips.

"Impossible," she murmured, her nostrils flaring as hot tears slipped from her eyes, rolling down her cheeks.

"Nothing's impossible," he said simply, dropping his

hands to the pickets at the top of the gate and resting them there. "I'll start with your house, but I want to fix more than that, Halcyon."

"I appreciate your sentiments, Ian, but life doesn't work like that," she said, trying to stay calm.

"Why not?"

Anger ignited inside of her, joining the rest of her roiling feelings. "Because you can't go back. You can't change the past. We live with our mistakes. Big or small, they're ours." *Yours.*

"I know that," he said. "The past is the past. Of course. But I can change the future. I can...I can change the *now.*" He reached up and rubbed his beard, his eyes glistening in the moonlight. "You hate me, right?"

"Yep." She stared at him for a moment, then shrugged. "Less today than when I arrived here, maybe. I'm grateful for your help, and you've been kind to my daughter. But by and large? Yes, Ian. I hate you."

He nodded slowly, and suddenly it occurred to her how far away they were from one another. Her gaze fell to the flat piece of slate at her feet, counting the twelve flagstones between them, until she reached the gate again and slid her eyes up to his. They were shiny and black in the darkness, though she knew that when morning gilded the skies, they'd be emerald green in the sun.

"I don't want you to hate me," said Ian softly. "I want to heal us."

Then maybe you shouldn't have betrayed me with Vicky-fucking-Lafontaine, her heart screamed, the many impenetrable parts of that organ single-minded in their protection of any softness that remained.

She was silent.

And sometimes, she had learned, silence was the strongest voice of all.

She didn't believe him.

She didn't *want* to believe him.

"I have to go," she said, stepping back, inside the doorway, into the house that had offered childhood joy and a shabby harbor for her battered soul. This was all too much. She'd been stalwart throughout her divorce, but now? Now she just wanted to curl up on the couch and cry.

He nodded. "Yeah. Of course. It's late."

"So um…good night."

"Good night," he said.

But as she was closing the door she heard him add soft words—"*Oíche mhaith agus codladh sámh, grá gael mo chroí*"—said plaintively into the night.

Good night and sleep well, bright love of my heart.

The same words he'd said to her every night when they'd parted that summer so long ago.

"Halcyon days are golden days," he'd once explained to her, playing with the literal meaning of her name. "The brightest of my life."

The door clicked shut, and she leaned back against it, closing her eyes and forcing air into her lungs as she rested her head against the door.

Her heart raced, sprinting as she recounted their conversation as best she could, but the words jumbled in her mind, boiling down, like simple sugar, into the words: *I don't want you to hate me. I want to heal us.*

She recalled the promise she'd made to herself last weekend on her drive to New Hampshire: to hate men—*all men*—until the end of time.

But the righteous indignation she'd felt then escaped her now, and more than anything, she just felt...sad.

Once, during a fight with Sergio, he'd said to her: "Sometimes I feel like you don't love me, *meu amor*. Sometimes I feel like you *wish* you could love me, but for some reason, you *can't*."

Since February, Hallie had felt furious with her ex-husband—angry at his betrayal of their marriage and family, and the way he ran away from their divorce, leaving her with his debt—and filled with righteous indignation, but as she thought about his words now, they rang with so much truth, she couldn't deny them.

She couldn't truly love Sergio, of course, because she'd never *stopped* loving Ian.

Pressing her hand to her heart, she took a shaky breath, because she knew—in the most profound reaches of her soul—that it was possible to love someone but *not* to have him.

Opening her eyes, she stuffed that useless, stupid, blessedly torpid, love back into the deepest vestiges of her heart, shook off their conversation, and resolved never, ever to fall for Ian Haven again.

"Fool me twice, Irish," she said aloud, turning off the light and heading to bed, "shame on me."

CHAPTER SIX

"Headed to Hallie's today?" Finian asked Ian. "Or needn't I ask?"

Fin sat down at the table on Saturday morning *without* scratching his balls, *buíochas le Dia*, likely because Brittany had come over earlier to make pancakes.

Brittany was good for Finian, Ian observed, the same way she'd been good for him. There was something about her that felt like a sister, even before she'd starting dating Rory, and her gentle, playful presence softened the rough edges of the Haven men.

"Yeah, Ian," said Rory with a shit-eating grin. "Headed to Hallie's?"

Ian grunted, picking up his coffee and taking a long sip to avoid the question. Since his visit to her place on Wednesday night, Hallie had become even more scarce than she'd been before.

While Jenny, wearing hot-pink rubber rain boots decorated with ladybugs, followed him everywhere, Hallie went out of her way to avoid being near Ian, even for a moment. He'd sort of hoped that sharing his need to make amends would make things more comfortable between them, but it didn't necessarily surprise him that it had backfired. He'd churned up hurt feelings in confronting her with his intentions.

That said, he remained undaunted in his designs.

Making amends required an attitude of humility, and Ian was ready to face and absorb whatever pain she still carried. And he wouldn't stop in his pursuit of peace for both of them until he'd exhausted every avenue.

Placed in perspective, he reminded himself, she had a right to her anger. Not only toward him, but toward her husband, and maybe even toward men, in general. The last six months of her life sounded pretty miserable, though the majority of his information was coming from his four-year-old, omnipresent sidekick.

"Hey, ladybug," he'd said on Friday morning, striking up a conversation with Jenny, who pulled weeds while Ian hammered down the loose flagstones on the front walkway with a rubber mallet, "you're a pretty good worker. Did you help your daddy with chores like this?"

"Nuh-uh," she said, pulling up some more of the unruly pachysandra. It had taken over every available inch of ground space in front of the cottage, but between his efforts and Jenny's help, they were getting it cleaned up so no one would trip and fall walking to the front door. "We didn't have a garden. We had a sidewalk."

"Well," said Ian, positioning the fourth piece of slate in the fresh dirt and hammering it into the dark soil. "What did your daddy like to do?"

"He liked to give me candy."

"Mm-hm."

"And he gave me Luna," she said, holding up the dark-haired doll she always had under her arm. "They play Luna on TV in Brazil. That's where Papa is. Brazil."

"Uh-huh."

"Once he met me to his special friend."

Startled by this unprompted revelation, Ian stopped what he was doing for a second, looking down at her. "His *special friend?*"

She didn't look up at him, just pulled another handful of pachysandra from the ground, tugging on the root. "The lady with the black hair. Like Luna."

"Oh. Huh. Where did you meet her?" asked Ian, swiftly gathering that her shit heel of a father had introduced his daughter to one of his girlfriends.

"She had a ice cream with us. She laughed at everything Papa said and smelled like a bathroom candle."

"Where was Mommy?"

"At work," she said, putting the pulled pachysandra in the black plastic lawn bag behind her. "At the hoppitul."

"What did Mommy think of your visit with the special friend?" asked Ian.

"Papa said Mommy would feel sad that she missed ice cream. So it was a secret."

"Huh." Wow. And he made his daughter keep his tawdry affair a secret? *Cac ar oineach.*

"Brazil is far," said Jenny, sniffling as she stood up and wiped her hands on her blue jeans.

A misty rain was falling, and Ian let his mallet fall to the ground, kneeling down in front of Jenny and reaching around her head to pull up the hood of her ladybug raincoat. It's not that he had any experience with kids, really, but common sense said that it was better for someone's head not to get wet and cold. Especially someone as little as Jenny.

He grinned at her gently. No matter who her father was, he was still her father. "You must miss him, ladybug."

She nodded, her blue eyes sad, her face way too serious

for so young a person. "Mommy fighted a lot to him."

"They fought a lot, huh?"

"She yelled a lot. And then she cried loud at the bathroom."

Ian winced, imagining all the times that Hallie had stood in the shower, her tears mixing with the bath water and slipping down the drain.

"Adults can get sad when they fight," said Ian. "I bet it made you sad too."

"Yeah."

"You know your mommy's trying to make a nice life for you here, right?"

Jenny shrugged.

"Hey," said Ian. "Did you know I knew your mommy when she was a teenager?"

Jenny shook her head. "No."

"Sure! We were good friends."

"Like Auntie Britt?"

"Different. But yeah. A little like Auntie Britt, I guess. We were all friends." *And we both loved your mom, though one of us really let her down.*

"I gotta tinkle," Jenny said suddenly.

Ian had blinked at her. "Well, I guess you better go, then."

As Jenny ran to the door, she turned around. "I'll tell you when Mommy makes the samiches, okay?"

Ian had grinned at her, nodding as he stood back up.

Noontime peanut butter and jelly sandwiches with Jenny was a daily occurrence.

On sunny days, they'd sit on the small patch of grass behind the cottage that looked out on the lake. And on rainy days, like today, they'd sit side by side in the director's chairs that Hallie had placed on the screened porch. Hallie never joined them, of course, though it felt sort of nice that she made him a sandwich too.

"It's a date," he'd said, and she beamed at him before slipping into the house to pee.

"...Ian?"

His head snapped up at the sound of Brittany's voice. "Huh?"

She was holding out a plate of three pancakes. "You were a million miles away."

"I was just...thinking."

Brittany searched his face, her eyes soft. "You're doing a kind thing for Hallie."

"It's the least I can do," he said, looking into Brittany's eyes and knowing that she remembered—as well as he did— the pain he'd inflicted on Hallie. He opened the maple syrup and tipped it, letting the amber goodness stream slowly onto his pancakes.

"You're making amends," she said.

Ian lifted his head to look at her. Had Hallie talked to Brittany about their conversation on Wednesday night? From the slight way Brittany's lips tilted up before she stepped back over to the stove, he guessed she had.

For a second, it irritated him that what he'd said to Hallie had been shared with Brittany; for him, their conversation had felt somehow...sacred. He shrugged off the thought and rejected the feeling. It wasn't his place to be annoyed. And it didn't change his commitment to showing her that he'd changed.

When he'd asked her if she hated him on Wednesday

night and she'd answered that she did, it hurt more than he'd anticipated. It's not that he didn't deserve her hatred. He did. But it still hurt to hear it articulated. That said, it gave him a starting place. Hate. Nowhere to go but up—all the way from loathing to healing.

Although his heart clamored every time he caught a glimpse of her face, he wholeheartedly believed that she could never love him again, and he'd never expect it. That ship had sailed a long, long time ago, and there was no getting it back. Any yearnings in his own heart would be borne, would be silenced, were not her problem, and would never become her burden.

But healing could take many forms, couldn't it? Hate was a corrosive that ate away at the vessel that contained it. If he could find a way to change her hate into acceptance, into peace, he'd be content. He'd have helped her. He'd have made his amends, and if she wanted him to leave her alone for the rest of their lives, he would.

"Ian? Ian?" Rory nudged his elbow. "Hey! Can you save some for the rest of us?"

Ian looked down at his plate, which was swimming in maple syrup, and quickly righted the bottle. "Sorry."

"Off in dreamland," observed Finian with a musical lilt. "Dreamin' of his lost love."

Ian sighed. "Jaysus, Fin. *Dún do bheal*, huh?"

"Ah, sure. I'll shut up." He threw his balled-up napkin at Ian. "Yer no fun anyway."

The kitchen was quiet for a few minutes—the smells of coffee, pancakes, and syrup mixing for a pleasing aroma. Ian thought about the day ahead, mentally answering the question Finian had asked before. No, there wouldn't be time to work on Hallie's cottage today. Tierney'd skin him alive if he missed the plans she'd made.

"Are we still on for today?" he asked no one in particular, spearing another bite of pancakes with his fork.

Rory nodded. "Family day for the Havens and Rileys. Should be interesting."

Before moving up to New Hampshire, Tierney's boyfriend, Burr, had invited his sister, Suzanne; brother-in-law, Connor; and young niece, Bridey, to come up for a weekend of fall fun.

"Are they here yet?" asked Ian.

Brittany nodded as she slid a plate of pancakes in front of an appreciative Finian. "They got in last night. Staying in Lady Margaret, of course."

"Yer a grand woman," said Fin, smacking his lips together.

"Yes, she is." Rory grabbed Britt around the waist and pulled her onto his lap, then turned to Ian. "We haven't met them yet."

"So what's on the agenda?" asked Ian.

"Oooo!" said Brittany, who loved planning anything. "Lots of fun stuff! There's a Pumpkin Fest down in Laconia with humungous pumpkins and crafts and kiddie rides. We're going for apple picking and hayrides at Stony Brook Farm in Gilford, and Rory said we could take out the pontoon boat to see the foliage."

Despite the heaviness on his heart where Hallie was concerned, it was impossible not to crack a smile for his brother's girlfriend. Brittany's enthusiasm was contagious.

"Want me to make a campfire for tonight?" asked Ian. "S'mores and a sing-along?"

"I brought me guitar," said Fin, "if you lads'll join me in a song or two."

"Yes yes yes!" screeched Brittany, bounding off Rory's lap and racing to the pantry. "I love it!"

"Woman," asked Rory over his shoulder, "what are you doing?"

"Seeing if Ian has graham crackers, marshmallows, and chocolate."

"If he doesn't, the kitchen does," said Rory. "Come back here and warm up my lap again."

"Oh, Lord," groaned Fin, "are you two gonna go at it again?"

"Jealous much?" asked Rory.

"Sick to me stomach much?" asked Fin with a snort. "I'd like to actually *enjoy* me breakfast without it comin' up while I'm eatin'."

"Oh!" cried Brittany, totally ignoring Fin. "I almost forgot." Her eyes slid to Ian. "I invited Hallie and Jenny to join in the fun today."

"Wait. You did what?" asked Ian.

Brittany shrugged. "Suzanne and Connor have a little girl about the same age as Jenny. I thought it would be fun for them."

But not for me, thought Ian.

As much as he liked being around Hallie, it was painful too, because she had nothing but disdain for him. To spend an entire day together? Doing fun things in a small group? It was going to be *beyond* awkward.

He pushed away from the table, giving his future sister-in-law a sour look. "Well, that's just great, Britt."

"I can't figure out yer brother, Rory. He obviously likes

the lass, but here he's lookin' down in the dumps that she's comin' along." Finian humphed. "She's a good-lookin' woman. Maybe I'll see if she's—"

"You do it and you'll lose teeth," growled Ian, flashing furious eyes at his cousin.

"Oh, ho, ho! Lookit that. Yer man ain't playin' now, eh?"

Ian cracked his knuckles. "Back off, Fin."

"Stand down, boyo." Finian held up his hands. "Too much baggage for me anyway…with that kid and all. I need a free-spirited lass."

Brittany's head whipped around and she stared at the Haven cousin for a moment, her eyes narrowing. "Is that right?"

"What's that mean, then?" asked Finian, looking nervous. "That's the look a woman gets when she's got ideas."

"Indeed," said Brittany, her grin widening. "Free-spirited, huh? That's what you want?"

"What? Uh. No. I mean, no thank you. I don't want nothin'. Shite. I gotta—I'm leavin'!" Finian's chair scraped the floor as he backed away from the table, grabbed his plate, and ran for the safety of his bedroom.

Ian chuckled. "He just got untangled from a girl named Cindy."

"Huh," said Brittany. "I wonder how he feels about the name Tate…"

"What're you up to?" asked Rory.

"Not a thing," said Brittany, turning to Ian. "Hey, would you mind heading over to Colby Cottage in in ten minutes? Rory and I have to go back to our place so I can get my purse, and we're all meeting in the parking lot at nine. It would help if you could go get the girls."

Rory's eyebrows knitted together. "What? Your purse is in the—"

"Shh!" said Brittany to Rory. "Ian? What do you say?"

"I promise you," said Ian, giving her a look, "Hallie would prefer *anyone else*—literally, *anyone else on the planet*—pick her up."

"Ah," said Brittany, taking Rory's hand and pulling him up from his chair, "but there *is* no one else, and I promised her a ride. Please, Ian. Be a love. For me?"

"Fine," he grunted, steeling himself for Hallie's perpetually wounded, disapproving face when he pulled up in front of her cottage.

As Brittany and Rory headed out, Ian went back to his room, brushed his hair into a neat ponytail and shrugged into his tan corduroy barn jacket. He grabbed his keys and headed downstairs, through the Summerhaven office, devoid of Mrs. T's presence on an off-season Saturday. When Tierney had asked to spend the weekend at Summerhaven with Burr's family, they'd decided to close the facility to any other guests.

Hopping into the truck, a feeling of anticipation made his belly flutter like a teenager. As he drew closer to her place, he couldn't deny the way he felt: happy to be close to her, even if she didn't want him there, and hopeful that maybe, someday, she wouldn't hate him quite as much as she did now.

Parking the truck by the front gate, he walked around the hood and stepped into the garden, looking up as the front door swung open. Jenny sprinted from the front door, hurtling herself against his legs and hugging him around the knees.

"Mr. Haven! I'm getting a new friend today!"

For the first time since Hallie and Jenny had moved to New Hampshire, Ian reached down and swooped Jenny up into his arms, grinning at her sweet little face, so close to his. "I know it! Her name's Bridey and I heard she's real nice."

Jenny's eyes sparkled with happiness. "Mommy said we're going to a punkin patch."

"Yep," said Ian, "and apple picking. Do you like apples, ladybug?"

"Yes!"

"And I think Auntie Britt said we're going on a boat ride too."

"Wow!" gasped Jenny, who hugged Luna between them. "I never been on a boat ride!"

"Never?" Ian acted shocked. "Well, you're going to love it."

"And then what?" asked Jenny.

"Well," he said, "I heard something about s'mores and songs around a campfire."

Jenny clapped her hands, then said, "I don't know what none of that is!"

Ian chuckled at her. "S'mores are sandwiches made of graham crackers, marshmallows, and chocolate. You like chocolate, don't you?"

"Yummy!"

"And a campfire is a big fire outside. People sit around it and sing songs."

"Like what songs?"

"Do you know 'The Wild Rover'? Or maybe 'Molly

Malone'?"

She crinkled her nose at him. "No! I don't know those songs!"

"Oh, wait a second!" said Ian, winking at her. "I know *your* favorite. It's 'Carrickfergus'!"

"I can't even *say* that!" exclaimed Jenny, placing her little hands on his bearded cheeks. "You know what, Mr. Haven?"

"No, ladybug. Tell me."

She lowered her voice, leaning forward until their noses touched. "I think you're magical."

Ian's breath caught as he looked into her blue eyes, so much like her mother's. Why these words moved him so deeply, he wasn't sure. Maybe because they were delivered so earnestly. Or maybe because it was a long, long time since he'd felt anything close to "magical." He hugged her close. "You too, ladybug. I think you're magical too."

She rested her cheek on his shoulder, and Ian caught sight of Hallie, who stood in the doorway, her eyes glistening with tears as she watched them.

Thank you, she mouthed, blinking her eyes against the gathered moisture.

Ian nodded, setting Jenny gently back down on the ground.

"I'm getting in the truck," she announced, racing down the flagstones and through the gate. "Let's go, Mr. Haven!"

"It's been a long time since I've seen her that happy," said Hallie, sniffling softly as her eyes tracked her daughter. "A *really* long time."

"She's a corker," said Ian.

"A *corker*," said Hallie, turning to close the front door

and lock it. She turned back around, and the bright fall sun shone on her dirty-blonde hair, making it golden. And Ian felt in his bones and blood, like it had always been there and would never go away, a deep and intense rush of love for her that had somehow survived their ten long years apart. "You used to call me that sometimes too."

He stared at her. "I might fall over dead if that's actually a *good* memory of me."

She scoffed, shaking her head. "If you die, you'll really disappoint my daughter."

"Speaking of her, you know what would be nice? Just for today?"

Hallie's chest rose under her cream-colored fleece jacket, and her eyes lost their short-lived sparkle, shuttering a little in wariness. "What?"

"A truce," said Ian.

"A truce."

He nodded. "We don't have to be friends. It's impossible. I know. But how about we just don't hate each other today?"

Her chest lowered as she sighed, and to his surprise, her lips tilted up just the tiniest bit. "Just for today?" she clarified.

"Full-on hate back in action tomorrow."

Her lips twitched again, and he held his breath as he waited for her answer.

"Okay, Irish." She held out her hand. "Just for today."

Irish.

His heart stopped for two reasons.

One, she hadn't called him that nickname since they'd resurfaced in one another's lives, and it felt so fucking good, he could barely contain the rush he felt.

And two, he looked down, hesitating for a moment. Touch. She was inviting him to touch her. His skin against hers. Her hand in his as it had been so many times before, as he'd never expected it to be again.

He reached forward, his eyes locked with hers as he enveloped her hand in his.

He'd be lying if he said he didn't feel the warmth of her touch from the tips of his toes to the tip of his ponytail and everywhere in between. And his heart beat out a primal and fierce rhythm. *Mine. Mine. Mine.* He held his breath and searched her eyes, watching as her pink lips parted, as though she felt the same jolt of energy pass between them.

"Umm," she murmured.

Her chest rose and fell rapidly between them and Ian fought to keep his eyes on her face.

"Halcyon," he whispered.

She jerked her hand away from his, wiping it on the thigh of her jeans, as though hoping it would erase whatever they'd just shared. She'd looked down as she pulled away, but now she glanced up at him again. Taking a deep breath, she schooled her face into a neutral expression, though there was nothing she could do about the two bright-pink spots high on her cheeks.

"I guess we should go," she said.

Ian nodded, gesturing with his hand toward the truck and hoping she didn't see the way it trembled.

***

Leave it to Brittany..., thought Hallie, sitting across from her friend at the roaring campfire.

"Mommy! Mr. Haven is showing me and Bridey how to

roast a marshmallow."

"Yum," said Hallie, reaching for one of her daughter's braids and tugging lightly. "Did you have fun today?"

Jenny beamed at her. "The best day ever!"

...to plan the best day ever. She finished the thought using her daughter's words, because they so similarly mirrored her own.

The day's adventures had included a visit to the Pumpkin Festival, where Bridey and Jenny had sat together on every ride, giggling like old friends while the adults looked on. Ian, Rory, Burr, Connor, and Finian had dunked for apples, with Burr, who basically drenched the entire upper part of his body, coming out as the winner, much to Bridey's delight.

They'd taken a hayride through an apple orchard and had cider donuts for lunch. And when they'd returned to Summerhaven in the late afternoon, they'd taken a two-hour cruise around Squam Lake, with the Havens, Brittany, and Hallie all pointing out their favorite spots while Suzanne and Connor snuggled under a blanket in the corner of the pontoon with mugs of beer and big smiles. Dinner had consisted of chili and cornbread in the dining room, with the Haven siblings and Finian giving each other a hard time and reminiscing about their shared childhood. And when there was a lull in the conversation, there was always Connor, Suzanne, and Burr, or Brittany and Hallie, to share a story of their own.

It had been a long, long time since Hallie had felt like she had a group of friends. Sergio was charming but not one for deep friendships, so they hadn't made many couple-friends during the course of their marriage. Hallie had friends at the hospital where she worked, of course, but they were the sort of friends you met for lunch in the cafeteria, not the kind you saw outside of work. Being an only child had only added to her sense of isolation. Once Hallie's parents moved to Florida, she was all alone but for Sergio, work friends, and—occasionally—Brittany.

So today? Feeling like a part of this big gregarious Irish family? It was heaven for her and for her daughter, who'd glowed all day, holding hands with Ian—or even, once or twice, with her. Hallie could feel their relationship mending day by day, hour by hour, and to see her happy, chatty little girl restored to her was worth everything.

Her eyes flicked up, watching Ian throw back his head and laugh at something the two little girls said, and Hallie couldn't help a small smile of her own, which—*damn it*—Ian managed to catch as his gaze slid to hers.

She looked away quickly, reaching for one of the blankets the Havens had left folded on logs around the campfire and pulling it across her lap.

She didn't want to care for Ian.

She wanted it less than anything else she could think of.

But since Wednesday, when he'd declared his intentions to "heal them," to "fix things," and to "repair them," she couldn't stop thinking about whether or not she wanted to be healed, fixed, and repaired. Hate had been her loyal companion for so long. Letting go of it felt dangerous, felt foolish, felt…scary.

And yet she watched this bear of a man with her tiny daughter—the way he paid attention to her and made her feel important, the way he'd intuitively gathered that she desperately needed a strong, kind male figure in her life, and had filled that position without being asked. Gently. Without a request for anything in return except for the chance to make peace between them.

It squeezed her heart in a way that frightened her.

"Penny for your thoughts," said Britt, sitting down next to Hallie and stealing half the blanket.

Hallie put her head on her friend's shoulder and sighed. "Life is complicated."

"Yes," agreed Britt, who'd had a tumultuous year of her own, but had managed to find a happy place for herself with Rory. "No doubt about it."

"Today was so nice," said Hallie. "We really needed it."

Britt took a deep breath and sighed. "He calls her 'ladybug.'"

"I know," she whispered, her voice breaking a little.

"I've never seen Ian around kids before, but wow, he was literally born for it."

Hallie sniffled softly. "Stop, Britt. Please."

"One more thing, and then we'll change the subject."

"What?"

"He *has* changed. I've been here since the day he came back, Hal, and he's…different. His life was pretty awful before he got here. But he committed to getting sober and look at him. He's over two hundred days clean now. I just…I feel like…he's not the same boy you knew. He's a man now."

And what a man.

His black hair was back in a sexy ponytail, and in the firelight, his black beard made him look fierce, like one of the Scottish warriors from *Outlander*. But his eyes. As green as summer ivy, they softened for Jenny, or for Brittany, or for…*her*. And then? She could barely keep track of what he was saying or what she was doing. And today? When she'd stupidly held out her hand to shake on their truce? She'd felt his touch everywhere in her body, parts of her blooming and opening for the first time in years, the unfamiliar feeling of desire making her dizzy and weak as she remembered those hands in her hair, on her face, in her body, wringing such pleasure from her that no man since had ever been able to compare.

She gulped softly. "It's confusing."

"I'm sure it is," said Britt.

"He hurt me."

"What he did was…"

Britt's voice drifted off, and Hallie filled in the blank with a million different words, including *unforgiveable*, *unpardonable*, *disgraceful*.

So why, after just a week in Ian's presence, were there whisperings in her heart about forgiveness and pardon and grace?

"Mommy and Auntie Britt! Look!"

Jenny suddenly appeared in front of them with her lips covered in sticky white marshmallow, a roasting stick holding a perfectly browned confection, and melting chocolate all over her fingers.

"You're going to need a bath when we get home," said Hallie, chuckling at her baby as she reached into her purse for wet wipes.

When she was clean, she pulled Jenny onto her lap, her heart full of gratitude when her daughter didn't immediately pull away.

Rory, Ian, Tierney, and Finian were taking seats across

the fire from where Brittany and Hallie were sitting, with the Rileys and Bridey to their right and Burr sitting beside Tierney to their left. Finian took out his guitar, tuning it softly as his cousins looked on in anticipation.

When Hallie and Brittany were teens, most of the campfire Fridays at Summerhaven had included traditional camp songs, but at least once every summer, the five Havens (with whatever cousins were visiting at the time) hosted an Irish jam session wherein anyone who played an instrument added to the gaiety, and between Irish songs in English and Gaelic, Mrs. Haven would tell tales and jokes about Ireland. It was one of Hallie's favorite nights of every summer, so she felt a mixture of nostalgia and excitement as Finian turned to his cousins and asked, "What're we startin' with, lads?"

"'Raglan Road'?" suggested Tierney. "It's an autumn day, after all."

"One vote for 'Raglan Road,'" said Finian, looking around the circle.

"Two," said Burr.

"Three," said his sister, Suzanne.

"Eh. Bloody Limerick's votin' too," said Finian, grinning at the O'Leary siblings, Burr and Suzanne. "Yeah, okay. Let's go."

The guitar accompanied those singing, and Hallie closed her eyes, feeling the sweet weight of her daughter on her lap, the kindness of her friend by her side, the warmth of the fire on her cheeks, and the gaiety of the voices singing.

Looking up toward the end of the fourth verse, her eyes sought out Ian's without permission, finding them easily as he gazed steadily across the flames at her.

"*Oh, I loved too much, and by such, by such, is happiness thrown away.*"

She breathed deeply, looking away as Jenny wiggled on her lap.

"Where are you going?" she whispered close to Jenny's ear.

"I wanna sit with Mr. Haven."

"Baby, he's singing."

"He won't mind. We're friends."

Loosening her arms, Hallie watched as her daughter walked carefully around the crackling fire, standing in front of Ian for a moment before he slid over a bit to make room between him and his brother. And Hallie had to chuckle because there was her little girl, looking so tiny, nestled between the two giant Haven men, and happy as a clam.

But even as she took pleasure in her daughter's happiness, it occurred to her that maybe she was making a mistake. Was it wise to let her daughter form a strong attachment to Ian? Would it foster expectations in Jenny that Hallie had no intention of meeting? There was no future for her and Ian, which meant that there was no long-term plan for Ian remaining in Jenny's life. Wouldn't she be devastated when the work on their cottage was finished and she didn't see Ian every day? They would always have a connection to the Havens through Brittany, and if they were to be neighbors, there was space for civility, she guessed, but an attachment? Maybe it wasn't such a good idea.

Tierney gave Bridey and Jenny tambourines and the little girls beat them joyously for the next song, "The Wild Rover," with all of them singing "*no, nay, never!*" when the choruses came around. Britt put her arm around Hallie's shoulders, rocking her friend back and forth, and if Hallie closed her eyes, she could have been fifteen again, harboring a wild crush on Ian Haven, the sweet smells of summer filling her senses.

Graham crackers were passed around, and more songs were sung until Bridey was asleep in her mother's arms and Jenny's head rested on Ian's thigh, her little shoulders rising and falling in slumber.

Finian turned to his cousins and said, "One last song? Any requests?"

"'Carrickfergus,'" said Ian softly, lifting his eyes to Hallie.

"Good one," said Finian appreciatively, strumming the opening chords on his guitar.

"*I wish I was in Carrickfergus only for nights in Ballygrand. I would swim over the deepest ocean, the deepest ocean, for my love to find,*" Ian sang, his baritone blending with his family's voices and creating a rich harmony.

And this time, too tired to fight, Hallie held his gaze, looking deeply into his eyes and letting herself remember how madly she once loved him.

"*My childhood days bring back sad reflections of happy times spent so long ago.*"

His lips moved to the words, his hand resting protectively on Jenny's sleeping head.

What would it have been like, Hallie wondered, if she hadn't found him with Vicky that morning? Would Ian have been Jenny's father? And would they have been as happy as her sixteen-year-old heart had believed they would be? Would he have still become an alcoholic, or would her love for him have saved him from that terrible journey?

The last notes floated away and they sat around the fire in silence for a moment before Brittany said, "I don't know about the rest of you, but this mama-to-be is exhausted."

Rory was up in a flash, sidestepping the campfire to get to her. "Why didn't you say something?"

She stood up, stretching her arms over her head. "Because the music and the company were so good."

Rory drew her into his arms. "Let's get you to bed. 'Night everyone!"

Connor stood up, leaning down to take Bridey from her mother's arms. "Thanks, everyone. Can't remember the last time I got to sing all of those old favorites."

Suzanne and Burr shared a hug, and he and Tierney walked his sister back to their cabin, leaving Finian, who was packing up his guitar, with Ian, Jenny and Hallie.

"Thanks for the music, Finian," said Hallie.

"Ah, sure. No worries," he said, flicking a glance at his cousin.

"Let me walk you home?" asked Ian.

"No," said Hallie. "There's no need."

But Ian was already standing up, holding a sleeping Jenny in his arms. "It's no problem. Let her sleep. I'll carry her back."

There was no way to refuse him without looking ungrateful and irrational, so she nodded, standing up and joining him. He walked slowly away from the campfire, effortlessly finding one of the paths that led through the woods to her cottage, even in the pitch dark.

And maybe it was the dark, she reflected later, that gave him the courage to say what he did.

"It was good having you two with us today," he said.

"Jenny loved every minute."

She put her cold hands in her pockets as the fall leaves crunched under their feet.

"She's a great kid."

"You're really good with her, Ian."

"Ha! That's a trick. I've never been around a kid this much."

"Well, you're a natural. She adores you."

They kept walking in awkward silence, their hips and elbows occasionally touching and sending a spark of recognition through Hallie's entire body. *He's not the boy you knew. He's a man now.*

"Brittany told me that you worked really hard to quit drinking."

He cleared his throat, the sound deep and low in the darkness. "Yeah. I'm, uh, six months sober now. Longest stretch since I started."

"When did you start?"

"Long time ago," he muttered softly.

She nodded, remembering the empty wine bottles in the barn loft that morning when she found him—found him with—

"Halcyon," he said, his voice interrupting her awful thoughts. "I want you to know something." He paused, the silence taut and heavy as she waited for him to continue. "I never stopped loving you. Never."

The words hit her hard, and stole her breath, leaving her lungs empty and her heart stuttering. Was he saying he loved her? Right here? Right now? How was that possible? And yet, she already knew. She knew because part of her still loved him too. Because, when you love as teens, as wildly and as passionately as they did, it's not something you ever forget or that dies an easy death.

But there wasn't room for an adolescent love in her adult life. What was she supposed to say? How was she supposed to answer?

After a few seconds had ticked by, she forced herself to breathe.

"Is this—is this part of making amends?" she asked.

"No," he said. "I don't think so. I think this is just…sharing the truth, without any expectations."

She gulped, her eyes stinging with tears. And what she'd been thinking about earlier at the campfire, about how Ian was getting too close to them too fast, skittered through her mind. It felt so comforting: a responsible and sound reason for pushing him away—and she clung to it, clearing her throat as they neared the front gate of her cottage.

"It's good there are no expectations, because I can't love you back," she lied, turning to face him, keeping her eyes averted from Jenny, who slept peacefully between them.

"I'm not asking you to."

"Good. Because it'll never happen."

"Hallie—"

"You can't make me forget," she continued. "You can't make me forgive. You can't fix something you broke ten years ago."

"I didn't—"

"Help me with my house. That's all the amends I need," she finished sharply, her voice ringing like a slap.

"Truce over," said Ian softly.

She nodded, opening the gate and heading for the front door. After it was open, she turned to face him, taking Jenny from his arms.

"Thank you for carrying her."

"No problem," he said, taking a step away from her, his eyes hooded.

"I think it's best if we avoid each other from now on," she added, ignoring the way her heart ached with every word she said. "Mr. Carlson should be free to help me by now. I could—"

"No," he said, taking another step away. "I'll leave you alone." He gulped softly, his face drawn and serious. "Let me finish up."

She sniffled, hating that her sinuses were filling from the tears deluging her eyes. She needed to get inside. Now.

"So um…I'll be back on Monday," he said.

"I'll leave a note in the mailbox indicating the roofer bid I'd like to accept."

"Great."

"Okay, then," she said, almost unable to see him, her vision was so blurry. She sniffled again. "Good-night."

"*Oíche mhaith agus*—" he started, but Hallie purposely closed the door before he could finish the beautiful words.

With tears streaming down her face, she put Jenny to bed and changed into her own pajamas, trying to convince herself that she'd done the right thing, while the words *I never stopped loving you* haunted her thoughts until she finally found sleep.

the plan

(Part 4)

Waking early on the morning of her seventeenth birthday, Hallie slipped down the stairs of Colby Cottage, careful not to wake up her parents, who were still asleep in their downstairs bedroom. They'd be up soon enough to drive back to Boston, but Hallie had already said her good-byes last night.

Tiptoeing through the cozy great room, she pulled her cardigan tighter around her shoulders before opening the front door. Even in the middle of summer, New Hampshire mornings were brisk.

When they'd arrived back at Colby Cottage after the cruise, Hallie had decided to stay overnight with her parents, at their family-owned cottage on the border of Summerhaven. She kept a change of clothes, pajamas, and toiletries in her room, and after all, if she stayed with her parents, she wouldn't risk waking up her Lady Margaret roommates who were already asleep.

This morning, she had woken up to thoughts of Ian, hoping that he wasn't too disappointed when Vicky told him she wasn't coming last night. She grinned as she walked through the misty morning woods, following the path back to Summerhaven. She wanted to find him right away to explain what had happened and to tell him that they could celebrate tonight instead.

As she approached the campfire ring, located near the

water in front of the Oxford Row cabins, she caught sight of Rory Haven securing the bowline of a canoe to the dock.

"Morning, Rory!" she called.

With the morning sun glistening off his black hair, he looked so much like Ian, her heart squeezed a little. She couldn't wait to see her love and make their plans for tonight.

"Hey, there, Hallie. Coming from your folks' place?"

She smiled and nodded. "Yeah. Stayed over last night."

Rory put his hands on his hips. "I'm bringing over canoes for the race this afternoon. You signed up?"

"Ha!" she exclaimed. "Have you seen me with an oar? It's not pretty."

"Well, find Ian sometime today. He'll be in charge of the cheering section, and I'm sure they could use your enthusiasm!"

Her heart leapt at Ian's name, but she was careful not to react. "Speaking of Ian, have you seen him this morning? I wanted to sign up to help with the talent show. As long as I'm already up, maybe I'll go track him down."

"Good luck with that." Rory chucked softly. "He never came home last night."

"What?" she asked, blinking at Rory. "He didn't—"

"Come home," he repeated, still grinning. "Left a note that he went to a party down in Weirs Beach and might stay overnight at a friend's, but he wasn't in bed this morning. And I happen to know he didn't have permission to stay out all night. So if you *do* run into him, tell him to get his story straight *before* he sees my mother, okay?"

Hallie forced a smile, though her mind was racing. *Why hadn't Ian come home last night?* "Um. Yeah. Sure."

"Gotta go get another canoe," said Rory, heading in the direction of the boathouse. "Reconsider the race!" he threw over his shoulder.

"Right," she murmured, turning away from the dock, toward the main path.

Her heart had started beating faster while talking to Rory. Yes, she understood why Ian left a note that he was going to a party in Weirs Beach and might not be home until morning. It was his excuse to cover being with her all night. But he *wasn't* with her. So…*where was he?*

Stopping by her cottage, which didn't stir with the sounds of her friends' voices yet, Hallie checked to see if there was a note for her thumbtacked to the bulletin board on the front door, but there was nothing. Her legs moved quickly as she headed up the path to the phone booth, slipping behind the rectangular structure to squat down and pick up the large flat stone where Hallie and Ian hid their messages to each other. But there was just dirt underneath. No note there either.

She stood for a moment, wondering what might have happened, and her mind slid seamlessly to her conversation with Vicky and Vicky's syrupy-sweet promise that she'd tell Ian that Hallie couldn't make it. Was it possible that Vicky had never told Ian anything? Maybe he'd waited for her all night, wondering where she was, worried or hurt, believing that she'd stood him up. Maybe he'd even fallen asleep waiting for her.

That *must* be what happened.

Half walking, half running toward the barn, she made quick time to the old wooden building, worried about Ian and eager to reassure him that she'd had no choice about abandoning their plans.

Damn Vicky Lafontaine for lying that she'd help out, but truly, what did Hallie expect? There was a reason she and Britt called Vicky and her crowd "the Fakes." And after this? There would be no love between Lady Margaret and Pembroke. None. That was for sure.

Hallie opened the barn door and stepped inside, looking around but finding nothing amiss. Dust motes floated in beams of morning sun that poured through high windows, and the sound of a meadowlark outside made for a soothing morning lullaby.

"Hello?" she called.

She scanned the room for signs of Ian but saw nothing, heard nothing, and was just turning to leave when her eyes landed on the stairs in the right corner that led up to the loft.

Of course.

Ian wouldn't have met her down here where anyone could have found them. He would have brought her upstairs for their intimate celebration.

She placed her hand on the bannister, taking the creaking steps one by one.

"Hello?" she called again. "Ian?"

Halfway to the top, she heard a sound. Loud breathing or light snoring, she wasn't sure, but a smile burst forth on her face, and she quickened her footsteps.

He stayed here all night! Waiting for me! Hoping I'd show up! Oh, Irish, I'm so sorr—

She stopped at the top of the stairs, her eyes falling to the jumble of blankets on floor. She stood frozen, all of the breath in her lungs expelled from her body as if she'd just taken a jump kick to the chest. Her lips parted. Her hands flew up to cover them as she blinked in shock and disbelief at the scene before her.

Candles lay on the floor in pools of melted wax.

Two empty bottles of wine littered the floor.

Various articles of clothing lay discarded.

And in the middle of it all, with a blanket covering his lower-half, was Ian—*her* Ian—completely bare-chested, with Vicky Lafontaine cuddled up beside him. Her cheek rested against the tan skin on Ian's chest, just over his heart, the strap of her bra drooping down her shoulder.

Hallie struggled to take a breath, but she felt like she was drowning or choking, the whole room spinning mercilessly as she looked for anything to steady her.

But there was nothing to grab on to.

There was nothing but an empty loft holding Hallie's sleeping boyfriend, the girl who'd spent the night with him, and the anguished crack of Hallie's heart breaking inside her chest.

She gasped, finally filling her lungs but left weak from the effort.

"Ian," she sobbed.

"Halcyon," he murmured, his eyes still closed, his voice ragged and raw.

Her eyes landed on something glistening beside Ian's head on the wood floor. The ripped, square, silver packet read *Troj.* A condom wrapper.

"Oh, my God," she whispered in stark and utter horror.

Her eyes, filling with tears, slid to Ian's face, watching as his eyes fluttered open. She lifted her chin and tried to blink back tears, but it didn't work. They coursed down her cheeks in rivulets. "*Why, Ian?*"

"Hallie?" he murmured, reaching up to rub his eyes with the hand that wasn't anchored under Vicky. He blinked at her, then winced before narrowing his eyes, like he was surprised to see her standing there over them. Like he was confused.

"*Why?*" she asked again, fisting her hands by her sides and letting her tears fall at will.

He blinked again then groaned, reaching up with both hands to rub his head, then quickly lowering his hands when Vicky sighed in her sleep, resettling herself on his chest. Ian reached for Vicky's head, touching her hair, before looking up at Hallie again. He reached toward her. "W—Wait. What's going—"

"Fuck you, Ian," she whispered, turning toward the stairs. Just before her descent, she pivoted and locked eyes with him. "Don't *ever* speak to me again."

And then she ran, as fast as she could, down the stairs, away from the barn, through the camp to the path in the woods, not stopping until she reached Colby Cottage. Her parents were outside, packing up the car to go home to Boston.

She was out of breath and dusty, her cheeks soaked, her nose running, and her heart broken. Barely able to form a coherent thought, she only knew one thing. She needed to get away. She needed to get as far away from Ian Haven as possible.

"Mom," she sobbed, falling into her mother's arms.

"What, baby? Sweetheart, what happened?" her mother asked, her voice filled with worry.

"I'm g-going w-with you," said Hallie between sobs. "I'm g-going h-home."

She backed out of her mother's arms, opened the car door, sat down, and pulled it close.

To her everlasting gratitude, they didn't ask her what had happened.

Not immediately. Not until she was ready to tell them.

She cried all the way home to Boston and every day thereafter, until August 15, when she boarded a plane bound for college in Palo Alto, determined, once and for all, to leave Ian Haven behind.

***

"*Ian.*"

He didn't know if he was still asleep or waking up, but the voice was Hallie's, and he sensed distress in its tone.

"Halcyon," he murmured with his eyes still closed.

Oh, God, his throat. So dry, it felt like scorched earth. There was no saliva to swallow, and Christ! His head. It throbbed like someone was hitting him in the skull with a hammer.

"*Oh, my God.*"

It was Hallie's voice again, but not close. Almost ethereal. And sad. Like she was trapped in a dream or far away. Wait. Was he still dreaming? Or was he awake? And where *was* he? Not at home. It didn't smell like clean cotton and dirty socks like his bedroom at home with Rory. It smelled musty. What the hell was going on?

He tried to open his eyes, but the clanging in his head intensified with the slight movement, and he winced.

Crying. I hear crying. Is Hallie crying? He powered through the pain in his head and forced his eyes to open, narrowing them as he tried to focus.

Ceiling beams.

Dust swirling over his head.

For the first time, he realized that there was a warm, heavy weight on his bare chest. Hallie? Was it Hallie's head over his heart? It had to be…

"*Why, Ian?*"

Wait. The voice wasn't coming from beside him. It was coming from *over* him. He needed to look around. Reaching up with the hand that wasn't pinned down, he rubbed his eyes.

"Hallie?" *Where are you? Why are you crying, baby?* He wanted to say more, but his mouth was like chalk, like sandpaper.

He looked around, blinking rapidly, and finally found a fuzzy figure standing over him. He tried harder to focus, but the slightest movement resulted in a pain so sharp, it was like eating a hundred freezing-cold ice creams at once. Sharp, sharp pain in his head that made him gasp in shock.

"*Why?*" she sobbed again.

This isn't right.

None of this feels right.

Hallie's crying.

Someone's lying on me, but it isn't her.

Goddamn it, what the fuck is going on?

His heart started beating faster, and his head ached in a way that was almost unbearable. Ian wiggled both of his hands loose, reaching up with both hands to hold his head.

The person resting on his chest sighed, rubbing her head against him, but it couldn't be Hallie, because Hallie's voice was coming from over him. *What the fuck?* Ian lowered his hands to her hair. Curly hair. Not straight and smooth like Hallie's.

It isn't Hallie, his brain whispered. *Try to keep up. Hallie's not lying next to you, she's standing over you. Someone else is lying beside you.*

His eyes slid back up to Hallie to find that her face was finally in focus.

But he'd never seen her looking like this—her cheeks wet with tears, her eyes flashing with fury and heavy with grief. She looked, well, *devastated* as she stared down at him like he'd done something…something…*unforgiveable.*

But the last he remembered, everything was set up for her birthday celebration and he was waiting for her to arrive. The candles. The flowers. The promise ring. The wine.

The wine.

The wine.

A sickening feeling overcame him, and his stomach revolted against it.

What happened?

What the fuck *is going on?*

He reached toward Hallie, wanting the reassurance of her hand in his, where it belonged, where it always belonged. "W—Wait. What's going—"

"Fuck you, Ian," said Hallie—*his* Hallie, whom he'd *never* heard swear. She moved out of view, the sound of her footsteps headed toward the stairs. They stopped for a second. "Don't *ever* speak to me again."

Wait. Wait wait wait! What are you talking about? We love each other! I love you! Wait!

"Hallie!" he cried, scrambling to sit up as the downstairs slammed shut.

Every movement hurt. Every sound echoed in his head like a gong. He groaned, reaching up to dig the heels of his palms into his temples to find relief.

"Hey," said a girl's voice. "Hey! Ian!"

He turned his neck to look at Vicky Lafontaine, who lay on the blanket beside him. She leaned up on her elbow and looked at him, her blonde, curly hair falling around her bare shoulders.

Staring at her in horror, he reached for the blanket covering them and whipped it off, only to find that neither of them was wearing more than underwear.

"What. The. Fuck?" he demanded.

She looked back at him with wide, innocent eyes. "What do you mean?"

"Why—why—why the *fuck* are *you* here? Why are we almost naked? What the fuck just—Hallie was just here! She left!"

"I guess she was probably looking for you," said Vicky, sitting up and holding her bent knees against her chest.

Ian shot up too fast into a sitting position and paid for it with another wave of nausea. He groaned through clenched teeth. "I'm gonna be sick."

"Wait a sec," said Vicky, scrambling across the floor in her bra and underpants for the picnic basket and thrusting it at him. "Use this."

Ian heaved into the basket, his puke dripping through the webbing at the bottom. It smelled sour and made him retch more as he struggled to try to remember what the hell happened last night. Why was Vicky here? And why the fuck was he only wearing boxers?

Reaching for the shirt he'd been wearing last night, he wiped his lips and turned to her.

"What happened?"

"You don't remember?"

"Did we fuck?" he asked, searching her eyes, feeling so disgusted, he thought he might vomit again.

Her lips tightened as she lifted her chin. "Would that be so bad?"

"So *bad?*" he bellowed. "It would be a fucking *nightmare!*"

Her eyes widened, then quickly narrowed, sliding to a point over his shoulder and lingering there for a second.

"There's the evidence, Romeo. What do *you* think?" she snapped.

As Ian twisted his body to check out what she was looking at, Vicky reached for her shirt and pulled it over her head. His blood went cold as he caught sight of a ripped-open condom wrapper. His hand shook as he flattened his palm over it, and his stomach sank to find there was nothing inside.

He gasped in horror, turning to Vicky, who was standing up a few feet away from where Ian still sat on the blanket. She had already pulled on her shirt and skirt and was slipping her feet into turquoise flip-flops.

"What...the fuck...happened here?" Ian demanded.

"A *nightmare*," she said sweetly, crossing her arms over her chest, a bitter expression on her face. "And fuck you, Ian. Fuck you very much. You're a total asshole."

Without another word, she headed for the stairs, the slap of her sandals softer and farther away with every step.

Alone, Ian ran his hands through his hair, trying to breathe, trying to think straight, trying to put together what the hell had happened here.

He remembered walking to the barn, picking flowers,

and setting up their cozy spot in the loft.

He remembered looking at the promise ring and thinking about Hallie coming home at Christmas.

He was nervous, and she was running late, right? Right.

He remembered opening one of the bottles of wine and pouring himself a glass.

Staring down at his hands, he tried to remember what happened next...

But his mind was a blank.

A total and complete blank.

Looking behind him, he picked up the condom wrapper, holding it up before crumpling it in his hand and throwing it away.

He picked up the two bottles, but there wasn't a drop of wine left in them and the smell inside the bottles turned his stomach again. Reaching for the picnic basket, he threw up again, then shoved it away. Jesus, what a mess. The candles he'd lovingly set up last night were all knocked over, with melted wax, in various, grotesque shapes, anchoring them to the floor. The cookies had been eaten. The flowers were wilted. The little white box had been kicked behind him, but Ian crawled over to it, relieved to see the ring still inside.

Fuck you, Ian. Don't ever speak to me again.

He reached for his shorts and pulled them on.

No. No, no, no.

He needed to talk to Hallie.

Now!

He had no idea what had happened here last night, but he had no feelings for Vicky Lafontaine. His heart was full of Halcyon.

As he raced down the stairs barefooted, he jammed his arms into the shirt that reeked of vomit, leaving it unbuttoned as he ran as fast as he could toward Lady Margaret. The camp was just starting to stir, and he garnered a mixture of curious and amused glances from campers as he raced to her cabin half-dressed.

Arriving there out of breath, he banged on the door.

"Hallie? Halcyon? We have to talk!"

The door opened and Hallie's roommate, Tate, stood behind the screen. "What the hell?"

"Where's Hallie?"

"Not here," said Tate in a sleepy voice, looking over her shoulder, then back at Ian.

He didn't believe her. Hallie was upset by what she'd seen, and Tate was covering for her. Ian opened the screen door and pushed around Tate, who cried, "Hey! Cut it out!" while Ian looked frantically around the cabin.

"Hallie? Baby, are you here? We need to talk!"

But Tate wasn't lying. The bathroom was empty. Brittany and Chelsea looked bleary-eyed as they sat up in their bunks to look at him. And Hallie's bed was empty and neat, like she hadn't slept in it.

"Sorry," he muttered to the girls, leaving the cottage.

Where are you? Where are you?

If you didn't sleep here, then...

Colby!

Yes, that's it! She's at her parent's cabin!

Running by the boat dock, around the campfire ring, and through the woods, he ignored the branches and rocks that cut his feet open, the desperate burning in his lungs, and the way his stomach heaved without mercy. He had to get to her. He had to talk to her before it was too late.

He heard the engine of a car in the distance and ran faster, choking on his own vomit as he ran out of the woods in time to see a car with Massachusetts plates stop at the end of the lane before turning onto the main road.

"Wait!" he tried to cry, but his throat was so dry. Almost no sound came out.

A whimper.

The saddest fucking noise that Ian had ever heard.

It turned into a silent wail as he slumped against the white picket fence in front of her house, rested his forehead on his knees, and wept.

chapter seven

For the three weeks after the Rileys' visit and before Rory's wedding, Ian continued to work on Hallie's cottage but stayed out of her way, as she'd expressly requested.

October turned into November with wee Jenny proudly showing Ian her Halloween costume (*"A turtle, Mr. Haven, 'cause there's a turtle on the Summerhaven sign."*) and Hallie avoiding every possible interaction with Ian, right down to pleasantries. When he arrived in the morning, she was on the phone, or in the shower, or had already taken Jenny to the store. He started bringing his own lunch so she wouldn't be troubled to make him anything, though Jenny still kept him company every day. And when it was time to go home, Hallie was scarce again, having taken Jenny on a walk or running errands or just nowhere to be found.

It made Ian ornery not to see her. It made him ache to arrive at her place every day without the promise of seeing her face or hearing her voice. It made him sad that there was no room for friendship between two people who had once loved each other so passionately.

But then he'd remember back to that day—when she'd found him with Vicky and left Summerhaven with her parents. He'd tried to call her, though he suspected they'd changed their phone number because of him. After a week, all he received was a busy signal and a recorded message that the number was no longer in service. He'd written her letters, pouring out his heart to her, but they'd been returned unopened.

Finally, Brittany Manion had pulled him aside one evening when they passed each other on the main path.

"Ian."

"Brittany."

"Stop trying to contact her," she'd said, her blue eyes cold.

"Can you get her a message?" he'd asked desperately.

"Are you crazy?" asked Brittany. "No! Absolutely not! You broke her heart, Ian. She hates you. Just leave her alone."

"I can't," he said. "Please. I have to talk to her."

"About what? Screwing other girls? No."

"*Please,*" he'd begged.

Brittany had shaken her head. "She doesn't want to hear from you ever again."

"It's not what she thinks."

Brittany had cocked her head to the side. "Oh, really? You *didn't* spend the night with Vicky? You weren't found naked, asleep in each other's arms? There *wasn't* a used condom wrapper by your head?"

Ian had gritted his teeth. "I can't even *remember*—"

"Well, isn't that convenient," she'd said, crossing her arms over her chest.

No! No, it isn't! It's awful!

But no matter how many times Ian tried to piece together what had happened, he'd come up empty. He'd completely blacked out. He had no memories—not one—of what had happened in that loft from the time he'd started drinking until the moment Hallie's voice had woken him up the following morning.

And Vicky Lafontaine, whom he'd tried to ask and who could fill in the blanks if she wanted to, told him to "fuck off" and threatened that if he bothered her again, she'd tell his parents what had happened and/or figure out a way to press charges against him.

Ian hadn't gone near her again.

So that night—the night that was supposed to be the best of his life—was a black hole of misery and despair, and Ian was drinking so much to numb the pain, it was probably scrambling his memories even more.

"*Please, help,*" he'd murmured, a desperate and pathetic plea.

"That's actually what I'm trying to do. Let her go, Ian," advised Brittany. "Move on."

He'd watched Hallie's best friend walk away, his heart throbbing with the terrible truth that any chance he'd ever had with Hallie was gone. And then he'd gone on his first two-day bender, with some high school friends from Sandwich.

"Mr. Haven?"

"Yeah, ladybug?" asked Ian, relieved to have a respite from bad memories.

"Are you almost finished fixing our house?"

Ian had hauled the dock out of the water yesterday, and today he was using a chainsaw to cut it into pieces. Jenny was allowed to watch him from a few feet away as long as she didn't get up from her pink plastic beach chair.

He looked up at the house—at the new screens on the porch windows; at the roof, which had been completed last week; and the shiny new glass on panes that had once been broken. The chimney had been cleaned out, the electric heat refurbished, and the water now ran clear. No mouse dared run amuck in Colby Cottage with the number of traps Ian had laid out, and he'd piped new insulation into the walls, then patched them, so the girls would stay warm this winter. Was it pretty? Not really. The house would need a new coat of white paint in the spring, some serious landscaping and a new dock. But for now? At least it was habitable.

"All I've got left to do is break down the dock and boat house. Once they're hauled away, ladybug, I think I'm done for now."

"And then you'll just come over to see me? We won't have to work no more?"

He was dragging a piece of the dock by her chair, but he stopped, staring at her hopeful face for a moment before dropping the wood to the ground.

Squatting in front of her chair, he smiled at her sadly. "We'll always be friends."

"I know!" said Jenny, reaching out to pat his beard. She had spoken to her father via Skype several times now, and between knowing he was alive and well, and settling into Colby Cottage, she seemed happy, which was the sole bright spot in Ian's life right now. "We can just have fun!"

Ian took a deep breath and sighed. "We'll have to talk to your mommy, okay?"

Jenny nodded gravely, remembering Ian's first and most important rule. "We always get Mommy's permission first."

He leaned forward to kiss her forehead, then reached for the rotten planking and dragged it around the house to the half-filled dumpster in the driveway.

Part of him would really miss coming by Colby Cottage

every day, but part of him would be relieved not to receive his daily shunning.

Help me with my house. That's all the amends I need.

An important part of making amends was not forcing your will on the object of your efforts. Sure, Ian would like to be friends with Hallie. Hell, he'd like to be a lot more than friends with her. He'd like the chance to love her all over again. He'd like to prove that the boy who betrayed her had grown up, and the man he'd become could and would, given the chance, love her until the end of time.

But that wasn't his call.

It was hers.

And she'd been clear: no matter how much he loved her, she wasn't able to love him in return. Shit. She was barely able to *like* him.

So be it.

When her house was finished, he'd leave her be. Or he'd try, at least. He'd try his best, and that was all a good man could do.

That said, they had a very real and immediate challenge ahead if she intended to keep her distance and he intended to leave her alone. With Rory and Brittany's wedding extravaganza commencing next Wednesday, he'd see quite a bit of her socially, and acting awkward around each other wouldn't be fair to the bride and groom, especially since Ian was the best man and Hallie was the matron of honor.

Maybe, he thought, *they could try another truce? This time for Rory and Brittany?*

But he quickly squashed the idea. It had fucked with his head for them to be cordial to each other the weekend the Rileys had visited. It had messed with him, making him hope, making him dream, making his desperate, fucking longing for her multiply with every second. Since that night at the campfire, he'd listened to "Carrickfergus" no less than one hundred times, remembering her steady gaze across the campfire—the way they couldn't look away from each other and the feelings it had stirred in him.

He couldn't have her.

But he couldn't help wanting her.

And the whole thing sucked.

A few mornings later, he stirred his coffee, his thoughts a mishmash of Hallie and Jenny and Rory's upcoming wedding, as Finian walked into the kitchen in flannel tartan sleeping pants and a white T-shirt.

"'Morning," said Ian. "Happy Thanksgiving."

"'Mornin'," said Finian, taking a cup for coffee. He turned to Ian, leaning against the counter and humming "The Death March" before taking a big gulp. "Two more days."

Ian couldn't help chuckling. "I don't think Rory feels as dreary about his wedding as you do."

"Eh. I don't feel dreary. Good for him."

"If memory serves," said Ian, "you like a party."

"That I do," said Fin, "and Rory asked me to play a wee song or two at the reception."

"What'll you play?"

Fin pulled out a chair, spun it around, and straddled it. "I was thinkin' of Carrick-bloody-fergus, but you've gone and ruined it for me."

Ian rolled his eyes, adopting a brogue. "Tell me somethin': are you stayin' in my house, lad?"

"I am."

"Then I can play whatever feckin' songs I feckin' want."

"Maybe you should do more than play songs," suggested Fin, lowering his chin to give Ian a look over the rim of his cup as he sipped his coffee.

"What does *that* mean?"

"Yer moony as a wee *buachaill*. Yer obviously in love with the lass. Why don't you do somethin' about it, then?"

Feeling unaccountably annoyed by Fin's accurate observations, Ian stared back at his cousin, crossing his arms over his chest.

Fin wasn't going to let it go. "She wasn't lookin' at me over that campfire, mind. Only had eyes for you."

Ian continued to stare, cracking his knuckles loudly.

"You rebuilt her whole bloody house for her, for Jaysus' sake."

Eh, it was no use. Fin wasn't going to be intimidated into dropping it, t' scrappy little bastard. Ian cleared his throat, taking a sip of coffee. "Doesn't matter how I feel about her. She hates my guts."

It was Fin's turn to stare. "Say what, now?"

"She. Hates. My. Guts."

"That's what I thought you said, and I have two things I need to say about that," said Fin. "Ready? Good. One, hate isn't the opposite of love. That'd be indifference. So maybe she hates you, but that means she still has *feelings* for you, and it's not such a long way from love to hate, Ian. And two," he scoffed softly, "no she doesn't. No woman looks like *that* at a man she hates."

"This isn't helpful," said Ian, even though his foolish, hopeful heart was already clinging to Fin's words like a life raft.

"I get it. The truth can hurt…"

"Shut up, Fin."

"…but that doesn't make it any less true," he finished, standing up, swinging his chair around, and taking his coffee back to his bedroom.

***

After such an exciting Thanksgiving Day, it was almost impossible to put Jenny to bed, but with Rory and Brittany's rehearsal tomorrow and rehearsal dinner tomorrow night, Hallie's little girl needed her sleep. Hoping it would help her drift off, Hallie lay down beside her.

They were still sharing the same bed that Ian had put together for them weeks ago, in the same room they'd slept in since arriving in New Hampshire. Although she could set up one of the upstairs bedrooms for Jenny, Hallie figured there was time enough for that after the new year. For now, she sort of loved listening to her daughter breathe in and out beside her, watching her sleep, grateful for the miracle of her life.

Britt had contacted Sergio several times over the past few weeks on Hallie's behalf, and Jenny had become accustomed to talking with him over Skype, which had seemed to reassure her that her father hadn't disappeared. Hallie was even considering Sergio's suggestion to meet in Miami next summer so that he and Jenny could spend a few days together. No matter how much Hallie despised him, he was Jenny's father and finding a place for him in Jenny's life was important.

As for the other man headlining Jenny's life, lately it felt like every one of her daughter's sentences started with *Mr.*

*Haven did this…*or *Mr. Haven did that…*and damn, but it was hard to put someone out of your mind when your child was so focused on him. But Hallie did her best to avoid Ian, to disappear when he was around, planning market runs and errands when he was on his way over and visits to Brittany when he was about to go. She didn't want to exchange pleasantries. She didn't want to run into him. She didn't want to encourage the feelings he had for her and she had for him. She just wanted them to go away.

On Friday, he'd left a message for her in the mailbox. She'd seen him leave it, standing in the upstairs window and watching as he closed the lid. He'd locked eyes with her and placed two fingers behind his ear just like he used to do. *I left a note for you.*

Then he'd dropped his hand with a frown and walked over to his truck.

After he left, she hurried downstairs.

But the note was maddeningly brief:

Halcyon,

The work's finished.

Thank you for letting me make amends.

Ian

She recognized the handwriting, running her fingers over the bold letters, her heart clenching with longing and telling her something she knew deep inside, and was now forced to acknowledge:

I don't want you to be finished.

I want more.

I shouldn't, but I do.

For weeks he had done everything possible to prove to her that he was a changed person. And for weeks she'd rewarded those efforts with avoidance and contempt. Was it fair? Was it fair that she was still making him pay for something a decade in the past? What was the statute of limitations on hating your cheating seventeen-year-old boyfriend? Just shy of forever?

She sighed, throwing an arm over her forehead and glancing at her sleeping daughter. Jenny had raced to Ian today at the Summerhaven Thanksgiving dinner, and he'd swooped her up in his arms after their five-day hiatus from one another. And after that, Jenny wouldn't leave his side.

Wedding guests had arrived steadily all day until most of the Oxford and Cambridge cottages were full, and the Thanksgiving dinner acted as the kick-off to Rory and Brittany's wedding weekend.

Hallie and Jenny had been seated with Mr. and Mrs. Toffle, Burr, Tierney, and Ian at Thanksgiving dinner, which made avoiding him that much harder. Especially when she kept catching him looking at her with that heartbreaking expression—the one currently worn by her heart, which was bursting at the seams with unrequited yearning.

Since he'd finished the work on the cottage last Friday, she'd felt indescribably lonesome for him. Every morning at eight, she listened for the sound of his truck, disappointed when she didn't hear it. Even though she'd avoided him, she'd been comforted by his presence, heartened at the thought of him improving her home, making it safer and warmer over the countless hours he'd selflessly given to her. He'd done thousands of dollars of work for nothing, and she was grateful. She was so very grateful. In fact, gratitude didn't fully describe her feelings anymore. They had grown beyond gratitude to tenderness, and the more she fought it, the stronger it held on.

"Mommy, I loved Thanksgiving today," said Jenny in a dreamy whisper.

"I thought you were asleep."

"Almost," said Jenny, opening her mouth to yawn. Her eyes opened sleepily. "Mr. Haven is my best friend."

"It was good to see him, huh?"

"I missed him, Mommy. On Monday and Tuesday and Wednesday. I missed him," she said, yawning again, unable to keep her eyes open. "I like it better when he's here."

"He can't come here every day," said Hallie. "He has other jobs he needs to do. But remember, he's our neighbor. He's just through the woods and up the path. Not far."

"Not far," repeated Jenny in a whisper, snuggling closer to Luna and falling back to sleep.

Not far enough, she thought, thinking of Ian's face across the Thanksgiving table earlier that evening, and what a slippery slope existed between hate and love. With such heavy thoughts weighing her down, it wasn't long before she drifted off into a deep sleep of her own.

The morning sun rose high and strong for November, and Hallie woke up, still dressed in her clothes from the night before. From the great room, she could hear the hum of Jenny's morning TV shows, and she checked the clock on the bedside table: 7:54 a.m. They had plenty of time before Rory and Brittany's four o'clock rehearsal in the barn, followed by dinner for the entire wedding party...including Ian, of course.

Ian, for whom her feelings were so confusing. She was still angry at him, of course, but her anger was quickly waning, outlapped by gratitude and tenderness.

You just need to get through today and tomorrow, she told herself. *After the wedding, Britt will leave on her three-week honeymoon, and you won't see another Haven until Christmas. You can do it. Just stay out of his way today, and for God's sake, Halcyon, don't keep looking at him. In fact? No looking. None. You're not allowed to look at Ian Haven today.*

Thus determined, she took Jenny for a long walk, spent the late morning cleaning the cottage, then took a long, hot shower. She dried and curled her hair with care, and chose a royal-blue Dupioni silk cocktail dress for the rehearsal and dinner.

When the doorbell rang unexpectedly around three thirty, she rushed from the bathroom to open the door, but Jenny got there before her.

"I'm Jenny. Who are you?"

"I'm Tate. Where's your momma?"

"Tate!" cried Hallie, beaming at her old friend as she hurried to the door.

"Hallie, Hallie, bo-Ballie!" said Tate, wrapping her skinny arms around Hallie and squeezing tight. "Look at you, beautiful!"

"When did you get in?" asked Hallie, pulling away from her friend.

Tate Jennings was one of those rare women who didn't age—she could pass for nineteen even though she was twenty-seven. Tan and petite, with platinum-blonde hair cut short like Michelle Williams and wearing stylish short-shorts on surprisingly long legs, she looked more like a pixie pin-up than a charter boat captain in the Florida Keys.

"Five minutes ago," said Tate in her strong southern accent. "I'm in Lady Margaret, but without any roommates, I was feeling lonesome. Thought I'd sneak through the woods and see how you're doing." She looked over at Jenny and smiled. "I've seen pictures of you, small fry…on Christmas cards. But you're *way* purtier in person."

Jenny grinned, half hiding behind her mother's back.

"Brought you a little something." Tate reached into her purse and pulled out a conch shell. "It's the ocean, Jenny." She showed Jenny how to put the shell up to her ear and listen. "You try."

Jenny's eyes widened with her smile as she took the shell from Tate and listened, racing over to Luna to give her a chance to listen to the ocean too.

"Well, *she's* beautiful," said Tate, pushing her sunglasses up on her head and unmasking her blueberry-blue eyes. She glanced up and down Hallie's trim form in her fitted dress. "And you look like dynamite, sister."

"Hair and makeup," said Hallie. She flicked a glance at her watch. "Speaking of which…we have to be at the rehearsal in twenty-five minutes. You coming?"

Tate shook her head. "No, thanks. Weddings make me itchy. I'll show for the dinner tonight, but tomorrow's nuptials will be more than enough monogamy for me."

Hallie cocked her head to the side. "Wait a second. Didn't Britt tell me you were dating someone down in Florida?"

Tate shrugged. "I've dated a *lot* of someone's. No one special."

"With all those wealthy businessmen booking charters, you won't be single for long."

"Unlike Britt, I ain't looking for anything serious. I'm only looking for fun."

"Someday you'll settle down, Tate," said Hallie, "won't you?"

"Ha! He'd have to catch me before he could keep me, and I ain't met the one who could catch me yet."

"Fair enough." Hallie laughed. That was Tate—the freest free spirit God ever created. "Want to come hang out in the bathroom while I finish getting ready?"

She shook her head. "Nope. Just came to say 'hey.' I'll see you at the dinner later, okay? I asked Britt to put us together."

"I'm so glad you're here. Can't wait to hear all your news!"

Tate waved good-bye, calling farewell to Jenny before heading out.

Hallie finished getting ready, helping Jenny into a light-blue party dress, with white tights and patented leather shoes, then rushing both of them into the car.

It wasn't until she was halfway to the barn that Hallie realized this was the first time she'd be back there since the morning of her seventeenth birthday. Suddenly she remembered that morning with blistering clarity: the dust motes in the air and the soft sigh of Vicky Lafontaine as she resettled her head across Ian's bare chest.

But another picture—one Hallie hadn't revisited in years—also developed in her mind: Ian's face that morning. Huh. For the first time in a long time, she thought about his expression. He didn't look caught, or sheepish, or sorry. He looked…surprised. Almost as though he was as shocked as she was.

"Mommy! Look! Look how pretty!"

From the top of the hill that led down to a car park

area, she looked at the old barn, which had been painted since her summer camp days. It was once barn red, but now it was bright white and sparkling, roped with white lights and flowers for Brittany's rehearsal. It was more than pretty. It looked like a magical fairy castle hidden in an enchanted wood.

"It's beautiful," she said, driving down the hill and pulling into a parking place.

Looking at the barn through her windshield, she felt a gladness—a mixture of relief and wonder—that the old place should be so transformed. It didn't look like the same spot where her dreams had been crushed and her heart broken. It looked different. And decorated for such a wonderful occasion, it hummed with warmth and hope. It was the perfect place for her best friend to practice her wedding to the boy she'd loved since childhood.

Jenny unbuckled herself from her seat and bounded from the car as soon as Hallie opened the door, no doubt looking for Ian.

Meanwhile Hallie walked slowly up to the building, remembering the last time she'd opened the door and walked inside.

Hello?

Hello? Ian?

She half expected to see sunlight filtering through the high windows and dust motes floating in her sightline, but happily, she was greeted with no such reminders. The inside of the barn had been as meticulously renovated as the exterior.

The floors shined with multiple coats of shellac, the walls and overhead beams were painted a bright white, and the old fireplace in the center had been rebuilt. The room had been split into two distinct areas tonight. Half of the barn had two rows of seats with a center aisle, and the other half had about six round tables—enough seating for sixty.

"Hallie! You're here!"

Beautiful Brittany, dressed in a pale-pink satin skirt and matching top, crossed the room, taking Hallie's hands and kissing her friend on both cheeks. "You look...stunning."

Hallie grinned. "Says the prettiest girl in the room."

"No. I mean it," said Brittany, extending her arms so she could look at Hallie. "You look hot. You curled your hair and—"

"You're making me blush," said Hallie, clapping her cool palms over her cheeks. "You're just used to seeing me in crumbling cottage mode."

"I guess. Been a while since I've seen you like this...dress, heels. Wow." She met Hallie's eyes, her own narrowing. "Couldn't be you wanted to look extra gorgeous for anyone in particular?"

"What? Of course not! No! I mean, *you*, I guess. It's *your* rehearsal. Oh, look! Rory's coming over."

She dropped Brittany's hands to accept a kiss on the cheek from Rory, and that's when she saw him—over Rory's shoulder, looking so much like his teenage self, her heart literally stuttered.

Gone were the thick black beard and long black hair that he'd kept back in a ponytail since their reunion in October. His face was clean shaven but for a dark shadow of scruff, and his thick hair was short. He looked...devastating.

"Ian," she whispered, unable to keep the words from passing through her lips, unable to stop herself from gawking at him when she promised herself she wouldn't.

With his eyes locked on hers, he crossed the room with long, confident strides, standing behind his brother as Rory pulled away from Hallie.

"Hey, Halcyon," he said softly.

"Hey, Irish," she answered, her voice a whisper, her heart racing.

Rory and Brittany took hands and left them alone without a word.

He was ridiculously beautiful, standing before her in a navy-blue suit with an unbuttoned white dress shirt beneath. There was a faint tan line around his jaw where his beard had hidden his face from the summer sun, and her fingers twitched at her sides, itching to trace the line on his skin.

"You shaved."

Ian smiled.

He *smiled* at her, and it almost blew her mind because she wasn't ready for the brilliance of it; for the megawattage of Ian Haven's smile without a thick beard hiding it. She gulped softly, reminding herself to breathe.

Reaching up to massage his jaw with his thumb and forefinger, he nodded. "For Rory. He's been on my case to shave it for months."

"You look…" *Familiar. Handsome. Heartbreaking.* "…good."

"You look *beautiful*," he said softly, his voice lowering so that only she could hear him. His smile faded away, the expression on his face changing until it almost appeared that he was in pain. But his gaze was so steadfast, she couldn't look away. Between them, his chest rose and fell, his breathing audible in her ears. Hers did the same, every cell in her body leaning into him, toward him, like a flower to the sun.

"I...I..." She didn't know what she wanted to say; too many words jumbled in her mind. *I wish things had turned out differently? Thank you for all the work you did on my house? Thank you for nurturing my daughter? I can't stop thinking about you?* But she couldn't seem to form meaningful words. Instead she just nodded slightly. "Thank you."

He took a deep breath then offered her a small smile and his bent elbow. "Well, like it or not, we're partners."

"What?"

"Best man and matron of honor. Partners."

"Oh," she said, dropping her eyes to his elbow and realizing that he was offering it to her. They were going to walk down the aisle together. And tomorrow, they were going to do it again, in a church, while his brother and her best friend bound themselves to one another until the end of time. "Right."

He searched her face, keeping his elbow extended. "Will you take it?"

And she felt it—right then, right there:

If you don't want him...if you never want him again, make an excuse to go find Jenny, or go talk to Brittany, or use the ladies' room. If you want to close the door on forever, say no. Right now, right here, say no and walk away.

Still looking deeply into his eyes, she reached up with a trembling hand and placed it in the crook of his arm, watching the worried lines smooth out on his handsome face and wondering if her heart could stand the risk of loving him out loud again.

chapter eight

While the beginning of the evening had started in a place of high and intense emotion, the rest of it had been light-hearted, full of fun, and uneventful.

They rehearsed the ceremony twice, then immediately filled the other half of the room to party. Cocktails were followed by dinner and then by toasts and singing.

Hallie and Jenny were seated at a table with some of Hallie's old friends from Summerhaven and a few acquaintances from Boston, while Ian sat with his sister, parents, cousin, and other visiting Havens several tables away. And yes, they did meet on the buffet line over the chicken piccata once, and he did catch her eyes once as Finian sang "Lock Up Your Daughters," but Tate had poked her in the ribs, stealing her attention away.

"Who is that?"

Hallie looked at the table where the Havens were singing, her eyes landing effortlessly on Ian. "Who? Ian?"

"No, Hal. I know who Ian Haven is. *He* hasn't changed a bit." She gestured with her chin. "The brown-haired one with the guitar. Some younger Haven brother we never met?"

Hallie shook her head. "Nope. That's their cousin. Finian."

"Oh," she said, nodding like she should have known. "*That's* Finian, huh?"

At about the same time, Finian had looked up too, still

singing his heart out—*Where girls are good-looking we're looking for fun! Oh, we'll chase them and catch them and love them! So lock up the last one*—as he grinned at Tate.

"He's *trouble*, huh?" she asked, a catlike smile on her lips.

Hallie shrugged. "I don't know him."

As the song wound down, Tate looked away from Finian, turning to Hallie. "I've been meaning to ask: what's it like being around that rat, Ian Haven, again?"

She didn't like Tate calling him a "rat" but set that feeling to the side.

Hallie took a deep breath. "Confusing."

Tate's eyes bugged out of her head. "*Confusing*? Why? What the Sam Hill are you *confused* about? 'Member Vicky?"

"I remember Vicky," said Hallie with a sigh. "But that was a long time ago."

"A leopard don't change its spots," said Tate, taking a sip of champagne. "If you're smart, you'll steer clear of him." She leaned over and kissed Hallie's cheek. "I gotta powder my nose. You coming?"

Hallie smiled at her friend and shook her head, turning to look at Jenny, who sat beside her, resting her weary, little head on the table. "Big day tomorrow, and my baby's fading. I think I better get her home."

"See you tomorrow, Hal."

"See you tomorrow, Tate."

Jenny had fallen asleep in the car, and Hallie carried her inside the cottage. After she was settled into bed, Hallie removed her makeup and changed into pajamas. For a minute, she thought about making a fire and pouring herself a glass of wine, but her weariness won the draw, and she got into bed instead, watching the shadows dance on the ceiling as she thought about her evening.

On one hand, there was Ian—handsome as hell, and so kind to her and Jenny. She'd taken his arm when she probably shouldn't have, but that damned tenderness inside of her was asserting itself, making itself known.

On the other hand, there were Tate's words—Tate, who'd been a witness to what had happened with Ian—telling her not to get tangled up with him again.

Unsurprisingly, perhaps, Hallie ended up dreaming about a gentle leopard who couldn't change his spots, no matter how much he wanted to. No matter how much *she* wanted him too. And when she woke up the next morning, she was still tired.

But today is Brittany Manion's wedding day, she reminded herself, smiling as she swung her legs over the side of the bed. *And God couldn't have offered a lovelier day for it*, she thought, walking over to the window. Sun sparkled on the lake, and puffy white clouds floated across the sky. It didn't look as warm as yesterday, but that was okay. It was a crisp, cool autumn day. Perfect for a wedding.

"Mommy!" exclaimed Jenny, running into the bedroom. "It's Auntie Britt's wedding day!"

"I know!" said Hallie, impulsively grabbing her daughter around the waist and picking her up for a cuddle.

And to her delight and relief, Jenny grinned at her mother, placing her little hands on Hallie's face. "I love you, Mommy."

An arrow to the heart.

I'm dead.

It had been months since Jenny told Hallie that she

loved her. Months of not speaking and anger and sadness. Months of Hallie second-guessing her worthiness as a parent. Months of wondering when and if her child would "bounce back" as the doctor had predicted.

Somehow it had happened. Jenny was restored to her. And it filled her heart with so much joy, she couldn't contain it. She squeezed Jenny close. "I love you too, baby. You'll never know how much."

"Mommy, you're hugging me too hard!" cried Jenny, and Hallie leaned back a little to look into her daughter's face.

"Sorry. I'm...I'm just so excited about today."

"We're getting our hairs done and our fingers painted."

"We sure are," said Hallie, thinking they'd better shake a leg because they needed to meet Brittany and Tierney at the beauty salon in Meredith in about an hour.

"And then Auntie Britt's going to get all dressed up like a princess."

"And you too, Jen-Jen."

"And you too, Mommy. Like last night."

"Last night?"

"You looked beautiful, Mommy. Mr. Haven said so."

"How do you know that?"

"He told me. He said, 'Your mommy is the most beautiful woman in this room.' Then he smiled and shook his head and said, 'I take that back. Your mommy is the most beautiful woman...in the *whole world.*'"

"Ian said that?"

"Uh-huh," said Jenny nodding with a chipper grin. "He likes you lots, Mommy."

"Jennifer Giovanna Silveira, are you playing cupid with

me and Mr. Haven?" she asked, trying not to smile back at her minxy little girl but losing the fight.

"Does that mean I want him to kiss you like Ariel and Eric?" she asked, referring to her favorite Disney movie. "Yes!"

Hallie shook her head at Jenny, making a silly face, then tickled her belly until they were both giggling.

Finally, Jenny wiggled out of her arms. "I'm making cereal. You come and eat breakfast, Mommy, okay?" Then she ran out of the room to go make two bowls of cereal.

Sitting on the bed, in the bright autumn sunshine, Hallie marveled at her mended relationship with Jenny. She recalled that the morning after they'd arrived at Colby Cottage, Jenny had slapped her bowl of cereal away. Several weeks later, here she was, cheerfully fixing them breakfast. It felt so good. And she breathed deeply, knowing that she had one specific person to thank.

He deserved to hear the words. He deserved to know how much he'd helped her.

In fact, all he'd done since she'd arrived back in Summerhaven was help her.

And what is love, if not helping someone you care for and expecting nothing in return?

"Mommy! Breakfast time!"

Scooting off the bed, Hallie joined her daughter for breakfast, then quickly got them both dressed and out the door, driving twenty minutes to the salon in Meredith and getting there just as Britt and Tierney were pulling in.

"Good morning!" called Brittany, who was holding a tiara and veil covered in clear plastic.

"Auntie Britt!" cried Jenny, running to her godmother.

"You're getting married today, and I'm a cupid!"

Hallie cheeks flamed as she caught up with her daughter. "Hi, ladies! What a beautiful day for a wedding."

"Or for playing cupid," deadpanned Tierney. She cocked her head to the side. "So it was *you*. All those years ago. *You* were the one."

There was no use denying it. Hallie nodded her head. "It was me."

Tierney winced, looking away from Hallie for a moment before turning to her again. "It destroyed him. Not that I blame you. I know he did something terrible to you. But whatever it was, he wasn't the same after it happened."

Hallie knew this because Brittany had filled her in on Ian's steady decline after she'd left Summerhaven Camp that July. At the time, she'd felt vindicated by his behavior—she felt that he ought to feel terrible about what he'd done. But now, it hurt a little to think of Ian spiraling down like that.

"He made a choice," she said softly.

Tierney held Hallie's eyes, her voice gentle, but insistent. "Maybe he made a mistake."

"Maybe," said Hallie, thinking about his face that morning—his shocked and confused expression, like he had no idea how he'd ended up in bed with Vicky. And she thought about the work he'd done for her, despite her cold treatment of him. What did it all add up to? She was still trying to figure it out.

"I think he still loves you," said Tierney carefully, her green eyes so much like Ian's, Hallie couldn't look away. "If you don't love him...if you *can't* love him...tell him that."

"I already have."

"Yeah." Tierney nodded as though she should have

already known that. "That's Ian. He might give up on himself sometimes, but he'll never give up on someone he loves. He once told Rory that of the three of us, Rory was the heart, I was the soul, and he was the entertainment." She chuckled softly. "He was right about everyone but himself. He *is* entertaining sometimes, but his purpose is deeper."

"What is it?"

Tierney offered Hallie a small smile. "Ian's the glue."

"Um...hello? It's my wedding day!" Britt, who was holding Jenny on her hip, grinned expectantly at her friends. "Are you two finished with Ian?"

"For now," said Tierney.

Not by a long shot, thought Hallie, though she kept the words to herself, following her friends toward the salon.

"I've never been here," said Britt, "but all the ladies in my book group said it's the best place in town. It just opened." She put down Jenny to open the door, leading the way to their morning of beauty.

Hallie looked up at the sign over the posh salon that read "The Fountain of Youth." With a bubbling fountain in the courtyard in front of the business, it was a pretty clever name. In fact, she was still musing over the wittiness of it when she suddenly realized that it had a double meaning.

Fountain.

Like Lafontaine.

Like *Vicky* Lafontaine, who looked up from behind the reception desk with a cheerful grin when they walked in.

"'Morning, ladies! Welcome to the Fountain of Youth!'"

"Vicky? Vicky Lafontaine?" asked Britt, her breathless voice telegraphing all of the shock that had made Hallie's blood run cold as soon as she matched the salon name with

Vicky's face. Brittany whipped her head around to look at Hallie, her expression horrified.

Hallie felt like a fish on land, her lips parted, her lungs empty. She wanted to run, but Jenny had taken her mother's hand and was looking up at her. "Mommy? Is that Auntie Britt's friend?"

She wanted to say no. She wanted to *scream* no. But all she could do was stare at the woman who'd once been the girl that shattered her dreams.

"Oh, my Lord! Is that *Brittany Manion*? Give me a hug! It's been years!"

Vicky bustled around the counter in her chic black cocktail dress and high heels, pulling Britt's stiff body into an awkward hug.

"I *never* stop by on Saturdays, but my receptionist called-in sick today so I came by to help! I had no idea you were coming in!" Vicky leaned away, her eyes landing on Britt's veil. "And it looks like it's a big day for someone!"

"I'm...I'm getting married."

"Here?" asked Vicky.

"At, um, Summerhaven. Um, do you own this place?"

Vicky nodded. "I do! *Fountain* of Youth. Get it? Fountain? Like Lafontaine? Although that's not my name anymore. It's Rodney. Victoria Rodney. I married a banker in Boston who had a lake house on Winnipesaukee. We bought *this* place over the summer. It's his little tax write-off and *my* little hobby."

Leave, thought Hallie. *Leave before she notices you! Just grab your child, turn around, and go. Britt and Tierney will understand. Go! Just go!*

But she was frozen in place, staring at Britt and Vicky's

unlikely reunion with a sort of horrified fascination.

"We come up every other weekend. Gabe likes to fish, and I was bored so he bought me this," she said, gesturing to the salon with an elegant hand. "Keeps me busy when we're up here in the wilderness," she finished, finally letting her eyes wander to Tierney, whom she looked at in surprise. "Is that Tierney Haven? Oh, my God! *You've* changed!"

The Tierney of their youth had been bookish and awkward, but there was no trace of her now. With long, black hair and huge green eyes, the adult version of Tierney Haven was a knockout.

"You haven't," said Tierney, taking a step back to stand beside Hallie.

Vicky's eyes slid to Hallie and her jaw dropped. "And—oh, my God!—Hallie? Hallie Gilbert? Is that *you?*"

"It is!" exclaimed Jenny. "My mommy's name is Hallie!"

Vicky stared at the child. "*Mommy?* Oh, my. Hallie had a baby."

"I'm *not* a baby," said Jenny with a frown.

Vicky dismissed Jenny with a shrug, her eyes trailing up Hallie's old Saint Laurent jeans and ivory cashmere boat neck sweater. "You always had style, Hal."

"Thanks, Vicks," she said without smiling, her voice relaying all the bitterness and hatred she felt.

She turned away from Vicky, catching Britt's worried eyes, which flicked to the door then back to Hallie. *Do you want to leave?* Forcing herself to think about someone other than herself, it occurred to Hallie that it would be impossible to find another salon with four available appointments for washes, blow dries, updos, manicures, and pedicures at the last minute. They were stuck. She shrugged, forcing herself to give Brittany a wan smile.

"Well!" exclaimed Vicky. "This is fun! Let me run back and make sure everyone's ready for you and we'll get started, okay?" Tossing her wavy blonde hair over her shoulder, she sauntered into the back of the salon, out of view.

Hallie finally took a deep breath, her shoulders slumping and her body weak. Vicky Lafontaine. Fuck. What a fucking nightmare.

"Unbelievable," she whispered.

"Hallie!" Britt grabbed Hallie's hands, holding them tightly. "You say the word and we'll go. I promise. We will walk out of here and—and—and well, we'll just do our *own* hair and nails."

Taking a deep breath, Hallie let it go through pursed lips. "No. I'm not doing that to you. I'm not letting *her* do that to *us*."

"Can someone clue me in?" asked Tierney.

"Can we tell Tierney?" asked Britt, and Hallie nodded, finally giving Brittany permission to spill the beans. She turned to her almost sister-in-law. "As you've already guessed, Ian and Hallie secretly dated the summer we were seventeen."

"So how does Vicky figure in?"

Brittany winced. "He cheated on Hallie with Vicky. Hallie found out, left camp, and they never saw each other again. Well…until last month when Hallie moved back up here."

"Oh, God. Oh, Ian, what did you do?" muttered Tierney, her voice laced with disgust. "*Come on*." She looked up at Hallie. "I'm so sorry."

"It's not your fault, Tierney."

Vicky returned with a flourish. "Britt, I have Nadia ready for you. Tierney, you're with Inga. And the child is with Stacey." She looked at Hallie. "Hallie, Johann is finishing up with another client. Can I get you a cup of coffee while you wait?"

Hallie shook her head, taking a seat in the reception area while Britt, Tierney, and Jenny were shepherded to the back.

Wow, thought Hallie, looking up at Vicky, who drummed her shellacked nails on the black marble reception counter as she reviewed an appointment log. *This is the definition of awkward.*

"So…" said Vicky, looking up and plastering a fake smile on her hot-pink lips. "How are things with you?"

"Why'd you do it?" asked Hallie, the quiet words slipping from her lips without permission, without notice.

"Excuse me?"

She had half a thought that she should pretend she hadn't spoken or pretend she was asking about something else. But the reality was that this woman owed her an explanation, and Hallie intended to have one.

"Why. Did. You. Do it?"

"Do what?" asked Vicky, her smile fading.

Hallie's nostrils flared. "Why did you sleep with Ian Haven on the night before my seventeenth birthday?"

"Oh, my! Were you always this tacky?"

"Goddamn it, Vicky, answer me!" she demanded. "Why did you *screw* my boyfriend?"

Vicky stared at Hallie for a moment, searching her face, before leaning closer, her lips parted in surprise. "Oh, my

God. You don't know."

"Know what?"

"What happened that night." She laughed softly. "*I'm* the only one who knows? Neither of you two ever figured it out? Oh, my!"

"Figured *what* out?" Hallie stood up, approaching the counter, fisting her hands at her sides and willing them to stay there and not, as she would prefer, slam them into Vicky's plastic-perfect face. "I asked you to tell him I couldn't make it. Instead, you slept with him."

"Right," said Vicky, nodding her head, her eyes laughing at Hallie. "*Slept.*"

"*Fucked,*" hissed Hallie.

Vicky took a step back, her face both surprised and offended. "That's an ugly thing to say, Halcyon."

"It was an ugly thing to see."

Vicky sat down on the high stool behind the counter and picked up an emery board. She began filing her nails like they weren't discussing the most devastating moment in Hallie's entire life; a life that included her ex-husband giving her a venereal disease.

"Hello?"

Vicky looked up and shrugged. "Calm down. It wasn't what you think."

"Oh. You *didn't* fuck my boyfriend?"

"No," snapped Vicky. "I didn't."

The.

  Room.

    Spun.

Around and around and around.

Feeling dizzy, Hallie reached for the marble counter in

an effort to steady herself.

Vicky put her nail file down on the counter between them and looked up at Hallie, her delicate eyebrows furrowing. "Let me get you a cup of water."

"I don't want any goddamned water," said Hallie. "I want to know what *happened*."

"Fine!" Vicky sighed with annoyance. "Lord, it was ages ago, but I think it went something like this…You asked me to relay a message to Ian, but I was already in my pajamas. I had to get ready, and it took a while. And then I had to walk all way across the whole campus to the barn. When I got there, he was drunk. Like, *drunk* drunk—lying on his back, on the floor, with a bloody forehead because he must have knocked it into something. I told him you weren't coming, and he got upset. *Really* upset, like on the verge of tears. He asked me to stay."

Hallie blinked back a sudden onslaught of tears of her own, imagining Ian in such a state. "Then what?"

"He kept getting confused and calling me Hallie and saying he loved me. Um, let's see. I think I sat down next to him, and we drank the rest of the wine, and—I don't know…I guess we—"

"You fucked him."

"Fat chance, sister. I already told you that didn't happen. He could barely *stand up*, let alone *get it up*."

"So how'd you end up half-naked, sleeping next to him?"

Vicky tapped her lower lip with one perfect nail. "As I recall, I took off my shirt and skirt, and helped him with his shirt and shorts. I figured, he asked me to stay…he was offering, right?"

"No! He thought you were me!"

"Whatever. When you're that drunk, any piece of ass will do."

"You're disgusting," Hallie whispered.

Vicky's eyes narrowed, and her next words carried a bite. "He was a *flirt*, Hallie Gilbert. A *bad* one. He had flirted with me all summer, raising my expectations, and—"

"He was *my* boyfriend, and you *knew* it!"

"Not my problem," said Vicky. "I was there. He was there. I was horny. He was hot."

Hallie took a step away from the counter, because she was *thisclose* to doing bodily harm to the bitch in front of her. "Then what?"

Vicky sighed dramatically like this entire conversation was exhausting. "Um…well, he was lying on his back—"

"With his underwear still on," Hallie blurted out.

"Yes. God!" She bugged out her eyes in exasperation. "Can I finish?"

Hallie nodded.

"…and I found a condom under the other blanket, so I ripped it open, and I was about to help him get it on when I realized he'd passed out."

"Passed out."

"Totally. I smacked his face, and he didn't make a sound."

"What then?"

"I might have pushed down his boxers and taken a look at the goods." She hummed something appreciative, and Hallie winced, shaking her head back and forth with pure disgust.

"I figured I might get lucky in the morning, so I laid

down next to him, pulled the blanket over us, and went to sleep. But instead, *you* woke us up in the morning, *he* freaked out, and I told him he was an asshole and walked home."

"And told everyone at camp that you'd fucked him."

Vicky shrugged, a slight smile teasing her lips. "I was out all night. People saw me walking home and made assumptions."

"And you let them."

Hallie stared at her nemesis, trying desperately to process this new information and find its place in events that had haunted her for years. But all it boiled down quickly to one important fact:

"You *didn't* have sex with him."

"Honey, I don't even think we *kissed*." She sniffed elegantly. "I'll see what's keeping Johann."

Slipping behind the desk and through a velvet curtain, Vicky disappeared, leaving Hallie alone.

He didn't have sex with Vicky.

He didn't betray me with Vicky.

Which meant that—and it crushed her soul to realize it—she and Ian had lost years with each other not because of an actual betrayal, but because a set of circumstances had colored a situation to appear like cheating.

He'd gotten drunk and assumed the worst of himself.

She'd found Ian and Vicky together and assumed the worst of him.

And the net result of their assumptions and distrust? Her stomach turned over as she added it up: a decade of alcoholism for him…and a loveless marriage and expensive divorce for her.

They'd ruined both of their own lives over things that

had never actually happened.

And it broke her heart all over again.

A curtain to the left of the reception desk parted, and a man with bleached-blond, spiked hair appeared. "Hallie? I'm Johann. Sorry to keep you waiting. Shall we?"

She nodded, too sad for words, alone in no-man's-land and wondering how in the holy hell she was supposed to tell Ian.

***

Although Hallie looked just as beautiful today as she had last night, Ian couldn't shake the feeling that something had happened. She was…different.

Last night she'd been almost playful—a little like the day they'd declared a truce back in October. She'd told him he looked good in his suit, and she'd taken his arm when he offered it to her. It had almost seemed like they were turning a corner of some kind into peace, and he'd been eager to embrace it.

But today?

Today she was quiet and grave, like he might behave if he'd received terrible, unexpected news. She seemed lost in thought and barely able to meet his eyes, while he couldn't keep his off of her.

Dressed in a pink dress that matched Tierney's, with her hair piled up on her head like a princess, she was so tragically beautiful, it hurt to look at her. It hurt to think that he could love her as much as he did—as much as he always *had*—and never stand a chance with her.

As Rory and Brittany recited their vows, promising to love, honor, and cherish each other until death, Ian thought to himself that he'd already made those promises to Hallie when he was seventeen. He considered her promise ring, which he still had, hidden in the corner of his sock drawer, a sign of his eternal love for her, of an unspoken promise to love her until the end of his days. It didn't matter that he'd never had the chance to give it to her and say those words aloud. Those promises had already been made in his heart, regardless of what happened with Vicky.

In this life, there was only Halcyon Gilbert for Ian Haven.

And so it would be until the end of his days.

Standing there in the First Congregational Church of Sandwich as his brother pledged to love and honor Brittany Manion until death, Ian had a crystal clear revelation of his own: he'd rather spend his whole life loving Halcyon, than force himself to shut off the purest feeling he'd ever known and move on. He'd rather love her unrequitedly and die knowing that he'd never given up on them.

She didn't look at him during the ceremony or afterward, her eyes downcast and sad until someone spoke directly to her; at that point, she'd smile, but her cheer was false. Something had happened between last night and now, and Ian wanted to know what it was.

Maybe her husband was making trouble for her? Or her financial situation had somehow worsened? It couldn't be about him, could it? Maybe she regretted today that she'd been friendly last night? Maybe she'd decided she wasn't ready to forgive him yet? He didn't know. But as soon as the wedding was over, he'd track her down at the reception and ask what was going on. He couldn't bear for her to be upset if there was anything he could possibly do to ease her worries and give her peace.

After the wedding, Ian stood in the receiving line outside the church, his glance occasionally flicking to Hallie and Jenny, who were talking with Burr in the church courtyard. He didn't feel jealous; he had it on good authority that Burr was going to ask Tierney a very important question very soon. He just wished that he had a few minutes to talk to her too.

Suddenly Jenny bolted away from her mother and beelined to Ian. Grinning at her, he squatted down, ignoring the guests who wanted to shake his hand. This particular guest was more important to him than all of them put together.

"Hey, ladybug. My goodness, you look pretty today!"

"You already said that to me!" she reminded him with a giggle. "Did you know that Bridey is coming for Christmas? Mr. O'Leary said so!"

"Is that right?"

"Yes! I get to have my best friend here for Christmas! Can you believe it?"

"I can. And you see that big hill over there?" Jenny turned to look over her shoulder, then nodded at Ian. "How would you like to go sledding?"

Jenny clapped her hands. "I would love it! I'ma tell my mommy!"

Ian reached out to give her a squeeze. "You do that, ladybug. You tell your mom and make sure—"

"—I get permission!"

He stayed low as he watched her scamper away, looking up to catch Hallie's eyes for a second. She gave him a grim smile before turning her attention to Jenny. Whatever she said to her daughter made her little shoulders slump, and a minute later, the twosome said good-bye to Burr and trudged to their car.

Again, Ian wondered, *What's up with her today? What's weighing so heavily on her mind?*

He was determined to find out.

Ian drove himself and his parents back to Summerhaven from the church, helping his mother into the main dining room. Nine years after her stroke, Colleen Kelley Haven still used a wheelchair, though her speech had improved mightily over the years.

She gasped as he wheeled her inside, and Ian had to agree: the event planner that Brittany had hired in Boston had done an amazing job. The large room was decked out with white flowers, bright-green ivy, and white-satin bunting. A twelve-piece swing band was set up in one end of the room with a temporarily installed dance area protecting the original wood floors. He counted twenty tables set for ten people each, marveling that Rory and Brittany even knew that many people. If Ian ever got married—not that it would ever happen, but if it did—the only people he wanted to be there were his family and a few close friends.

"Ian," said his mother over her shoulder in her strong Irish brogue, "are you well, son?"

"I am, mum," he answered, pushing her to Table Two, and sitting in an available chair beside her as guests started filing into the huge room for the reception.

"Yer clean now?"

"Yes. I'm sober," said Ian. "Haven't touched a drink since March. Go to meetings faithfully."

"Tierney's kept me updated, but I didn't want to get my hopes up," she said, reaching out to cup his cheek.

"I don't plan on ever going back," he said, leaning into his mother's touch. "I'll do whatever it takes to stay sober."

"We're proud of you, son," said his father, sitting down on Colleen's other side. "We prayed that you'd find your way."

"I have, Dad. I'm going to be okay. I'm sorry for what I put you through."

"You've already said all that," said his mother, waving away his apology. "We're just relieved you're healthy again."

Ian smiled at her, then glanced over at the door, hoping for a glimpse of Hallie. But when it opened, Fin walked in, hurriedly tucking in his shirt and smoothing his hair. Ian watched, a bit bemused when, a second later, Hallie and Britt's friend, Tate Jennings, walked in reapplying her lipstick. *Hmm. I suspect shenanigans.*

"What're you grinning at, now?" asked his mother.

"Finian," said Ian.

"Yer man's trouble. Me sister was always too lean on the punishment."

"But not you, Mum."

"Boys need the spoon sometimes," she answered, giving him a dry look. "Especially boys whose names end in 'ian.'"

Ian chuckled. "Well, trouble or not, he's done the work of two men over the past month. Wish he could stay longer than six months; this old place would be running like the Ritz."

She grinned, though the paralysis of her face made it appear endearingly lopsided. "I guess he's found his callin'."

When the dining room door opened again, Ian's heart swelled, because Hallie and Jenny entered, standing side by side. Hallie leaned down and said something to Jenny, and she ran over to the place card table, where Tate was still composing herself. Tate grabbed two cards from the GS row and handed them to Jenny, who took them to her mother.

Ian already knew where they were seated—Hallie with him and the rest of the bridal party at Table Three, and Jenny with the rest of the children in attendance at Table Six, which was set up with arts and crafts and a hired babysitter to help the little ones stay busy.

"Mum, I have to go."

His mother nodded, looking over at the door where Hallie stood, her eyes trained on Ian. "She's grown up to be a beautiful woman."

"You remember her?"

"Halcyon Gilbert? Oh, yes. I always liked her. A cut above some of the others."

Ian nodded. "I agree."

"And her daughter's very cute."

"Right again."

She cleared her throat, lowering her voice. "Where's her father?"

"Out of the picture."

"Officially?"

Ian nodded. "They were divorced over the summer."

"I see." His mother sighed, smiling again for Ian. "Then I guess you have somewhere you need to be, don't you, now?"

Ian leaned forward and kissed her forehead. "*Tá grá agam duit*, Mom."

"Ah, Ian. I love you too, son," she said, squeezing his hand before letting him go.

CHAPTER NINE

Ian crossed the long room, steadily holding Hallie's eyes as he approached her.

Ten years and four months ago, he'd crossed this very floor, staring into those same eyes, touching the soft skin behind his ear to confirm she'd gotten his note and would be meeting him later. He'd been nervous that night but so full of hope and love.

He wasn't nervous tonight, but he'd be lying if he said he wasn't filled with hope and love.

Hope for them.

Love for her.

A second chance, his heart whispered. *Please give us a second chance.*

"Mr. Haven!"

"Hey, ladybug," said Ian, glancing down at Jenny with a smile.

"Guess what! I'm sitting with the big kids!"

"You are? Well, you better get over there," he said.

"Can I, Mommy?"

"Of course," said Hallie. "I'll be at Table Three if you need me, baby…" But Jenny was already halfway across the dining hall, racing to be with the other kids.

Hallie stared at Ian's throat for a minute, gulping before lifting her eyes to his. The expression in them was grave, though he couldn't decipher more than that.

"Halcyon," he said softly, taking a step closer to her. "What happened?"

She held his eyes for a moment, then shook her head, looking away. "I can't. Not here."

He reached for her hand, wrapping his fingers around the soft, cool skin, relieved when she didn't pull away. "Come with me."

Leading the way, he pulled her to a door hidden in the wood grain of the wall and opened it. Once inside, they walked down a dim hallway and through an open doorway. Ian reached for the light switch and flicked it on to reveal a small, windowless room with a table, six chairs, and six lockers against the wall.

"I didn't even know this was here," said Hallie.

"The hallway connects it to the kitchen. In the early days, this was a kitchen-staff dining room. Now it's just a break room."

She nodded once, then withdrew her hand from his, looking up at him like she had something to say but didn't know how to say it.

"You know you can say anything to me," said Ian. "*Anything.*"

"I don't—I don't know…" She crossed her arms over her chest and looked away from him, her voice trailing off.

Taking a risk, Ian dropped his hands to her shoulders. "Please, baby. Tell me. Talk to me."

She lifted her face when he called her "baby," blinking at him in surprise. Her lips tilted up in a sad smile. "What would have happened? For us? If Vicky hadn't…I mean, if we'd…"

"I know what you mean," said Ian, removing his hands

at the mention of Vicky Lafontaine. He let them fall to his sides, his shoulders drooping with regret.

"I *really* want to know," said Hallie softly. "I want to know what you think would have happened between us."

He pulled out a chair for her, holding it as she sat down, then pulled out another for himself, turning the back to her and straddling it to face her.

"I know what I *wanted* to happen."

Her eyes were glistening, but she didn't cry. "What? Tell me. What did you want?"

"You, Halcyon. I wanted you," he said. He took a deep breath and let it go slowly. "That particular night, I wanted to make love to you. I...I wanted to be with you, to touch you, to watch your face when you...when we..." He took another breath, but it was shallow and ragged this time. His voice was low and gravelly when he continued. "I wanted to feel you next to me afterward while we fell asleep."

She nodded at him in encouragement, reaching up to wipe away a tear.

"Beyond that night," he said, thinking about his plans for them, "I wanted to stay together. I had this idea that you'd go to Stanford and I'd go to BU, and we'd write and call and see each other at Christmas. I felt like..." He scrubbed his hands over his face, grateful to finally have a chance to tell her these things but overwhelmed by them too, by the rawness of his feelings as he told her everything that had slipped through his fingers that night. "I felt like that night was the beginning of forever for us. I wanted...I wanted *forever*, Halcyon."

A small, sad sob escaped through her lips, and she bent her head, clenching her hands together in her lap. Unable to bear it, Ian bolted from his chair to kneel before her, taking her hands in his as she cried.

"I am *so sorry*," he said, barely able to see their hands through his own tears. "I am so sorry, Halcyon. So sorry, *mo chroí*."

"My…heart…" she whispered through tears.

"Yes." Ian squeezed her hands, staring back at her and nodding. "*Mo chroí*. My heart."

"Do you…" She took a ragged breath, raising her head to meet his eyes. "Do you think we would still be together?"

Without hesitation, Ian nodded. "Yeah."

She nodded too, her face crumpling into more tears. "Me too."

Letting go of one of her hands, he reached for her cheek, brushing away her tears with the pad of his thumb before palming the soft skin. He searched her eyes. "Is it too late, Halcyon?"

She leaned into his touch, her eyes closing for a moment as she took a deep, shuddering breath. But just as she was about to answer, his phone started buzzing.

Buzz. Buzz, buzz.

"Ignore it," he said.

She shook her head. "It might be Rory. It's his wedding day."

Honestly? Ian had all but forgotten where he was and what day it was. But she was right. It *was* Rory's day. Still holding her hand, he dropped his other hand from her face and took his phone from his breast pocket, hitting "Answer."

"Yeah?"

"Ian? Where are you?" Rory, just as she'd suspected.

Shit. Think fast. "Uh. Had to go to the john."

"They're about to announce us. Can you finish up and get over here?"

"Yeah."

"And if you see Hallie, tell her we need her too!"

"Will do." The line went dead, and Ian pocketed the phone, looking up at Hallie. "They're about to announce the bride and groom. We need to get back in there."

She nodded, slipping her hand from his so she could swipe the tears from her cheeks. "Oh, God. I've been crying. I'm a mess!"

"I've never seen you more beautiful," said Ian, standing up and offering her his hand. "Can we finish this conversation later?"

She took his hand, rising from the chair and smoothing her dress. "Yes. Or maybe tomorrow. Another time. Tonight isn't—it's not the right time."

This answer frustrated Ian, though he had to agree with her. Stealing random minutes at his brother's wedding wasn't ideal for such an important conversation. He'd already waited ten years for this talk; he supposed he could wait another day.

"Ready?" he asked, squeezing her hand.

She looked up at him, and he hadn't been lying before: she was so beautiful in his eyes, it gave him the shivers. "I'm ready, Irish."

They left the little break room, and Ian changed his grip on her hand, lacing his fingers through hers, his heart swelling when, instead of pulling away, she pressed her palm flush to his. His body reacted too, his blood heating, tearing through his body and pooling below his belly. He wanted her as much today as he had that night—more, maybe. For the last ten years, he'd missed her so desperately, every drink he took trying to mask the pain of losing her. But now? In this moment? For the first time since that terrible morning, the future felt…hopeful. Like maybe, just maybe, there was another chance for them; like maybe fate wasn't finished writing their story.

They slipped from the hallway back into the reception, and Ian was grateful that the crowd around the door was thick and deep so they could blend into the mass. He tugged on her hand, moving them toward the front door. Just outside, through the windows, he could see Tierney and Burr holding hands, ready to walk into the dining room after being announced. But what struck Ian the most was the look on his sister's face.

Happiness.

Such pure happiness, he knew that Burr had jumped the gun and asked her to marry him.

Turning back to Hallie, he caught her eyes and grinned, relieved when she smiled back at him. It felt good to see her smile, like maybe their talk had lightened some of the burden she'd been carrying around all day.

"Excuse us," he said to a couple standing between them and the door.

They moved aside and Ian pulled Hallie outside with him, letting the door to the dining hall close behind him. Tierney looked up at him, and Ian beamed at her. He didn't need a peek at her finger to know that there was now a ring on it.

"*Comhghairdeas*, Tierney," he said, leaning down to press a kiss on her cheek. "*Tá grá agam duit*, little sister."

She smiled up at him. "I'm engaged!"

"I could tell the moment I looked at you." He turned to Burr, who stood beside Tierney with his arm around her shoulders. "Congrats, brother."

"I promise to make her happy," said Burr, drawing Tierney's hand to his lips and kissing her knuckles.

"You already do that," said Tierney, standing on tiptoes to swap her knuckles for her lips.

"Ian!" yelled Rory from behind Tierney and Burr. "Can you please get in here? They're going to announce Tier and Burr, then you and Hallie, then us. *We're* going to dance, and then they'll tell you guys to join in. Got it?"

"Got it," said Ian, looking down at Hallie as he slid into line between his brother and sister. "I guess we're going to dance."

"I can't remember the last time we danced."

"I can," whispered Ian, leaning down close to her ear. "Fourth of July. After the fireworks."

She looked up at him, her eyes luminous in the light reflected from the dining hall, and smiled. "That's right. You have a good memory."

"Where you're concerned, I do."

"...the groom's sister and the happy couple's friend, Tierney Haven and Burr O'Leary!"

Tierney and Burr stepped forward through the door, walking into the reception to the roar of clapping and cheers.

"We're next," said Ian, untangling her fingers from his and placing them in the crook of his elbow to escort her inside.

"...the groom's brother and the bride's best friend, Ian Haven and Halcyon Gilbert!"

The door opened again, and Ian walked into the reception with Hallie on his arm to the cheers of the guests, who made an aisle for the wedding party that extended from the front door to the dance floor. Ian and Hallie took their place in front of the band by Tierney and Burr, waiting for Rory and Brittany to join them.

"And now...for the first time, may we introduce to you...Mr. and Mrs. Rory Haven—Rory and Brittany!"

Rory and Britt took their place in the center of the dance floor as the band started playing "I Love You (For Sentimental Reasons)," with the lead singer giving an excellent Sam Cooke–style cover.

Though his eyes were focused on his brother and truly, in the depths of Ian's heart, he was overjoyed for Rory's happiness, he was hyperaware of the woman standing beside him with her fingers curled into the black fabric of his tux. The energy between them hummed, a galvanizing gathering, and Ian could *feel* it like a palpable, living thing.

I love you, I love you, I love you, I love you, I love you, I love you, I love you...

The words were everywhere.

Coming from the voice of the singer.

In Rory's eyes as he gazed at his wife.

In Tierney's as she smiled at her fiancé.

And in Ian's heart as he reached for Hallie's hand and covered it with his.

Love.

Everywhere.

"And now we'd like to invite the wedding party to join Rory and Brittany on the dance floor!"

Ian took Hallie's hand, his breath catching when she

looked up at him to meet his steady gaze. She offered him her hand and he took it, reaching for her waist to pull her closer. Her other hand landed on his shoulder, her fingers curling a little into the fabric as they had in his elbow. Sliding his hand to the middle of her back, he tightened the distance between them so that her chest grazed his with every movement, so that he could feel her breathing, so that he could almost feel the beats of her heart.

He bent his elbow to draw her hand to his chest, flattening it over his own heart, then covering it with his and holding it there as he stared deeply into her eyes.

It's beating for you, Halcyon.

It's only *beating for you.*

He felt her quick intake of breath as she leaned forward, brushing her cheek against his jaw and resting it on the collar of his shirt. His eyes closed slowly, soaking in this moment and committing it to memory, should it be the final time he ever held her.

All too soon, the song ended. His eyes opened slowly as she lifted her head.

"Thanks for the dance," she said.

"Halcyon," he said, "I want—"

"Mr. Haven! Me next!"

Hallie's lips tilted up in a grin, and they looked down at the same time to see Jenny standing beside them, tugging on the bottom of Ian's jacket. And even though he was dying for more time alone with her mother, Jenny never failed to get a genuine smile from Ian.

"Are you asking me to dance, ladybug?"

"Yes, I am!" she said, reaching her arms up so he'd lift her.

Still smiling, Hallie let go of his shoulder and released his hand so he could dance with Jenny to Billy Joel's "The Longest Time."

For the rest of the reception, Ian's heart felt lighter than it had in years.

It wasn't that Hallie had necessarily said anything reassuring to him or given him actual hope for a second chance, but it felt like something important had changed between them. At the wedding, her mood had felt like sadness to him, but since talking to her, it felt different, like moving forward. And the way she'd let him take her hand, and how they'd danced together? Hate didn't seem to be a part of the equation anymore. And damn but he was eager to talk to her about everything and find out what had changed, but he was also eager to enjoy the changes: the way her eyes caught his over dinner, the way she danced with him twice more, the way she asked him—toward the end of the night when she found Jenny asleep at the kids' table—if he'd walk them home.

Maybe that was the biggest miracle of all, he mused as he carried her sleeping baby in his arms through the dark, cool Summerhaven night. She'd asked him for help. Him. When she could have asked anyone else. She asked *him*.

They made small talk as they walked, speaking of the wedding and the reception and the little girl in Ian's arms.

"She's going to sleep well tonight," said Hallie, her heels crunching over leaves as they made their way through the woods to her cottage.

"Are you going to the brunch tomorrow?" asked Ian.

"We're planning on it. You?"

"Yeah. I want to say good-bye to Rory and Britt."

"Three weeks in Ireland," said Hallie. "Sounds like heaven."

"Have you ever been?"

"No," she said. "To England, yes. Never to Ireland."

I'll take you sometime, he thought, then grimaced at his eagerness.

His heart was flying after tonight, and he needed to slow down. Did it feel like things were changing? It did. But one, he didn't want to get his hopes up too much. And two, Ian knew well that change was a funny thing. It could happen in fits and spurts. A lot of change today, then none for a while as they both acclimated. No sense in wanting more than she was able to offer. Best to move at her speed.

"It's beautiful," he said. "When I was a kid we went every other year. And all of us studied abroad in Ireland."

"I studied in Paris," she said.

"I didn't know," he said, suddenly realizing how much he wanted to know. He'd like to spend a million hours learning the secrets of Hallie.

The light over her front door came into view—a spark of brightness in the darkness of the evening, and their conversation drifted off as she opened her purse to find her keys. They jingled as she adjusted them in her hands.

Last time he'd carried Jenny home—after the campfire with the Rileys—Hallie had reached for Jenny and taken her from his arms. This time, she unlocked the door and opened it, preceding Ian into her house and closing the door behind him. He followed her through the great room and past the kitchen to the back bedroom that she shared with her daughter. As gently as possible, he placed her little girl on the bed, then bent down and kissed her forehead.

"'Night, ladybug," he whispered.

He straightened up to find Hallie looking at him intently, her eyes liquid and vulnerable, her lips parted.

"Before," he said, "at the reception...I asked if you thought it was too late for us." The need to touch her was so overwhelming, he reached for her face, cupping her cheeks reverently, his heart racing when she covered his hands with her own. "I need you to know...it's not too late for me. It will *never* be too late for me because even after everything that happened, I still believe in us. I—I *believe* in us, Halcyon. And if I love you hard enough, and long enough, with my entire heart and my entire soul, I believe you'll love me back. You'll find a way to love me again."

Bright blue and shining, her eyes searched his face, tracing the lines wrought from years of drinking and sadness, her gaze finally landing on his lips.

And maybe he should have leaned forward and kissed her on the forehead as he had Jenny, but that wasn't what he wanted. He wanted to kiss her like a man kisses the woman he loves. And if that wasn't what she wanted, she could push him away and he'd go.

He drew her face closer, angling it up to his, and let his lips fall, with unerring precision and infinite tenderness, to hers.

She gasped softly as he brushed his lips over hers. Once. Twice. His hands slid gently down the column of her neck, over her shoulders and down her arms. They encircled her, pulling her body against his as he kissed her again, sealing his lips over hers and tracing the seam of her lips with his tongue.

They opened to him with a soft moan, and his tongue

swept inside to find hers, his body reacting to this kiss that he'd dreamed of for years and years—tasting her again, remembering the soft stroke of her tongue sliding against his, the way her breasts molded against the hard lines of his chest.

He groaned, holding her tighter, wanting her to feel his arousal, to remember the way it had been between them once and could be again. She arched her back and pressed her body against his, their chemistry familiar, yet new, as undeniable as it was unrivaled; there was no woman on earth whom he wanted, had ever wanted, or would ever want, as much as she.

"Mommy?"

A sleepy voice interrupted them, and Hallie instantly pulled away from Ian, blinking at him in surprise as she reached up to touch her lips, her breasts heaving with every shallow breath she took.

"I'm here, baby," she said, still looking up at him.

"So slee-py, Mom-my," murmured Jenny.

Ian looked at Jenny over Hallie's shoulder to see that her eyes were closed.

"I know, honey," said Hallie, sitting on the bed beside her daughter. She brushed the hair from Jenny's forehead tenderly, leaning forward to kiss her in the same place that Ian had. "I love you, baby."

"Love you...Mommy..."

After kissing her once more, Hallie stood up and took a step back, staring at Ian.

Should he stay? Did she want him to stay?

"Ian..." she started.

She didn't. He could tell from the stilted way she said his name, and whatever she was going to say next, he probably didn't want to hear it. He couldn't bear hearing that the kiss they'd just shared was a mistake.

"I'm gonna go," he said quickly.

She gulped, then nodded, wringing her hands together. "That's probably best."

"Good night, Halcyon," he said softly, turning quickly and leaving the room, and her home, before she could try to undo what had already been done between them.

***

HALLIE: Britt, Jenny is so tired today, I don't think we'll make brunch. I'm so sorry and I hope you understand. Have the best honeymoon and post tons of pics on Facebook! See you in three weeks.

BRITT: Of course I understand. Rest up and give my goddaughter a kiss from me. Love you two!

Maybe skipping the brunch was cowardly, but Hallie was in no condition to see Ian Haven again so soon.

So much had happened yesterday, she could barely get her head around all of it.

She needed time. She just needed a little bit of time to process everything she'd learned, and everything that had happened so quickly between them. She needed to be certain that her life was headed in a direction she *wanted*. She had been through too much—and put Jenny through too much—to just allow her life to take unexpected detours without her express permission.

So instead of attending Britt and Rory's brunch, Hallie stayed in her fleece pajamas on Sunday morning, making a fire in the fireplace and pancakes for her and Jenny. When Jenny asked why they weren't going to the brunch, she lied and said it had been canceled, but that they'd see Auntie

Britt and Uncle Rory when they returned home from their honeymoon in mid-December. Hallie just wasn't up for a quarrel, and there was no way Jenny would skip a chance to see Ian and the rest of the Havens if she knew the brunch was still happening.

As her daughter played LEGOs on the living room carpet with Luna by her side, Jenny lay back on the couch, staring at the ceiling and thinking about yesterday.

For ten years, she'd believed that Ian had willingly had sex with Vicky. Learning that he hadn't even kissed her that night was...well, earth-shattering. Not only had Ian not betrayed her, but it actually sounded like he'd been so drunk and confused, he'd possibly believed that Vicky *was* her.

It hurt to think of him waiting for her that night.

It hurt to think that he'd probably assumed she wasn't coming.

And it hurt to think of his eyes filling with tears when Vicky told him that she definitely wasn't.

Suddenly his expression the next morning—shock and confusion—made sense to her. He was shocked to find Vicky beside him and confused that it wasn't Hallie.

And Vicky, who'd been rejected by Ian, had perpetuated the lie that she'd slept with him. She'd let it happen. She'd even encouraged it with her silence.

It made Hallie's eyes burn with tears to think of the injustice of it, of the way her love for Ian, and his for her, had been ripped away from them. And *why*? Because of her parents' surprise visit...and Ian getting drunk...and Vicky's hurt pride...and Hallie's assumptions. Circumstances had worked against them, and by not examining those circumstances, they'd been complicit in the destruction of their relationship.

She rolled to her side, staring at the fire and sighing.

She had no doubt that Ian was still in love with her; he'd said as much last night before kissing her. *Oh, God.* They'd *kissed.* She closed her eyes as her heart raced at the memory of his lips on hers. It had felt so right, so perfect, so very much what Hallie wanted and needed. His hands on her body, his lips pressed to hers, his tender words of love and hope in her ears.

Is this what I want? Is Ian Haven what you want, Hallie?

"Mommy! Look at my tower."

"That's great, baby," said Hallie, turning to look at her daughter's colorful creation and mustering a small smile.

"Barbie and Wonder Woman are roommates with Elmo."

"Wow. Progressive. Good for them."

"Elmo steals the cookies that they buy."

"Does he give them to Cookie Monster?"

"No," she said, lying on her belly with her back to her mother. "He eats them."

Hallie laughed softly. "Did you have fun yesterday?"

"Yes. Know what, Mommy?" she asked, still focused on her LEGO figures.

"Nope. Tell me."

"I love it here. I love it better in Hampshire than Boston."

"*New* Hampshire," said Hallie. She took a deep breath. Since they'd left Boston, she hadn't spoken of Sergio directly, worried that it would trigger a negative reaction in Jenny. But now she decided to try. "Hey, Jen-Jen…do you miss Papa a lot?"

"Yeah." Jenny shrugged her little shoulders. "I miss him sometimes."

"You know he'll always be your father, right? And he'll always love you. No matter where he is. No matter what."

"I know," said Hallie, picking up the Elmo figure. "Elmo and I are going to go steal Oreos from the kitchen so we don't make Barbie and Wonder Woman mad."

Hallie nodded. "Just two, okay?"

Well, that went surprisingly well, she thought, watching Jenny go.

She maneuvered onto her back again, throwing her arm over her forehead and remembering the promises she'd made to herself the day they'd driven up to New Hampshire so many weeks ago: *No more men. No more lies. No more betrayal. No lovers. No male friendships. Nothing. No one. No more.*

But Ian wasn't "men"; he was *Ian.*

And since the day she'd returned, he'd been honest and forthright with her, even when it was painful or awkward.

And contrary to what she'd believed all these years, he *hadn't* betrayed her.

She took a deep breath and thought of all the hours he'd worked on her cottage to make amends. She thought of the way he treated Jenny, and how much his presence in Jenny's life had healed her daughter's fractured heart. She thought of the way it felt to hold his hand, or lean against him as they danced, or—*oh, Lord, yes*—the way it made her entire body shiver and ache when he kissed her.

I want his friendship.

I want his love.

I want everything that we were cheated out of having.

I want a second chance.

Giggling softly to herself, she whispered the words aloud, "A second chance."

Tomorrow, she would walk over to Summerhaven with Jenny and see if Mrs. Toffle could watch her daughter for an hour while Hallie looked for Ian. She needed to talk to him.

He wanted to give them a second chance?

She couldn't wait to tell him that she did too.

CHAPTER TEN

Crash!

The roar of wind and a loud burst of shattering glass woke Hallie from a deep sleep.

Her eyes flashed open, and even though she was disoriented, she could tell right away that something was very wrong. Biting cold nipped at her face, and a frigid wind whipped through the room.

Grabbing her phone from the bedside table, she looked at the time: 3:25 a.m.

She grappled for the pull chain on the lamp, though the wind was making it hard to grasp. As soon as light brightened the room, she sat up straight in the bed and looked to her right where a tree branch had smashed through the double windows in the bedroom she and Jenny shared.

"Jenny," she whispered loudly, putting her hands under her daughter's shoulders and pulling her away from the branches looming over the bed, "wake up, baby."

"Mommy?" whimpered Jenny, half opening her eyes before closing them again.

Snow swirled around the room from the gash in the windows and Hallie pulled Jenny onto her lap, swinging her legs over the side of the bed and standing up with Jenny in her arms. She fumbled for the doorknob, closing the bedroom door behind her and beelining into the great room.

Outside, all she could see was white. Swirling white snow. Their first major snowfall of the season...unpredicted and unexpected.

Laying Jenny on the sofa, Hallie covered her with two warm blankets from a basket beside the fireplace, then looked out the windows at the lake. Waves whipped up two or three feet high, but at least they still had power...for now. Living in such a wooded area, however, with high-speed winds and wet, heavy snow, meant she probably wouldn't have it for much longer. One tree had already fallen. Another would surely follow soon.

Hallie raced back into the bedroom for her phone, trying to assess the damage, and realized that it was as bad as she feared. The windows were shattered and part of the wooden window frame had been smashed by the trunk. She moved as close to the branches as she dared, realizing that they weren't on the top of the tree, but in the middle part of it, which meant...

She turned ran upstairs, pivoting left at the top of the stairs and flicking on the hall light, but she already knew she was in trouble from the cold air blasting into the hallway from under the bedroom door. Bracing herself, she opened the door to find that the upper part of the tree had fallen onto her roof. Branches at the midpoint of the tree had broken through the downstairs window, and the trunk had smashed into the roof of the cottage.

It wasn't quite as bad as the hole she'd found in the other bedroom—the one that had *just* been fixed a few weeks ago—but still, the bedroom ceiling was cracked from the weight of the trunk now leaning on it.

"Damn it!" she cried, staring at the damage. The tree

would need to be removed and both the roof and ceiling would need to be repaired. "Why can't I catch a break?"

Ian had warned her that this could happen again, but she'd decided to wait on tree removal until the spring. Now she was going to pay mightily for that decision.

Tears gathered in her eyes as she looked at the room. She hadn't decorated it yet, but it had a bedframe and mattress that were covered in broken ceiling plaster and other debris. And just when it felt like nothing could get worse? The hallway light went black. She'd lost power. "Aw, *come on!*"

Backing out of the room, she closed the door, turning on the light on her phone and making her way down the dark hallway to the stairs. The stairs were icy cold, and now that the electricity was gone, it was only going to get colder. Fast.

Checking on Jenny, who was still sleeping, she glanced at the fireplace, wondering if she should make a fire. But then she remembered her father once telling her that opening the flue to create a necessary draft actually made everything colder in a house, not warmer.

Still gripping her phone like a lifeline, she tapped on the "Phone" icon, and then on her phone book. Britt's cell number was first in her list, but useless, since Brittany was en route to Ireland right now, probably halfway over the Atlantic. Hallie bit her lip as she looked at the rest of the numbers in her phone: her parents, fast asleep in Florida, and a few friends in Boston who'd be concerned but utterly useless in this particular situation; Tate, who'd gotten a ride with Fin to the Boston airport this morning, was probably back in sunny Florida already; Tierney and Burr, who lived twenty minutes away…and Ian.

Her heart clutched.

Ian.

Without thinking about it, she touched his name, lifting the phone to her ear.

Ring. Ring, ring.

Ring. Ring, ring.

Ring. Ring, ring.

"You've reached Ian Haven, Co-Manager of the Summerhaven Event and Conference Center. I can't get to the phone right now. Please leave a message and have a great day!"

She waited for a tone, then said, "Ian? It's Hallie. I know you told me to have the trees dealt with, but…well…I didn't, and another one fell tonight, and the power's gone, and it's a mess here. Can you—I'm so sorry to bother you—but, can you call me?"

She pressed "End," backing up to sit on the couch beside Jenny's feet and feeling so terribly alone, she couldn't help the tears that slipped down her cheeks.

Being an only child had had its advantages—her parents' undivided attention, no one to fight for the remote control or the cupcake with the most frosting—but it had had its disadvantages too. The main one was loneliness. No brother or sister to pal around with on family vacations or call in times of need. No one to hold onto her memories or be extended family for her daughter. She had Brittany, of course, and thanked her lucky stars for her "sister from another mister," but in times like this, when the world was, figuratively and literally, dark, Hallie felt a deep longing for someone to stand beside her.

Sergio hadn't been a great husband—they'd only known each other a few weeks when she discovered she was pregnant with Jenny, and he'd "done the right thing" by asking her to marry him. He was handsome and charming, and even though Hallie didn't love him, she'd said yes. They were going to have a baby, right? Maybe they would learn to love each other, and anyway, she was tired of being alone, tired of dating, tired of wishing for someone beside her. Here was someone asking to marry her, she'd reasoned. Surely they'd come to care for one another, right?

Right. They *did* come to care for each other, but love was elusive, perhaps because their relationship was never very deep or because Jenny's impending arrival had forced Sergio to propose. Hallie and Sergio hadn't shared an understanding of each other's hearts. They didn't have long conversations into the night. They didn't share their secrets. They didn't laugh at the same things.

They co-parented Jenny with love, watched a few of the same TV shows when they both happened to be home, and enjoyed decent sex now and then. But it didn't take more than a year or two for Hallie to start feeling lonelier *with* Sergio than she'd felt without him.

She wanted to be *loved.*

She wanted to be *understood.*

She wanted to be *needed* and *wanted.*

She wanted something that felt like what she'd been building with Ian Haven so long ago, and there was no one—least of all Sergio, with whom she'd never connected with on a deeper level—who could take Ian's place in her heart.

The only time in Hallie's life when she hadn't felt

utterly alone were the moments she'd spent with Ian. Ten years ago...and, it occurred to her, *now*; in these past few weeks, even when she was so resentful of Ian's help, she had come to rely on it.

Why? Easy.

Ian made her feel loved.

Ian made her feel understood.

Ian made her feel needed and wanted.

And all she wanted right now...*right this minute*...was Ian.

Bang. Bang, bang.

Her head whipped up as a fist slammed against her front door.

"Halcyon? Hallie?" *Bang.* "Hallie! Are you two okay? It's Ian!"

"Ian!" she cried, leaping from the couch and running across the room to the door. She whipped it open to find him—fully dressed in a parka, hat, and gloves—standing outside, his fist raised to bang again. Grasping at his glove with both hands, she pulled him inside. "You're—You're *here*."

"I'm here," he said, his face only illuminated by the ambient light on the screen of her phone. "I got your message, got dressed, and jumped in my truck. You're not staying here. You're coming home with me."

And just like that, her shoulder sagged with relief, because she wasn't alone anymore. She didn't know if it was smart idea to stay with Ian—there was so much unresolved between them—but right now, she didn't care. He'd come to her rescue. He'd keep her, and her daughter, safe. That's all that mattered. They could work out the rest. Heck, if she was staying with him, they'd have ample time to talk and—

"Halcyon. Baby," he said gently, interrupting her thoughts.

"Huh?"

"Don't overthink it." When he looked into her eyes, it was as though he could read her mind. Taking off one of his gloves, he cupped her cheek with a warm hand. "It's going to get wicked cold in here. An hour from now, you'll see your breath. In two hours, you won't feel your toes. Just…come home with me."

Come home with me.

Oh, my heart.

"Yeah. Okay."

He smiled at her. "Okay."

"I'm in my pajamas," she said, pointing to her T-shirt and fleece pants. "And Jenny's asleep."

"I don't mind pajamas," he said, sweeping his eyes down her body with appreciation and making her feel warm all over despite the dropping temperature. "I'll carry the ladybug to the truck while you grab some things for the next few days. Deal?"

"Deal. She's on the couch," said Hallie, pointing toward the great room, "covered in blankets."

"I'll get her settled. Meet me outside?"

Ian's snow boots thudded across the floor as he headed for Jenny, and Hallie hurried in the other direction to the bedroom.

He was right—she could already see her breath. Opening the closet, she grabbed a duffel bag, filling it with underwear, socks, jeans and shirts from the dresser. She grabbed a few sweaters, plus Jenny's parka from the back of the closet, then shrugged into her own.

She didn't know where her snow boots were but guessed that they were probably still in a box in the basement. Because this first snowstorm was a surprise, she hadn't unpacked all of their winter things yet. Grabbing her sneakers instead, she pulled them on, shoved her phone charger, tablet, and Luna into the bag and zipped it shut.

When she returned to the door, Ian was waiting.

He frowned at her feet. "It's snowing."

"I know," she said, "but I think our boots are still packed in the basement—whoa!"

Ian swept her into his arms like she weighed no more than Jenny. Looking down at her face, so close to his, his breath kissed her cheek when he said, "The snow's too deep for sneakers."

Snug in his arms, she had no words. All she could do was smile up at him.

"I'll come back for your bag after I get you in the truck. Give me your keys too so I can lock up."

With the snow falling on his dark hair, he looked almost mythic, like some great, protective giant from a kingdom far away, ferrying her from peril to safety.

"Thank you for coming," she said. "I don't know what I would have done without you."

"*Mo chroí*," he said softly, "I would do anything for you. That's how it is when you love someone."

When you love someone.

Her breath shuddered, and overcome with too many feelings to name, she leaned her forehead into the crook of his neck as he carried her down the path and through the gate to the warm truck. He opened the door and slid her gently onto the passenger seat beside Jenny, who was still asleep. Hallie fumbled for the keys in her coat pocket, holding them out for Ian.

"I'll be right back."

She watched through the window as he trudged back to the house. He hauled the bag onto his shoulder, locked the door, then returned to the truck. A moment later, they were on their way back to Summerhaven.

"Fin usually stays in Tierney's old room, but he got caught in Boston. I'm in the room Rory and I used to share. That leaves my parent's old room for you and the ladybug, okay?"

"That's great," she said, rubbing her cold hands in front of the heater. "I'm so grateful."

Fifteen minutes later, Jenny was snuggled under a down comforter in the Havens' old queen-sized bed, and Hallie was sitting on the couch in the living room with her slippered feet resting on the coffee table. Ian had offered to make them each a cup of warm milk before bed, and she was only too happy to accept his kindness. After the craziness of the last hour, she needed to unwind a little before going back to sleep.

The microwave beeped, and a moment later, Ian stepped into the room with two steaming mugs. He set them on the coffee table, then sat down next to Hallie. And the first thing she thought was: *Closer. Sit closer to me, Irish.*

He was dressed in jeans and a wrinkled T-shirt that looked like he'd plucked them from the floor in his haste to rescue her, and suddenly she wondered if there had been underwear lying on the floor too or if he'd ignored them in his rush to pull on some clothes and get to her. Her eyes dropped to his lap, and she stared at his crotch, weirdly turned-on by the notion that the only thing between her eyes and his skin was a brass zipper.

Her cheeks flushed as she remembered long summer nights, half-naked in each other's arms. Ian was big. Everywhere. And her body tingled with the sensory memory of his erection in her hand, wanting it in her—

"So uh…" Ian cleared his throat, and she snapped her neck up to find his eyes wide and lips twitching as he held back a smile. "Was there something you, um…*needed?*"

She blinked at him, caught between sharp embarrassment and a fit of giggles. And whether it was the way he was looking at her, or the sheer absurdity of her thoughts, or the burst of rightness she'd felt to find a snowy Ian at her door ready to save her, there was something wonderful about giggles winning the draw. As they subsided, she turned her head slightly to look at Ian, who was grinning at her, a question still lingering in his dilated eyes.

"No," she said. "Not right now anyway."

"Another time," he suggested.

"When I'm not delirious with exhaustion," she teased.

He leaned forward to grab their mugs, offering her one. She sat up, taking it from him and cheers-ing his with a soft clank.

"I haven't had warmed milk since I was little."

Ian took a sip. "Sometimes when I wake up in the middle night and want a drink, I make some."

"Does it help?"

"Not really," he said, chuckling ruefully before lowering the cup. "Maybe a little. But it's probably just *doing something* that helps."

She looked at him over the rim of her mug. "I was an ER nurse in Boston, and I can't count the number of alcoholics I met during my work there. It broke my heart every time. It's so hard to break free from addiction."

"It is." Ian nodded, then nailed her with an earnest look. "But I have."

"How long has it been?"

"Two hundred and forty-two days sober as of tomorrow—er, today."

"That's amazing, Ian. Congratulations."

He nodded, taking another sip of milk but otherwise remaining silent.

"You don't want to talk about it?" she prodded gently.

If discussing his sobriety was important to him, she wanted him to know that he could talk to her about it any time. He didn't need to keep it to himself or protect her from it.

"I was an alcoholic. Now I'm recovering. I'll never go back." He shrugged. "That's my past, present, and future right there, Halcyon. Nothing more to it."

"Well, I'm here if you ever need to talk," she said. "I'm proud of you, and I support you, and this milk is better than any other drink I ever had."

"You were always a bad liar," he said, grinning at her. He stared at her for a moment before cocking his head to the side. "I missed you at the brunch yesterday."

She winced, looking away from him.

"Fuck," he whispered. "I know that look."

"What look?"

"Rejection," he grunted softly.

Hallie leaned forward, placing her mug on the coffee

table and shifting on the couch to face him. "Ian, look at me."

He did, and around his eyes, she could see the wear and tear of the last decade etched into his face. She reached out, gently tracing the lines that spoke of his struggles and demons and everything else he'd fought in order to get here today.

"You're wrong," she said softly, caressing the face she loved so well. "That look was confusion. That look was fear. That look was shame from cowardice. But nowhere in that look was there rejection, Ian. I promise you."

Somehow her hands had ended up cradling the scruff on his jaw, and she held his face steady as she leaned forward and pressed her lips to his. His mug landed on the table with a loud clunk, and suddenly his hands were under her arms, lifting her onto his lap. She straddled him, and he pulled her closer—as close as possible, so that the only thing between her unbound breasts and the hard wall of his chest were their T-shirts, and his erection throbbed at the apex of her thighs.

He growled into her mouth, his hands trailing down her back to the hem of her shirt, then underneath, sliding up the bare skin of her back. She rubbed her breasts against him, her nipples hardening into tight points as a delicious heat pooled into her stomach. And lower, her muscles tightened and released in anticipation, and a rush of wetness soaked her panties.

Moaning softly, she dug her hands into his hair as his tongue tangled with hers. She rolled her hips against him experimentally, then with more purpose when his hands clutched her waist, urging her to do it again.

His lips skated down the column of her throat, pressing

and licking, sucking lightly and nipping at the sensitive skin as her breathing grew quick and shallow. She leaned her neck to the side to give him better access, whimpering softly when he sucked so hard she knew she'd have a mark in the morning.

Mark me, she thought, dragging her fingers through his hair. *I'm yours.*

"I've waited for you so long," he said, his voice thick with emotion, with love and longing. His lips continued their journey to her collarbone, and he reached up, shoving her shirt aside so that he could lean his forehead against her shoulder. His arms tightened around her body. "I never thought I'd hold you like this again."

Wrapping her arms around him, she closed her eyes and leaned her cheek against his head. "Me neither."

"Don't go away again," he implored her, his voice gravelly and deep.

"I'm not going anywhere," she said, gently stroking the hair on the back of his neck as tears welled in her eyes.

"I can't lose you again," he whispered so softly, she wondered if he meant to say it aloud, but then he added, "I wouldn't survive it," and she knew that he was speaking to her, that he was expressing his most honest and painful truth: that losing her had almost broken him.

It had almost broken her too.

"On Saturday, you asked me for a second chance," she said, her heart fluttering and racing as she spoke. He didn't say anything, but every breath he took pushed his chest into hers, and she could feel the pounding of his heart against her own. "Ian...I want that too."

His hands, which had been flat and rigid on her back,

trembled lightly as his fingers curled into her skin. "You mean it?"

"I mean it." She let her hands trail from the back of his neck to under his ears, drawing his head up so she could look into his eyes. "And there's something else I need to tell you: Ian, you didn't sleep with Vicky."

He flinched, looking into her eyes with confusion. "What?"

Hallie shook her head, ignoring the tear that slid down her cheek. "You didn't have sex with her. You didn't even kiss her. You passed out before anything could happen."

"What are you talking about?" he asked, still holding her but leaning away a little, his body rigid and shocked, his eyebrows furrowed in confusion.

"There's a new beauty salon in Meredith, and it turns out she owns it. I saw her there on Saturday, and—God, I don't know what made me confront her, but I wanted answers about what had happened that night and—"

"That's why," said Ian in a breathless voice. "That's why you were so distant on Saturday morning. That's why you asked me if I thought we'd still be together."

"Yes." She nodded, sniffling as more tears flooded her eyes. "I made assumptions that morning. The morning I found you two asleep. I—I decided you'd betrayed me, but you...you didn't. You didn't have sex with her, Ian."

He winced, closing his eyes and keeping them shut for several minutes before opening them again, his chest heaving as he put all of the pieces together. "I still lost you."

"We lost each other."

"But we didn't...I mean, I didn't..." He reached up and covered her hands with his, his eyes wide and vulnerable as they searched hers for the truth. "I didn't cheat on you?"

She shook her head. "You didn't. You got drunk and—well, I guess she got there to tell you I wasn't coming, and you were upset...and she said that she was hoping something would happen between you two, but you passed out before anything could."

"Why'd she let everyone think—"

"I think her feelings were hurt," said Hallie. "I think she felt rejected by you."

He winced again, his face contorting with pain and anger, "Fuuuuuuuck!"

"Ian," said Hallie, hurting for his hurt, knowing what he'd suffered, because she'd suffered it too. "Ian, look at me."

He looked at her, but she could tell he was about to explode with anger, with the intense frustration of lost chances and the fierce cruelty of being split apart when they had been so fucking in love.

"Listen to me."

His lips were pursed, and his nostrils flared with every breath he took.

"Listen!" she demanded.

"What?" he yelled, blinking at her like he was trying to break out of a trance.

"I'm. Here. Now." She searched his eyes frantically, waiting for her words to sink in. "I'm here now. I'm here with you."

"But we lost—Jesus, we lost years, Hallie, we lost...we lost..."

"No, Irish. We win," she said, increasing the pressure on his cheeks so he'd stop cycling through his anger and hear her. "Don't you see? Nothing could keep us apart. Not really. Not forever. It took a while, but we found each other again."

Finally, his eyes met hers, *saw* hers, and understood what she was saying: that despite years apart that included a bad marriage and a battle with alcoholism, what they had, what they shared—the love they *still* shared—was stronger than anything else.

"I love you," he breathed, pressing his forehead against hers. "I never stopped loving you, baby. I love you so much."

And Halcyon Gilbert, who hadn't said those words to anyone but Jenny in over ten years, took a deep breath and said,

"I love you too."

"You do?"

"I never stopped either," she said.

"What? You *hated* me."

"I sure did," she said, leaning forward to nip at his lips and loving that they were hers again. "But hate is so close to love, Ian."

He chuckled softly, the rumble welcome after such an intense conversation. "That's what Fin said."

He kissed her back, his hands sliding under her shirt to rest flat against her skin and hold her against him. When he drew away, his eyes were smiling.

"You love me?"

"I love you, Irish," she said.

"I love you, Halcyon, my golden girl, *grá gael mo chroí*."

"Bright love of your heart," she said, nuzzling his nose with hers.

"Always," he whispered.

She licked her lips, then caught his lower lip between hers, tugging lightly before shifting her head so that her mouth fit perfectly over his. Gently, Ian changed their position, lowering her onto the couch and lying down on top of her. She held his face in her hands as they made out like the teenagers they'd once been...until the first light of dawn brightened the room and the clouds that bore hours of angry snow cleared to make way for the sun.

And in those first beams of morning light, they shifted onto their sides, Hallie's back to Ian's front, and entangled in one another's arms, they slept.

chapter eleven

The next morning Ian went over to her house and came back with his verdict:

"It's a mess, baby."

"How bad?" Hallie asked, taking two pieces of toast out of the toaster and buttering them.

Ian sighed, shrugging out of his parka and hanging it on the back of a kitchen chair. *Really fucking bad.* "Well, that tree needs to be removed. Then the windows, walls and siding on that side of the house need to be repaired. The roof is fragile at best. We'll need to fix that too."

"Let me give this to Jenny," she said, "and then you can tell me the rest."

Jenny was sitting on the couch in Ian's living room watching TV, and as Hallie handed her the plate, Ian overheard her say, "Mommy, I love it here with Mr. Haven. Can we stay here forever?"

Hallie shushed her daughter, whispering something he couldn't hear, but all he could think was, *I hope so, ladybug. I sure hope so.*

When she came back into the kitchen, her cheeks were pink, and he grinned at her. "You can stay as long as you need to."

"I know," she said, sliding onto his lap in her pajamas and winding her arms around his neck. She leaned forward and pressed her lips to his. "Thank you."

A miracle.

That's what it felt like to have her in his apartment, to hold her in his arms, to know that she wanted to be with him as much as he wanted to be with her.

After a decade of hell, she was his very own slice of heaven.

"I love you," he whispered.

"I love you, too," she whispered back, nuzzling her warm nose against his cold one before standing up. "Coffee?"

I'd rather have you back on my lap, he thought, but after being outside in the cold for over an hour, coffee sounded mighty good too. Besides, it felt so fucking good to have her here—to watch her move around his kitchen like it was hers too. "Yeah. Thanks."

She poured him a cup and sat down across from him at the table. "What else?"

"Windows. Walls. Siding. Roof. Upstairs ceiling." He took a sip of coffee. "And the other tree? It hit a transformer—blew it out and burnt the wires. That's why you lost power. And unfortunately, it's not owned by the utility company. It's private—owned by the lake association where your cottage is located. It's going to be out for a while before they get someone out to fix it, Hallie. A week at least. Maybe two."

"Two weeks?" she asked, her eyes widening as she started understanding the damage last night's storm had wrought. "Oh, my God."

"I took a chainsaw and some tarps over to your place this morning. I cut through the trunk by the house, but I can't move it on my own. Got the window and wall sealed up in your room, so no animals will get in. We need for the snow to melt off a bit, and then I can start fixing the rest. But it's New Hampshire. Could be a few months before there isn't snow on the ground."

She clenched her eyes shut, folding her hands together so tightly on the tabletop that he could see the whites of her knuckles.

"Tell me what's going on in your head," he said.

"I don't know what to do. We can't live there. I'm getting low on money. I only had so much when I moved here. The roof and the basement cost so much and even with you doing so much for me, it's…well, I—I was going to wait to find a job until after the holidays, but I think I'm going to need to start looking sooner rather than la—"

"Hallie." Ian reached across the table, covering her hands with his. "Your turn to look at me."

She looked up, and he could see the glistening in her worried eyes, which made his heart ache. She'd been through so much this year. He wanted to spare her as much heartache and sorrow as he could. "Your place is rent-free, and you won't have much of a utility bill next month, I'm guessing. I'll get Rory, Fin, and Burr to help me move the tree, and as soon as it's warm enough, I'll get started on the walls, siding, and windows."

"I don't know how much I can afford."

"Then let me help."

"You're *already* helping. I can't let you pay for all of the supplies too. A new window? Double-sized? That's six or seven hundred dollars, not including the—"

"Then stay here," he said, squeezing her hand. "Just stay. Get the rest of your stuff and move in here with me for as long as you need to. Get a job when you're ready. And when you're able to buy what you need to restore the cottage, I'll get started on the labor. Free of charge."

"I can't do that to you. I can't—"

"*Please* do that to me," he said, his voice low and fervent. "*Please* lean on me. *Please* let me help you. *Please* let me take care of you two."

Her eyes were weary as she searched his face, trying to determine his sincerity.

"*Grá gael mo chroí*," he said. "If I could have anything in the world, it would be for you to stay."

Her smile started small, but grew steadily, brightening her eyes with happiness until they shone with so much love, it would have blinded him if he didn't need it, want it, so badly. "You're sure?"

"Never been more sure about anything," he said. "Stay."

She took a deep breath and nodded. "Okay. We'll stay awhile. Thank you."

"Stop thanking me," he said gruffly, squeezing her hand before letting it go. "You have no idea how much I want you here. I'm being selfish."

"You're being wonderful," she said. "You're being you. The glue."

"The glue?" he asked. "What does that mean?"

"Tierney said it. She said that Ian might give up on himself now and then, but he never gives up on the people he loves. You hold us all together."

He laughed softly. "Sounds like something Tier would say."

"I envy you three," said Hallie, sipping her coffee.

"We're not perfect."

She shrugged. "I was an only child. I *wish* I'd had a sister or brother. Someone to call in the middle of the night when a tree crashes through my bedroom."

"You've got me for that, baby."

"I do." She grinned at him, nodding. "But also, I bet birthdays and vacations and holidays were extra fun. I missed out on all that."

Ian smiled at her, cocking his head to the side. "Speaking of the holidays, this place needs a Christmas tree and some decorations. You think you and the ladybug would be game for helping me choose a tree today?"

"Oh, Lord," said Hallie. "I think she'll be over the moon."

"Hey, ladybug!" called Ian, holding Hallie's eyes. "Wanna go get a Christmas tree today?"

They grinned at each other when they heard her loud gasp from the living room. "Yes! Yes, yes, yes!" she cried, racing into the kitchen to jump up and down by Ian's chair. "Can we? Can we really go and get one, Mommy?"

"Since Christmas is in four weeks, I think we better!"

Jenny danced around the kitchen with Luna. "A Christmas tree! A Christmas tree! We're going to get a Christmas tree!"

"Why don't you go get dressed, and we'll get started, huh?"

As Jenny ran down the back hallway, Hallie leaned across the kitchen table for a kiss. "Thank you for making her feel so important...and loved."

Ian reached for her face, cupping her cheek gently as his tongue slid against hers, marveling at the fact that he could touch her, he could love her, that he'd see her face every morning and every night for the foreseeable future. His body hardened at the thought of tonight, wondering—*hoping*—that their physical relationship would make the same amazing headway.

"Don't take this the wrong way," said Ian, dragging his lips across her cheek to her ear. He took the lobe between his teeth, biting lightly, feeling her gasp in his groin, "because the ladybug is my favorite kid in the whole world, but, um, when does she go to sleep?"

Hallie chuckled breathily. "Eight."

He winced. "I have a meeting at eight."

"When are you back?"

"Nine. Which means we have a date on the couch at nine-oh-one," he growled, kissing her hard to seal the deal.

"Nine-oh-one," she agreed, her blue eye dilated, her lips red from kissing, and looking so damned sexy, Ian didn't know how he'd make it through the next twelve hours. "It's a date."

Eleven and a half hours later, there was a tree up in his living room, he'd taken "his girls" out to lunch, and they'd roped the tree with lights and hung decorations to the festive warbling of Bing Crosby. Hallie had made them spaghetti and meatballs for dinner and told him she'd clean up so he could make his meeting on time.

He glanced at his watch. Fifteen minutes to go.

"Hey," whispered Shandie, who was sitting next to him. "Can I talk to you after the meeting?"

It took all of his willpower not to grimace, not to wince, to keep his expression level and open. All he wanted to do was get back in his truck and race home to Hallie. But it was an unspoken AA rule. If someone needed you, you said yes.

"Of course. Everything okay?"

She shrugged. "I just need a pep talk."

Hopefully, a quick one, thought Ian. "Sure."

Standing by their cars in the parking lot, Shandie shared that her husband's new company was having a Christmas Party on December 22nd, and even though it was almost three weeks away, she was already trying to figure out how to avoid the bar, the passed drinks, and the toasts. Ian reminded her that alcohol was a part of everyday life for most people but not for them.

"Dale doesn't drink, does he?" he asked.

Shandie shook her head. "No. But it's awkward, you know? If his bosses and coworkers are drinking wine or beer, it's awkward for us to order Cokes."

"Why does anyone need to know you're drinking soda? Have Dale go to the bar and get two lowball glasses of club soda with a lime in each. Looks like a gin and tonic. No one will say anything."

"That's a good idea," said Shandie earnestly, nodding at Ian.

"Or you could say you're on antibiotics," he suggested. "Everyone leaves that excuse alone."

"Yeah. Yeah, maybe I'll do that. What else?"

"This is important: you need to leave the second you start to waver, Shandie. Fake a stomachache or say the babysitter called. But if you feel weakness coming on, you need to go."

"Right. Yeah. I know all of this," she said, clenching her jaw with frustration. "It's just…it's hard."

Ian nodded. "I know. But you've got this. You can do

it."

"Any other advice?"

"Don't linger. Plan to leave on the early side."

"But Dale's the newest associate."

"I know it's hard, but you can't risk your recovery, and if you're sitting in a barber's chair, sooner or later, you're going to get a haircut. Bars, clubs, and parties are hard for us. Don't make it harder by staying late."

"Okay." She gulped, then nodded. "Thanks, Ian. You're the best."

"All good?" he asked.

"Yeah. Better. I'm not freaking out as much."

She leaned forward, and Ian realized that she wanted a hug. Generally not one to withhold a hug, especially from a fellow addict, he felt a little funny hugging her back as he thought of his golden girl waiting at home for him. Rationally, he knew he wasn't cheating on Hallie, but he still ended the hug as soon as he could and pulled away.

"Get home safe, now," he said.

Shandie waved as she headed to her car, and Ian looked down at his watch.

9:16.

Damn.

Their date had begun sixteen minutes ago, and he was missing it.

He turned the key in the ignition and stepped on the gas.

***

Hallie put another log on the fire and checked the digital clock on the microwave. 9:10. Hmm.

Ian said his meeting ended at 8:45, and that he'd be

home by 9. She wondered what was keeping him, then chided herself for being silly. Maybe he met a friend and stayed after to chat. Maybe meetings ran long at the holidays. Maybe he needed to pick up something on the way home.

She sat down on the couch, her nerves making her jumpy, and though she wasn't a big drinker, she wished she had a glass of wine to calm them. But she'd already checked—Ian's apartment held no trace of alcohol. Not even cooking sherry in the kitchen or cough syrup in the bathroom cabinet. And while she admired his abstinence and would support it wholeheartedly, in this *particular* moment, she would have loved a drink.

After she'd gotten Jenny settled in her bed, Hallie had taken a quick shower, shaving her legs and under her arms and rubbing honeysuckle-scented cream on her skin. She didn't have any sexy pajamas, so she'd decided on a pair of pink-and-white-plaid flannel pants and a tight, white cotton tank top. Underneath both? Nothing.

But now? Sitting on the couch, counting down the minutes, and waiting for Ian, she wondered if she was being too forward. Maybe she should go put on a bra and some undies? *Oh, God. You're being crazy.* She leaned over the back of the couch and looked at the clock again. 9:16.

She was assuming that tonight was the night they'd do the "deed"—as Brittany had called it so many years ago—but maybe she was being presumptuous? Or hasty? They'd been reunited for several weeks now, and it was clear that their feelings for each other were genuine, even after all this time. But the reality was that Hallie hadn't slept with anyone in a long time. In almost a year. And she was a little nervous about that.

By her calculations, Sergio had infected her sometime in January, she'd had the STD diagnosed and treated in mid-February and was given a clean bill of health by the end of February. Which meant that the last time she'd had sex was in January, and it would be December in exactly two days. Almost a year. A year. And let's face it, the sex with Sergio had been of the "slam, bam, thank you, ma'am" variety.

The last time she'd had emotional, loving sex? The kind that opened your soul to the other person? The kind that made you cry because the connection you felt to the other person was so deep? The kind wherein the act and the emotions were so profoundly entangled, one was just an extension of the other?

"Oh, God," she whispered as a shiver shot down her spine.

It had been a long, long time. If ever.

What about Ian? He'd had a few sexual partners, she knew, before their scheduled night at Summerhaven. What about since then? Had he been with a lot of people? People he loved or random people? Had he been careful? Had he been tested, and was he clean?

She stood up from the couch and paced across the living room, hating the way her stomach dropped when she glanced at the clock and saw that it was 9:25.

The butterflies in her stomach had multiplied over the long minutes of waiting. Twenty-five minutes, to be exact.

Damn, Ian. Have you never heard of a phone?
Oh, wait! Maybe he called or texted!

Her phone was in the bedroom. She fast-walked down the hallway, opened the door, and tiptoed into the dark room where Jenny was sleeping. Plucking her phone from the nightstand, she unplugged it and backed out of the room, closing the door behind her.

Flipping over the phone, certain to be greeted with a message from Ian, her eyes watered—actually *watered*—when she saw there were none. Not to mention, as she was staring forlornly at her phone, the time changed to 9:30.

Half an hour late.

Or maybe, she had to admit to herself, *he's not coming back at all.*

Maybe he doesn't want to be with you and he's trying to figure out a way to say it.

Maybe he feels like everything is moving too fast and he wants to slow down.

Maybe something happened to him.

At this final thought, her heart started racing in earnest. The thought of losing Ian after finding him again was so painful, so fucking unbearable, the tears in her eyes doubled and she leaned against the hallway wall, holding her breath and praying that—

"Hallie? Halcyon?"

Ian!

She turned and raced down the hall, running through the living room and into his arms. He'd taken off his parka on the stairs, and his arms were warm as they hugged her against his sweet, solid chest.

"You're back," she sighed, clenching her eyes shut and willing away her tears and worries. "I didn't—I mean…you're late."

"Remind me to always be a little late if this is the greeting I get," he said, leaning away from her to look at her face. His sparkling eyes met hers, instantly clouding over, worry lines appearing around his mouth and between his brows. His hands captured her face. "What is it? What happened? Why are you crying?"

She shrugged. "Because I'm an idiot."

"Because I was late," he said, bending down to kiss her forehead. "I'm so sorry, baby. A friend from AA needed a little extra support. We talked in the parking lot. I wouldn't have been late, but I couldn't—I couldn't say no."

She dropped his eyes, feeling embarrassed. "It's not your fault. Like I said, I'm an idiot."

"Halcyon," he said, waiting to speak again until she looked up at him. "I know what it feels like to have a scheduled date with someone you love...and to wait and wait and wait for them to appear...and to worry about them and wonder where they are and trick yourself into thinking they're not coming. I was there too. You're not an idiot."

She sniffled softly. "Yes, I am. I'm—"

"This is important, baby, so listen up, okay? I will *always* come back to you," he said, interrupting her with a firm, but gentle, promise. "*Always*." She nodded, but he searched her eyes like he was looking for something—for that expression, that "look" that said—*I believe you.* "Sometimes I might be late. Sometimes I might get detoured. Sometimes it might take a little extra time," he said, no doubt thinking about the last ten years they'd spent apart. "But I will *always* come back to you, because I love you, Halcyon. And because, in the whole wide world, the only place I want to be...is with you."

Her heart burst with the tender sincerity of his words, and she threw her arms around his neck, pulling his head to hers, desperate to feel his lips on hers. He slipped his hands under her backside and she was lifted up, her ankles locking around his back as he groaned into her mouth, walking down the hall toward his bedroom.

As he carried her, their tongues tangling as he walked, she reached for the buttons on his flannel shirt, her fingers working furiously to have them undone by the time they reached his room. When they got there, he set her gently down, reached behind his neck and pulled off his shirt and T-shirt with one yank before drawing her back into his arms.

"Wait," she said, pushing him away. She looked up at his face, at his confused expression. "I want to see you."

Her mouth watered as she started at his shoulders, running her fingers over the ridges of muscle on his still-tanned pecs, the black wiry hair over his abs tickling the pads of her fingers as she moved her hands to the middle, tracing his tiger line to the button of his jeans.

"My turn, golden girl," he growled softly, reaching for the hem of her tank top.

Hallie raised her hands over her head, letting him smooth the cotton over her stomach, over her breasts, and over her head until it dropped to the floor with a light *whoosh*.

Staring at his throat, she heard his tight hiss of gasped breath and looked up to see his eyes, almost black, staring at her breasts. An unaccountable panic washed over her, and her gaze darted away, afraid she'd see disappointment in his eyes.

"I—I had a baby," she whispered, raising her hands to cover the breasts that weren't anywhere near as perky as they'd been ten years ago.

She gulped as his hands shot out, his fingers wrapping around her wrists to stop her from hiding herself. Gently, so gently, he lowered her arms, bringing her hands to her sides.

"Look at me, Halcyon."

Taking a shuddering breath, she raised her eyes to his, and all she saw there, to her relief, was a worshipful tenderness.

"You're so beautiful *now*, I can barely remember what you looked like when we were kids." Releasing her wrists, he raised his hand, extending his index finger and touching a small brown mole over her left nipple. "Aw. This little spot." She looked down at his finger, which brushed gently over the beauty mark. His eyes looked up and caught hers as he leaned forward slowly, reverently, exchanging his finger for his lips.

Staring down at his black head, she held her breath as his lips slid lower, until he sucked one puckered nipple into his mouth. When his hot, wet tongue swirled around the throbbing bud, she gasped softly, unaccustomed to careful lovemaking.

Reaching for the globe of her other breast with his hands, he lifted it as his lips skimmed across her chest, sucking and licking her warm skin, making fields of goose bumps rise all over her body as the rasp of his beard tickled places that hadn't been gently loved in far too long.

She closed her eyes, thinking about the first morning he arrived at her dilapidated cottage—how angry she'd been at him and how desperately she didn't want him there...and then suddenly she remembered his face as he helped her sixteen-year-old self off the bus—the warmth of his hand and the twinkle in his eyes. She saw him sitting on her back lawn side by side with Jenny, eating peanut butter and jelly sandwiches and talking about loons...and then the picture changed yet again, and he was lying beside her on a raft, staring up at the stars as they counted down the minutes to curfew. Then and now. The past and the present merging together.

"I *missed* you," she whispered, feeling the hot sting of tears on her cheek.

He raised his head and sighed. "I know. I missed you too."

"I'm spoiling this."

"You're not spoiling a thing."

His reverence for her. His gentleness. It was so foreign after years of being unloved, and yet it was familiar because it was him. But it made her feel so…*overwhelmed.*

"Ian, I just—I just want to cry my eyes out."

"So cry your eyes out," he suggested.

She nodded, letting go, letting her tears fall in torrents, sliding down her face so fast that his face blurred before her.

"Don't freak out," he said. "I'm going to get us both naked, but it's just so I can hold you, Halcyon. Nothing else. Not for now. Okay?"

She nodded, and he tugged on the drawstring of her pants. They fell over her hips, pooling on the rug around her feet. She heard the clank of his belt buckle hitting the floor, and then he took her hand and led her to his full-sized bed. He pulled the comforter and top sheet aside. "Come lie down with me."

She slid into bed, lying on her side, feeling his weight depress the mattress behind her, and then, there he was, lying beside her. His body was huge and warm, and a thick, muscled arm fell over her waist, pulling her against his chest.

"Cry all you want, baby. I've got you. I've got you now."

His lips would occasionally press against the back of her neck or her shoulder as she wept, but otherwise, he held her. Just held her. He had a slight erection, yes, but he didn't poke it into her back with unspoken expectations. It was pressed against her because it was part of him, not because he was demanding anything from her.

Holding her like this was as far as they'd ever gotten as teenagers in love—it was where they'd left off, and it felt so good, and so right, just to be held in his arms, skin to skin, his front to her back, his arm around her, his legs tangled up in hers; it comforted her more than he could ever know. In a life that had felt unfamiliar for years, here was something familiar. Here was something she wanted.

"Listen," he said after a while, "you're safe here. You're safe with me. I will never hurt you, baby. I will never leave you. I will never stop loving you." He paused. "You came here broken, Halcyon. You weren't loved by the man you married. You weren't cherished." He paused again. "But you will be now. For the rest of your life I'll cherish every minute I have with you."

She reached up and curled her fingers around his arm, taking a deep cleansing breath and letting it go.

"And think of this," he whispered, his voice low and sweet and intimate by her ear. "You have Jenny. No matter what else happened with your ex, you got that beautiful little ladybug for your troubles."

"I did," she said, her tears starting to let up now.

"And now you've got me too." He was quiet for a second, like he was thinking that over, and when he spoke again, his voice was raspier than it had been. "Maybe…well, you might think I'm a bad deal, Halcyon, because in some ways, I'm damaged goods, but I promise I'll—"

No one ever whipped around so fast in someone's arms as she did in his.

"Stop right there," she demanded.

"Huh?"

"A *bad deal?*" she asked.

"Well…"

"*Damaged goods?*"

"The truth is—"

"The *truth* is that you're mine, Ian Haven. You belong to me now. And you are the *best* deal, and *perfect* goods. Perfect for *me.*"

"When you met me I was a kid with my whole life in front of me," he said, sniffling softly. "It got bad, Hallie. I lost my job. I lived on the street at one point."

"I know," she said, her heart aching for him. "Britt told me."

"I'm a recovering alcoholic. I'll *always* be a recovering alcoholic."

"And I'm a divorcée with a kid." She reached for his face, making him look at her in the beam of moonlight that fell across his bed. "I know what you've battled, and I know you've gotten your life back on track. I know you're sober. I know you'll fight to *stay* sober." She leaned forward and kissed him gently before drawing away. "I know *exactly* who you are, Ian. And I want you. All of you. You take my imperfect and I'll take yours. That's what love is, Irish. That's the deal. You're the glue. We'll stick together."

Clasping his head in her hands, she demanded his lips again, arching her back so that the sensitive points of her breasts rubbed against his chest. With a roar of want, he flipped her onto her back, bracing his weight on the elbows he planted on either side of her head, and kissed her passionately, fiercely, with a raw and instinctive claim.

The truth was, she'd been his all along, and he'd been hers. They'd just had a long-ass detour on the way to forever.

"I want you," she murmured as his lips skimmed her jaw.

He bit her ear and she moaned, spreading her legs and thrusting up to push against his long, thick erection.

"I don't want to wait anymore," she added. "I need to feel you inside of me."

He groaned. "I want it to be good for you. I should—God, I should go down on your first. I had this whole plan…"

"You had a plan for going down on me?" She chuckled softly, a mixture of happiness and surprise. They'd never gotten quite this far, so they were in new territory, which felt…*exhilarating*. "If we fast-track to sex *now*, can we come back to your original plan *later*?"

"I wanted to be sure you were ready," he murmured near her ear.

"Irish," she said, licking her lips and feeling a little naughty. "I'm so wet, you'll slide inside like I'm oiled."

"Fuuuuuuuuck," he sighed, leaning up to look down at her. "For real?"

"Want to give it a try?" she asked.

"We need a condom," he said.

She looked up at him. "I'm clean. And I'm on the pill. You?"

His eyes held hers. "I haven't…"

"You haven't what?"

"I haven't been with anyone since…"

"Since what?"

"Since…"

"Ian, tell me."

"Since Vicky," he admitted on an exhalation of breath.

Her lips parted in shock. "You weren't *with* Vicky."

"Doesn't matter, Halcyon. I was waiting for you."

"College?"

He shook his head. "No. I mean, I was with women, I fooled around…but I didn't sleep with them."

"After?" she asked, her voice so soft it was barely audible.

"Even when I was shithouse drunk, no. It was the only line I never crossed." He took a deep breath, and his chest pressed against hers, his heart beating into hers. "I told you…there is *only* you for me, *mo chroí.*"

This fact exploded in her head like fireworks: the reality that when this beautiful man said that he was hers, he literally meant that he hadn't been with anyone else since the day he fell in love with her, since the day he'd lost her.

"Irish," she sobbed.

"I didn't want anyone else," he said. "Only you."

Her hands skimmed down his back, and she curled her fingers into his ass. "Then take me. I'm yours."

He rose up a little, positioning himself at the entrance of her sex. She felt the thickness of his head as it pushed forward, relaxing her muscles to accommodate him. As he slipped through her tight lips, she cried out softly, feeling the walls of her sex stretch, sucking him forward until he was fully embedded inside of her.

"*Fuuuck*," she moaned, reaching over her head to curl her fingers around the spindles of his headboard. "Irish, you are so *big*."

"You are so *tight*," he panted. "You did *not* have a baby."

"Cesarean," she sighed, managing to grin at him through a haze of pre-orgasmic tremors.

"*Awwwesome*," he groaned, withdrawing a little before pressing forward again. "I'm not sure how long I can…"

"Ian, I'm more than halfway there," she whispered as the head of his cock massaged her G-spot again. Her eyes rolled back in her head, and a whimpering noise escaped from her lips as the hot, hard muscle of his cock slid against every nerve ending inside of her.

He reached for her face, cupping it in his hands. "I love you. I'll do better next time."

"Better?" she asked, whimpering again as he rocked all the way into her. "You'll kill me."

"No, baby," he said, quickening the pace and depth of his thrusts. "You'll live through this a million times."

Her breathing was quick and shallow now, a gathering of flutters that had started in her stomach, now strengthening, spreading to every muscle in her pelvis as he pumped into her, filling her, loving her, using her body like it was meant to be used by the only man she wanted.

"I'm coming," she cried, the swirling in her body taking her higher and higher and higher until her hands slid from the headboard and landed on his back. Her fingers curled, her nails drawing blood as she clawed her way to perfect light.

"Halcyon!" he yelled as his body started to shake. For a

split-second, he froze, and then he came in waves and quakes, like a full-body heartbeat that she felt in every cell of her body. Pumping his seed deep into her, he collapsed against her shoulder, murmuring, "*Tá grá agam duit, grá gael mo chroí*" close to her ear.

***

As he came down from the high, he registered the gentle scrape of her nails against his back, rhythmically, absently, slowly, and softly.

"Baby?" he panted, rolling to his side and taking her with him.

"Mmm?"

"Did the world just move?" he asked, pulling her closer. He was still deeply lodged within her body and in no hurry to change that.

"Mmm-hmm."

"*Fuck*," he muttered, laughing softly with satisfaction. "Did you come?"

She laughed. "You couldn't tell?"

Honestly, he couldn't. Once his own orgasm hit, he'd been so carried away with his own pleasure, it was like the rest of the world had slipped away.

"It was okay?"

"Irish, if you've got more than that in the arsenal, it's going to be hard to get me out of your bed."

He grinned in post-orgasm happiness, clasping her closer. "Good. I don't want you to go anywhere."

"What did you say?"

"What do you mean?"

"In Irish. What did you say?"

He breathed deeply. "*Tá grá agam duit*. Literally, it means

'*Tá* There…*grá* love…*agam* I…*duit* you.' But it's 'I love you' in Irish."

Hallie, who was still on her side, smiled at him. "*Here. Love. I. You.*"

"How did this happen?" he whispered.

"Fate," she answered.

"Nah. Fate's a jealous fucker. He kept us apart."

"Silly Irish," she said, rolling to her back and breaking their physical connection. "*She* brought us back together."

And like every man on the face of the earth, all he wanted was to be back inside of her warm, wet body now that they were apart. He leaned up on his elbow. "What next?"

"Happiness," she said, her eyes dreamy.

"What do we tell the ladybug?"

"Nothing official yet," said Hallie. "But we can tell her that we'll be staying here for a while."

"*A while?*" he said, frowning at her.

"*More* than a while," she assured him, and while he'd have preferred the answer "forever," he'd take this for now.

"What do we tell everyone else?"

"They'll know just by looking at us," she said, rolling to her side to face him. "I'm sure your brother and sister already do."

"Halcyon," he said, his eyes starting to close, like he'd come to the end of an exhausting journey and it was finally safe for him to let down his guard now and rest, "if this is a dream, I don't want to wake up."

"It's not a dream. I'll see you in the morning," she said, her voice light and soft and tinged with love and humor. He tightened his arm around her and pulled her closer, into the spoon of his body.

"I love you," he said, drifting off to sleep.

"Here, Irish," she answered softly, "love I, you."

chapter twelve

One week of happiness turned into two, into three, until Hallie barely remembered the dark days that had led her to New Hampshire in the first place.

Living with Ian had turned out to be the best decision she'd ever made. Not only was his apartment Christmas Central, with nightly holiday movies, a never-ending supply of hot cocoa, and crackling fires every night before bed, but he was as good as his promise, loving her body to perfection every night and leaving her breathless for more come morning.

For the second time in her life, Halcyon Gilbert was deeply in love.

For the first time in her life, she could visualize a future so happy, so right, she woke every day feeling more whole, more strong and certain about her life, than she ever had before.

She became accustomed to Ian being away every weeknight between eight and nine, after they put Jenny to bed together. Two nights a week, he had hockey practice, but on the others, she looked forward to nine, knowing that when he returned, he'd carry her to bed, and they'd talk and laugh and make love until dawn.

Ten days after the nor'easter that had knocked out her power, it came back, but they'd already sealed up her cottage for the winter. After the spring thaw, in March or April, they'd see about repairs. Until then, Hallie had agreed to live with Ian, and the more comfortable she and Jenny were at his place, the more Hallie wondered how it would feel to stay with Ian forever.

Not that they'd discussed marriage, but the idea slipped into her mind now and then. Hallie Haven. Ian's wife. Britt's sister-in-law. A real family for Jenny. Imagining herself as Ian's wife was like a dream she never thought would come true. It made her heart swell with happiness and longing, though there was another side of her—a very small side— that she also had to acknowledge: a thread of trepidation at the thought of a wedding.

Her first marriage had been such a terrible mistake— she'd married Sergio for all the wrong reasons, which had made her wedding a trap, not a treasure. Next time she said, "I do," she wanted it to be for all the right reasons and forever; and she wanted to do it her own way.

On a Saturday morning, a week before Christmas, Hallie woke up alone in Ian's bed. She turned to her side, naked under the covers, and sighed. His pillow was cool. He'd been gone for a while.

Though business at the Summerhaven Event and Conference Center slowed down over the holidays, they did have a couple of groups still coming in to use the facilities. Tonight, there was a Christmas party in the main dining room for the Lakes Region Chamber of Commerce, which meant catering for over two hundred guests, and no doubt Ian was up early to salt and sand the dirt paths, parking lot, and walkways leading to the event.

Hallie stretched, swinging her legs over the side of the bed and reaching for the nightgown she'd worn for about ten minutes last night. Today was also exciting for another reason: Rory and Brittany would be home this afternoon. Their flight landed at three o'clock, and Britt had hired a car to drive them home to New Hampshire, where they'd spend the next two weeks celebrating Christmas and New Year's with the Haven clan.

In fact, Christmas would be a rather large celebration this year.

Mr. and Mrs. Haven planned to drive over from Dartmouth. Finian was still here, Burr's sister and parents were coming up, and—though she still couldn't believe it, because her parents loathed the snow and cold—Hallie's parents were coming up from Florida to spend a few days at Summerhaven too.

It was the first Christmas in a long, long time that Hallie was feeling that marvelous childlike anticipation again, and sharing her excitement with Ian and Jenny just multiplied it exponentially.

"Mommy! Are you up?" asked Jenny, bounding into the room Hallie shared with Ian. Though they would, at some point, probably trade rooms with Jenny so that theirs was the larger one, it seemed a premature conversation for now, so they were leaving things as-is.

"Good morning!" she chirped. "How's my girl today?"

"Auntie Britt and Uncle Rory are coming home today! And they're bringing me presents!"

Hallie pulled Jenny onto her lap, kissing her face and neck all over. "You taste delicious!"

"Mommy, stop!" Jenny insisted, amid a flutter of giggles. "We have to get dressed and go help Ian."

This was another development over the past few weeks.

At some point, Jenny had started called Ian "Ian" instead of Mr. Haven. At first, Hallie had been tempted to maintain propriety and insist that her daughter use a respectful address, but Ian had seemed so pleased by the informality—and they were living with him, after all—so Hallie let it slide.

"Ian is salting and sanding, ladybug," she said, letting her wiggling daughter go, "and you can't help with that. So how about we have some breakfast instead, huh? And then we need to do some grocery shopping, because we are out of everything."

"Ian eats like a bear," said Jenny, rolling her eyes.

Hallie hooted with laugher. "He does. But he's *our* bear, isn't he?"

"Yes, he is." Jenny nodded earnestly. "I'ma go get dressed!"

After breakfast, they bundled up in their parkas, the boots Hallie had finally found in the cottage basement, hats, and mittens and headed down to Center Harbor for some grocery shopping. With Christmas carols on the radio and Jenny singing along from her car seat, all felt right in the world, and Hallie, for one, was going to let herself enjoy it.

***

When Shandie had texted Ian early this morning, asking to meet him at the Starbucks in Center Harbor, he'd grimaced.

First of all, he wasn't her sponsor—she *had* a sponsor: an older woman named Maevis who'd been sober for thirteen years and lived in Sandwich—but for whatever reason, maybe because of their high school connection, Shandie had chosen to lean on him lately.

He didn't want to refuse her or let her down, and God forbid he didn't meet with her and she backslid, but there was a reason that AA preferred for a person's sponsor to be of the same sex. The intimacy of sharing your fears with someone of the opposite sex could foster affection, leading to expectations that the other person wasn't prepared to meet. Not to mention, Ian had been doing the steps for less than a year. Most of the time, a sponsor was someone who was well-seasoned in AA with a ton of tools in their toolbox. Ian was still relatively new.

Second of all, he had a lot of work to do today. With tonight's dinner group coming in, he still needed to freshen up the pine roping in the dining room, check the strings of white lights around the window frames and bannisters, and make sure there was a playlist of Christmas music three to four hours long. Yes, Chef Jamie would handle the food and waitstaff, and Doug could take care of the driveways and parking lot, but Ian would prefer to be at Summerhaven this morning, not sitting by the window at a Starbucks waiting for Shandie to arrive.

Maybe it was time to—gently—build a boundary with her. He would remind her to call Maevis and that AA encouraged newbies to lean on their sponsors. Maybe he'd even mention Hallie and tell Shandie that now that he was in a committed relationship, it felt funny for them to meet alone. But damn, he didn't want to negatively impact her recovery either. It was a conundrum.

"Ian!"

He looked up from his coffee to see Shandie walking into the café, a sparkly red gift bag in her hand.

"Morning," he said, offering her a half smile as she put the little bag on the table and took off her coat. It felt like she was a little overdressed for morning coffee in a red sweater with a plunging neckline, a necklace that drew his eyes to her cleavage, and matching bright-red lipstick. He cleared his throat. "You doing okay?"

"Great!" she said, beaming at him. "The Christmas party was last night. I did everything you said, Ian. You would have been so proud of me." She hadn't sat down yet. "Mind if I get a drink? I'll be right back."

He was about to say that yes, he did mind, because while he was glad she'd had a successful night, he really had a lot to do today and didn't have time to sit around drinking coffee, but she was already walking up to the barista to place her order.

Ian took out his phone and looked through his messages. There was a new one from Rory saying that he and Brittany were boarding their flight and should land in Boston by three. And one from Tierney saying that the Rileys were arriving on the twenty-third and could Ian and Doug have two of the winterized cottages ready for them?

He didn't bother writing back to Rory, who was halfway over the Atlantic by now, but he told Tierney he'd have Lady Margaret ready for the Rileys in time. Putting his phone back in his pocket, he grinned to himself, thinking about Christmas morning with Hallie and Jenny. It had been a long time since Ian had had Christmas morning with people he loved. It had hurt his parents and siblings to see the addict version of himself, so he'd declined their invitations to Christmas for years. But this year? He was making up for all of that. This year, he was spending Christmas with his whole family, the love of his life, and her adorable daughter. He felt like a kid again. He couldn't wait.

When Shandie returned to the table, she smiled at Ian,

stirring some sugar into her coffee and pushing the red bag toward him. "Thank you so much for meeting me, Ian. This is for you."

He looked at the bag, then back up at her. "What is it?"

"It's a gift, because you've been so amazing to me."

Ian sat back in his chair, looking at her, leaving the bag untouched on the table between them. "Shandie, why aren't you meeting with Maevis?"

She looked surprised, her smile fading a touch. "She's great, you know? I just…I don't know her all that well, and *we've* known each other forever."

"Yeah, but you have a sponsor for a reason."

"Can't I have friends too?"

Ian nodded. "Sure."

"So…? Open your present!"

He glanced at the bag but didn't touch it. "Does Dale know you're here?"

"He saw me go out."

"Where did you say you were going?"

"It's Christmastime!" she said. "Can't a girl run some holiday errands?"

She was getting defensive, and Ian didn't want that, but facing the truth was an important part of the steps. He leaned forward, folding his hands on the table. "Shandie, you're meeting with an unmarried man and giving him presents."

"I'm meeting with an old friend and thanking him," she said, reaching for his hands and covering them with one of hers, while the other nudged the bag toward him.

Ian looked down at her hands, then gently slid his away. "This just doesn't feel right to me."

She frowned at him, leaning back in her chair and folding her hands in her lap. "I can't talk to Dale about things. He doesn't get it."

"That's what meetings are for. That's what Maevis is for."

"That's what *you're* for," she said. "I want…I want *you* to be that person for me. I thought you wanted that too."

"No, Shandie. I'm sorry if I gave you that impression, but that's not my role. It's not a role I'm comfortable taking on." He reached for his coffee, finishing it up and letting his words sink in. "I'm with someone. She wouldn't like me meeting you like this. I don't think Dale would like it either."

"Dale doesn't know!" she blurted out.

"Exactly," said Ian. He cocked his head to the side. "I'm going to sit here with you while you call Maevis."

Shandie blinked at him, lifting her chin. "I don't need to call her."

"Yeah, you do," he said softly, crossing his arms over his chest.

"Why can't you—I mean, can't you just—"

"No," said Ian. "Call your sponsor. I'll wait."

Blinking back tears, Shandie reached into her purse and pulled out her phone. Dialing a number with one touch, she only had to wait a second. "Maevis? Yeah. It's me. Uh-huh. If it's not too much trouble. At the Starbucks in Center Harbor. Thank you. Okay. I will. Thank you again." Shandie looked up at him, her once bright smile gone, her eyes flat. "She's coming."

Ian nodded, reaching into his pockets for his gloves and putting them on. "Good. You're doing the right thing."

"Doesn't feel like it," she said softly, tracing circles on

the table, the gift between them an awkward reminder of her misguided intentions.

Ian sighed, pushing away from the table. "I'm going to get going now."

"I'm sorry, Ian," she whispered.

He reached for her hand, squeezing it gently before letting it go. "Merry Christmas, Shandie. Be good, okay?"

Still staring down at the table, she nodded. "I'll do my best."

***

The parking lot was packed with holiday shoppers, so Hallie parked in the back, unbuckling Jenny from the car seat and taking her daughter's hand as they walked toward the strip mall that had a pizza place, a mani/pedi salon, a hardware store, a Starbucks, and a grocery store.

"Mommy, look," said Jenny, pointing to a dark-green truck. "Ian's truck!"

Hallie glanced to the side, doing a double take and stopping in her tracks. It *was* Ian's truck. Huh. She didn't remember him saying anything about running errands this morning—when he went to town, he usually asked if she needed anything.

"Maybe he ran out of salt," she said, looking up ahead at the hardware store.

"Let's say hi to him!" Jenny suggested, pulling her mother toward the shops.

They'd been heading for the grocery store, but now Jenny steered them across the Starbucks to the hardware store. Hallie looked up at the Starbucks as they passed it, her heart dropping when she saw Ian at a table beside the window.

A shot of adrenaline blasted through her body making her fingers tingle and shake as she stared at him. He was holding hands with a woman in a low-cut red sweater. She smiled at him, in an intimate way like she'd known him forever, pushing a red Christmas bag toward him with her free hand.

"Who's that lady, Mommy?" asked Jenny, who had stopped walking.

"I…I don't…" She cleared her throat, her heart racing painfully as she watched Ian pull his hand away but stay seated at the table. "I don't know."

"She looks a little like Papa's special friend."

Hallie whipped her gaze away from the window to look down at her daughter. "What? Who?"

"The lady with the black hair who laughed a lot. In Boston."

Hallie grabbed Jenny's hand, turning them both around and marching back to her car. She was trembling all over, her eyes stinging with tears, her stomach churning up the toast and coffee she'd eaten this morning.

When they reached the car, she squatted down in front of Jenny, gripping her daughter's upper arms firmly. "What are you talking about?"

"Papa's special friend. We went out for ice cream."

"Fuck!" Hallie muttered, shaking her head back and forth. Her husband had introduced *their daughter* to one of his fucking whores? She practically shook with anger, wondering what else Jenny had seen and heard while Sergio was cheating on her.

"Mommy, you look so mad," said Jenny, tears welling in her eyes. "Like before. You're hurting my arms. It's scaring me."

"Oh, baby! I'm sorry!"

Hallie lunged forward, hugging Jenny tightly, her mind whirling with past and present revelations: notably, that her ex-husband was a worse asshole than she'd given him credit for and that Ian, whom she had started trusting again only recently, had some secrets of his own.

"We're going home," she said.

"We didn't go shopping."

"We'll…uh, we'll go tomorrow. I forgot my wallet," she lied, helping Jenny into the car.

As they drove back up to Summerhaven, Hallie desperately tried not to let her suspicions and fears run away with her, reminding herself that Ian had not cheated on her with Vicky and that since she'd returned to New Hampshire, he'd been nothing but good to her.

She'd lost Ian ten years ago because they hadn't unraveled the truth—she couldn't, *she wouldn't*, let that happen again. That said, however? They needed to talk as soon as possible. She needed to know who that woman was, and why Ian hadn't mentioned meeting her.

As they turned into Summerhaven twenty minutes later, Hallie took out her phone and texted Ian.

HALLIE: *Are you around? I need to talk to you.*

IAN: *Had to run into town. I can be there in 10 min. Everything okay?*

HALLIE: *Yeah. I'll meet you at the apartment.*

She took some quiet comfort in the fact that Ian wasn't trying to hide where he'd been, though she was eager to set the matter to rest once and for all. After she parked the car, she walked Jenny into the main office.

"Hey, Mrs. Toffle," she greeted the elderly receptionist, who was on duty today in preparation for tonight's event.

"Hello, dear. And hello to you, Jenny."

"Hi, Mrs. T.," said Jenny.

"Mrs. Toffle," said Hallie, "is there any way you could keep an eye on Jenny for a little bit? Ian and I need to…to talk."

Mrs. Toffle's eyes scanned Hallie's face for a second, no doubt taking in her flushed cheeks and overbright eyes. "Of course, dear." She turned to Jenny. "Want to help me lick some stamps and envelopes?"

Jenny nodded, eyeing the lollipop jar on Mrs. Toffle's desk.

"Take your time, dear," said the older woman with a comforting nod.

Hallie headed upstairs, grateful for a few minutes to compose herself before Ian got home, though it was hard to shake her worries.

"Calm down," she said. "Maybe she's an old friend. Heck, Hallie, she could be his cousin! You didn't even think of that. She could be *family*."

She fanned her face with her hand as she paced the living room, trying to get her emotions under control, but the more she thought about it, the more her heart sunk. Rationally, she knew that Ian hadn't cheated on her with Vicky but rewriting a history she'd held as true for ten years didn't happen overnight. And Sergio? He'd proven himself to be a rat bastard, with new revelations this morning about how low he would stoop: introducing their daughter to a woman who might have been an escort or prostitute.

She recalled her promises to herself on the drive up to

New Hampshire—*no more cheating, no more lying, no more men*—but she'd fallen head over heels for Ian Haven all over again, and the thought of losing him now was…unbearable.

When she heard his footsteps on the stairs, she took a deep breath and lifted her chin, turning to face the door.

***

Her text had unnerved him.

Not that Ian had a lot of experience with women, but the proverbial "we need to talk" line generally didn't bode well for those of his sex. What had happened?

When he got to Summerhaven, his anxiety increased to find Jenny downstairs with Mrs. Toffle, who gave him a dry look, glanced at the stairs, then returned her gaze to him with a pinched expression.

Okay.

She's upset.

He took the stairs two at a time, pulling off his hat, mittens, and coat before he got to the door and dropping them in a heap on the floor when he entered.

Halcyon stood across the room, clenching her hands together, her eyes wide and worried, her lips pursed, exuding a barely restrained panic that sent his own emotions into overdrive. What the hell was going on?

"Halcyon?" he said. "Are you okay?"

She nodded once, her nostrils flaring as she stared at him.

"What's going on?"

She gulped, remaining stock-still as she faced him. "I took Jenny to the grocery store this morning. She saw your…truck, um, in the parking lot. I saw you…with…with…um, a woman. At Starbucks, um…"

269

His heart started racing like a gun had just been shot beside his ear. Holy shit. She'd seen him with Shandie. Of course she was upset.

Covering the distance between them in two strides, he pulled her stiff body into his arms, his heart thundering with sympathy for her. He saw exactly what this looked like through her eyes: first, her boyfriend cheats on her, then, her husband cheats on her, then, her boyfriend cheats on her again.

"It's not what you think," he said.

"What do I think?" she whispered, her voice breaking, her body still stiff in his arms.

"I would never cheat on you. Never."

"That's not enough, Ian. You need to tell me everything. Who is she? Why were you—"

"Wait. I need you to hear this: You think that you're the girl that men cheat on, baby, but it's not true. I never cheated on you. Your husband is a well-established asshole, but you are rid of him. You're with me now, and I will *never* do that to you, Halcyon."

His words calmed her, though questions remained to be answered. "Okay, fine. Then tell me what I saw."

Leaning away from her, he took her hand and led her to the couch, pulling her down beside him. "Remember a few weeks ago when I came home late from AA on a Monday night?"

She nodded.

"That was because a friend needed some encouragement. The friend was Shandie, whom I knew in high school. And she texted me again today—last minute, no notice—to ask if we could talk again."

Hallie's shoulders, which had been tensed up around her ears, relaxed a little. "So that's what you were doing? Meeting a friend from AA?"

He nodded. "She went to a Christmas party last night, and she didn't drink. I'd given her some advice on how to handle social situations, and she wanted to thank me."

"*Thank* you?" scoffed Hallie. "She was dressed like she wanted to do more than thank you."

"I have no control over how she dresses," said Ian, keeping his voice gentle and even. "She brought a gift and said she wanted to thank me."

"Yeah. I *saw* the gift bag," scoffed Hallie.

"I have no idea what was in it."

"Wasn't it for you?"

"It was, but I wouldn't accept it. I told her that I was with someone now, and I couldn't accept a gift from her. I waited with her while she called her sponsor. Then I told her that I couldn't be the person she called anymore—that I wasn't comfortable with that role, and I didn't think my woman would be comfortable with it either."

"Your woman?" she asked softly, the slightest smile tipping up her lips.

He pulled her onto his lap, relieved when she straddled him and scooted closer to press her breasts against his chest. "My woman."

"Anything else?"

"I think she has a crush on me. To be clear, I do *not* have a crush on her. I am one hundred percent in love with you."

Her smile grew a little wider, and Ian felt it in his heart, how much he loved that smile. "Is that everything?"

"That's everything," he said. "I promise."

"I believe you," she said.

"Thank you," he said, sighing with relief.

"I'm sorry I doubted you," she said, leaning forward to brush her lips against his.

"It probably looked pretty suspicious. But baby, I'm *so glad* that you came to me," he said, reaching up to caress her cheek with the back of his hand. "Thank you for respecting me enough to ask. Thank you for not believing the worst and leaving."

"There will still be moments…sometimes," she said, "when my doubts get the better of me. But I promise to come to you when they do. I promise never just to leave you without a word…without fighting for us first."

"That's all I ask, *mo chroí.*"

She breathed in, her hardened nipples rubbing against his chest as her smile deepened and her eyes darkened. "You know…Mrs. Toffle still has the ladybug. The apartment's free…"

Standing up with her legs locked around his waist, Ian stared into her eyes as he walked into the bedroom, throwing her down on the bed, unbuttoning her jeans, and tugging them off with her underwear. He knelt between her legs, loving her clit until it was pebble hard, and when he entered her body, it was slick and hot like it had been oiled, just as she'd promised the night they first made love.

Later, when she was lying naked, sated and soft in his arms, with her head resting over his heart, a feeling came over him, so strong and true, it wouldn't be denied, and something he'd been planning to do on Christmas Day suddenly needed to happen now.

"Halcyon," he asked, lightly running his fingers up and down her arm. "How do you feel about…forever?"

"From where I am right now? Pretty good."

"Okay. More specifically…how do you feel about marriage?" he asked, holding his breath when the words left his mouth.

She leaned up on his chest. "Honestly? A little scared."

He exhaled, feeling slightly deflated.

"In fact, I wouldn't even consider it again," she said gravely, making his heart plummet until he caught the glimpse of a twinkle in her blue eyes, "except with one man."

Relief flooded him, and his lips quirked up in a tentative smile. "Do I know him?"

That made her laugh, and the sound of it filled his heart with so much joy, he leaned to the side a little, opening the drawer of his bedside table and withdrawing the little white box that held a *promise* ring, a *Christmas* ring, an *engagement* ring, made expressly for her.

"You stay there," he said, easing her head from his chest and sliding out of the bed to kneel down on the floor beside it.

He held up the little box, flat in his palm.

"I bought this over ten years ago." Opening the top, her listened to her sharp intake of breath as she looked at the tiny, sparkling gems in the simple silver setting. "It's a ruby for you and an emerald for me," he explained. "I was going to give it to you that night—a promise ring, to let you know how much I loved you and that what we shared was just the start of something wonderful."

"Ian," she sobbed, sitting up and covering her breasts with a sheet as she stared at him, one hand over her mouth.

"I held onto it, I think, because I never gave up hope of someday giving it to you." He gulped softly, reaching for the hand covering her lips. "I love you. I *have always* loved you, and I *will always* love you. There will never be a day that I don't belong to you, and I promise to spend the rest of my life making sure you know how precious you are to me. I promise to be a good dad-figure to Jenny and to any other kids we might decide to make. But most of all, I promise I'll never give you reason to doubt me, Halcyon, my golden girl, *grá gael mo chroí*."

"I love you so much," she whispered through tears.

"I'm glad to hear it," he said, "because I want you to be my wife. Will you marry me?"

Tears streamed down her cheeks as she nodded at him, and Ian slipped the ring on her finger.

"Yes," she said, nodding and laughing and crying all at once. "Yes, Irish, I'll marry you."

He climbed back into bed, pulling her into his arms, kissing her senselessly, and thinking that maybe fate wasn't such a fickle friend after all.

The girl he'd lost was the woman he found.

The girl he'd adored was the woman he loved.

The girl of his dreams was the woman who held his future in her hand.

Amends had been made and conflict cast away.

And all was very, very right with the world.

Three months later

"I was thinking," said Ian.

"What were you thinking, Irish?" asked Hallie, turning to grin at him over her shoulder from where she stood on a ladder, thumbtacking shiny green shamrocks to the beams running across the ceiling of the barn.

"I was thinking that Jenny should have a little brother or sister."

Hallie turned around to look at him, raising her eyebrows with a saucy grin. "I'm loving the practice, but don't you think we should wait to get pregnant until we're actually married?"

"Yes," said Ian, "which is why I think we should get married this weekend."

She put her hands on her hips, her eyes widening in surprise. "This weekend is the St. Patrick's party."

"I know," said Ian, stepping over to the ladder and reaching for the sides so his fiancée was trapped. He looked up at her. "And I think it's perfect, because your parents are coming up, mine are driving over, Tate's coming, plus the Rileys and O'Learys. Heck, Fin's only got a few more weeks before he's got to go back to Ireland. I thought it over. Everyone who means anything to us will be here this weekend. We should do the deed."

"Just like that?"

"Baby," he said, "it's a second wedding for you, right?"

"Uh-huh."

"And last time you wore a white merengue in a huge Catholic church and had three hundred of your parents' closest friends at the reception, right?"

She grimaced, remembering the wedding day of her *un*dreams. Her mother had taken charge of the details— hiring a planner who took care of the location, flowers, catering, and favors. Even Hallie's dress had been narrowed down to four choices, and she chose the least offensive of the bunch. It hadn't really been about her and what she wanted; more, it had been an opportunity for her parents to network and show off for their friends.

"Right."

"So this time," said Ian, his hands landing on her waist and pulling her down from the ladder. "It can just be about us."

She grinned up at him. "A wedding here at Summerhaven?"

"But not in this barn," warned Ian.

"In the dining hall," she suggested, remembering the way he'd look at her from across the room when they were teenagers.

"Yes!" He nodded. "Super simple. You and me in jeans. Ladybug in her rain boots. Whatever flowers we can find already growing…"

"Now you're pushing it," she said. "There's still snow on the ground."

"Okay. We'll grab some flowers from town."

"We could write our own vows," said Hallie.

"I love that," said Ian.

"I, Halcyon, take thee, Irish…"

He grinned at her. "I, Ian, take thee, *mo chroi…*"

She took a deep breath, thinking it over, loving it more and more as the idea settled in her head. "Do we tell anyone first?"

Ian shook his head. "Nah. Britt and Tier would make too big a deal."

Tierney. Hmm. "Tierney won't be mad? If we get married before her and Burr? I don't want to upstage her plans."

"First of all, she'd not getting married until June. Second of all, she's having a big, Irish wedding at Moonstone Manor with Celtic dancers and bagpipes. Our Dad's flying our cousin, Father Michael, over from Killarney to do the service. Plus, I think a whole bunch of Burr's folks from Limerick are coming too." He shrugged. "Ours would be nothing like that."

"Just a simple gathering with close friends and family, huh?"

He nodded, pulling her closer, his emerald eyes shining. "You want the truth, Halcyon Gilbert? In my heart, we're already married. In my soul, you're already my wife. Saying the words in front of friends and family just makes it legal."

Because she felt the exact same way, her heart took flight and she reached up to cup his face between her hands. "I'm in. Let's do it."

"Really?" asked Ian, dropping his lips to hers for a quick kiss. "You mean it?"

"I mean it…and you know what else?"

"Tell me."

She bit her lower lip suggestively. "I love that other idea you had."

"Which one?"

"The one about giving Jenny a little brother or sister."

"Good idea, huh?"

"*Great* idea," she said, sliding her hands under his T-shirt. "In fact, I don't have to pick up Jenny at nursery school for another half hour, so if you're willing…"

"Baby, I'm *always* willing," growled Ian, grappling with her shirt and lifting it over her head.

But suddenly his hands stilled as he looked around the old barn where they were supposed to be together for their first time, but instead, where their love story took an unwanted intermission for ten long years.

His eyes slid back to hers. "Here? You're sure, *grá gael mo chroí?*"

"Bright love of my heart," she whispered. "I love you."

He put on a heavy brogue. "Ah, and that there's her downfall, poor lass: loving Irish."

"Silly man," she said, leaning up on tiptoes to kiss him again. "Loving Irish is her greatest treasure."

THE END

ALSO BY KATY

THE SUMMERHAVEN TRIO

Fighting Irish
Smiling Irish
Loving Irish
Catching Irish

THE BLUEBERRY LANE SERIES

THE ENGLISH BROTHERS
(Blueberry Lane Books #1–7)

Breaking Up with Barrett
Falling for Fitz
Anyone but Alex
Seduced by Stratton
Wild about Weston
Kiss Me Kate
Marrying Mr. English

THE WINSLOW BROTHERS
(Blueberry Lane Books #8–11)

Bidding on Brooks
Proposing to Preston
Crazy about Cameron
Campaigning for Christopher

THE ROUSSEAUS
(Blueberry Lane Books #12–14)

Jonquils for Jax
Marry Me Mad
J.C. and the Bijoux Jolis

THE STORY SISTERS
(Blueberry Lane Books #15–17)

The Bohemian and the Businessman
The Director and Don Juan
Countdown to Midnight

a m o d e r n f a i r y t a l e
(A collection)

The Vixen and the Vet
Never Let You Go
Ginger's Heart
Dark Sexy Knight
Don't Speak
Shear Heaven

Fragments of Ash
Coming 2018

Swan Song
Coming 2019

STAND-ALONE BOOKS

After We Break
(a stand-alone second-chance romance)

Frosted
(a romance novella for mature readers)

Unloved, a love story
(a stand-alone suspenseful romance)

About the Author

New York Times and USA Today bestselling author Katy Regnery started her writing career by enrolling in a short story class in January 2012. One year later, she signed her first contract, and Katy's first novel was published in September 2013.

Almost forty books later, Katy claims authorship of the multititled *New York Times* and *USA Today* bestselling Blueberry Lane Series, which follows the English, Winslow, Rousseau, Story, and Ambler families of Philadelphia; the six-book, bestselling ~a modern fairytale~ series; and several other stand-alone novels and novellas, including the 2018 RITA® nominated, *USA Today* bestselling contemporary romance *Unloved, a love story*.

Katy's first modern fairytale romance, *The Vixen and the Vet*, was nominated for a RITA® in 2015 and won the 2015 Kindle Book Award for romance. Katy's boxed set, *The English Brothers Boxed Set*, Books #1–4, hit the *USA Today* bestseller list in 2015, and her Christmas story, *Marrying Mr. English*, appeared on the list a week later. In May 2016, Katy's Blueberry Lane collection, *The Winslow Brothers Boxed Set*, Books #1–4, became a *New York Times* e-book bestseller.

Katy's books are available in English, French, German, Italian, Polish, Portuguese, and Turkish.

Katy lives in the relative wilds of northern Fairfield County, Connecticut, where her writing room looks out at the woods, and her husband, two young children, two dogs, and one Blue Tonkinese kitten create just enough cheerful chaos to remind her that the very best love stories begin at home.

Sign up for Katy's newsletter today

Upcoming (2018) Projects

Fragments of Ash, a modern fairytale

Connect with Katy

Katy LOVES connecting with her readers and answers every e-mail, message, tweet, and post personally! Connect with Katy!